Quiller Solitaire

Quiller Solitaire

Adam Hall

William Morrow and Company, Inc.
New York

Library of Congress Cataloging-in-Publication Data

Hall, Adam.
  Quiller solitaire / Adam Hall.
    p. cm.
  ISBN 0-688-10730-3
  I. Title.
PR6039.R518Q52   1992
823'.914—dc20
                                                        91-31060
                                                        CIP

Printed in the United States of America

First Edition
1 2 3 4 5 6 7 8 9 10

For
Dale and Sally

Contents

Chapter 1

Hit

I dropped the bundle onto the desk and pulled the string and opened up the crumpled newspaper and Tilney stood looking down at the stuff I'd brought in, the two blackened number plates, wristwatch, bunch of keys, ring, metal cigarette lighter, the upper jawbone, the lower one, while the reek of burned flesh began filling the little room, sickening me, sickening him too, I would imagine, Tilney, looking down at the stuff and then bringing his head up.

"That's all?"

"That's all."

"What does he look like?"

"Cinder."

It was cold in here, or it felt like it. I shrugged a bit deeper into my coat.

"Nothing recognizable?" Tilney asked.

I gave him a dead stare. "The object of the exercise," I said, "was to remove all traces of his identity. I did that."

I suppose I would have put it differently if the rage hadn't been in me, burning in me like that bloody car, burning half the night out there among the trees.

In a moment: "Have you had any sleep?"

He'd caught my tone, the far faint echo of the rage. Others wouldn't have noticed.

"No. I had to watch over things." A vigil over the dead, you could call it, but let's not be too dramatic.

"You could have phoned for someone."

9

"I didn't want anyone out there." It would have meant headlights arriving and everything, attracting attention. Things had been bad enough with the fire, though nobody had come running: last night was the Fifth of November, with bonfires all over the countryside. Trust McCane to get himself blown into Christendom on Guy Fawkes Night.

Tilney wrapped the things up in the newspaper again and jotted a note on a pad and said, "Let's go along to my room, shall we? We need to debrief, then you'd better get some sleep."

The clock on the wall said 6:21. There was still dark in the windows.

In the corridor I asked Tilney, "Who was running him?"

"Shatner. But there's no actual mission on the board."

"Is he in yet?"

"Yes." Tilney was giving me quick sidelong glances, still catching things in my tone. I couldn't do anything about that. "They got him on the phone when your signal came in, and he—"

"I want to see him."

Tilney broke his step and looked at me directly and said, "You can, eventually, but first I'm going to debrief you on McCane's death." He opened his door and waited for me to go through. Tilney has been known to put you in your place less gently than that, but he wanted to humor me, I think. He didn't know what was on my mind, why my control was so thin; I'd seen people killed before, and he knew that. "Take a pew," he said, and got behind his desk, pushing some stuff to one side. "Spot of tea?"

"No."

He got a tape recorder from a drawer and set it going. "So what happened?"

I still felt cold, though the radiators were on: you could hear the water gurgling in the pipes. "He phoned me in my car. He said he was going to Reigate, and asked me if I wanted to follow him up."

Tilney watched me, not looking away much, a thin man

with glasses and ginger hair and pale freckled hands, straight out of some redbrick university, you would have said, the science department. We'd been in this bloody place for years, he and I, and we got on well enough, even when the signals room was running hot.

"He asked you to follow him up. Had he tried to phone you before, at your flat or anywhere?"

"I don't know," I said.

"I mean, how important was it to him? Did he sound worried?"

"He just said it offhand."

"But he must have been expecting some sort of attack? To have asked you to follow him up?"

I didn't want to talk about it, but it was no use telling him that. "Not necessarily attack. Perhaps surveillance. Wanted to know if there were any ticks on his tail."

Tilney looked at me. "McCane was a top shadow. He didn't need anyone to help him find out if he was being *surveilled*. If he—"

"All right, then he was expecting someone to try killing him, if you like, I don't know, how can I?"

Tilney looked away. He knew the score now: McCane had thought someone was liable to have a go at him and he'd asked me to cover his rear and I'd done that but I hadn't done it well enough and he'd ended up in a burning car and I was trying to think of some way of ever getting any sleep again.

"What actually happened?" Tilney asked quietly.

"He was about a hundred yards in front of me, most of the time, and just this side of Redhill when we were on a straight stretch another car came up from behind me and went past like a bat out of hell and cut across McCane's bows and he swerved and went into the trees and the tank burst and the whole thing went up."

Tilney's eyes were wandering around the cluttered room. "He would have been wearing a seat belt, and therefore wasn't thrown clear, and the fire started so fast that you

11

didn't have a chance of reaching him in time. Wasn't that it?"

"I should have—"

"There was *nothing* you could have done, obviously." He was watching me again now.

"I should have been ready for it."

Tilney looked down, folding his pale hands on the desk beside the tape-recorder. "It's going on record that in my opinion and from what you've described, there was quite clearly nothing you could have done to help McCane last night."

I left it. "The other car," I said, "kept on going. They hit the brakes once—I was waiting for them to turn and come back and make sure they'd done the job, but when they saw the tank go up they must have known he hadn't got a chance."

"What kind of car did they have?"

"A dark Mercedes. I didn't see much of it—I was watching McCane's."

"Of course. Then you phoned Signals?"

"Yes. I told them to pass it on to whoever was running him. I didn't know it was Shatner."

"Did anyone—" He stopped, tilting his head; there'd been the slam of a door. He picked up the intercom phone and I waited, my body heavy in the worn leather chair, my eyes wanting to close. But I wasn't going to catch up on my sleep until I'd seen Shatner. There was only one thing, really, I could do that would get me at least some of the way out of this appalling sense of guilt, almost of betrayal, and Shatner could help me do it. But I'd have to be *very* careful.

"You just come in?" Tilney was saying on the phone. "Listen, there's some things on the desk in the storeroom downstairs, the one next to Clearance. They're in some newspaper; you'll see what they are. I want you to deal with them." He put the phone down and looked at me and asked, "Did you get any instructions to blot out McCane's identity for us?"

Blot out. I could feel the cold going through to the bone.

"No. I did it as a matter of routine."

McCane had been a high-echelon shadow executive, and when one of us hits the ground there's immediate smoke put out. We're known to a dozen major intelligence networks and whether a given agent is alive or dead is strictly our own business. The essence of intelligence is secrecy, of all and any kind.

"You were there all night," Tilney said, and waited. The yellow pencil he'd picked up to play with was nibbled almost down to the lead, but I'd never seen him at it.

"The crash was soon after nine. Everything was too hot to touch until the early hours."

The embers glowing and the smoke drifting in thin gray skeins among the trees, the smell of pinewood, and frost, and the other smell, from the thing inside the car, sitting there like a charred scarecrow, a human sacrifice to gross incompetence, rub the salt in, let me rub it in.

"And you don't know where he phoned you from," Tilney was saying.

"No."

"No kind of background noise, that you can remember? Was he in his car, or maybe a pub?"

"I didn't hear any background." It was something you're trained to listen for; it can tell you a lot.

Tilney had the pencil between two fingers, and was swinging it up and down; it was getting on my nerves.

"You didn't see much of each other, did you, in the ordinary way?"

"I was in Budapest with him once, setting up a courier line. We did some infiltration work in Beirut a couple of years ago. He was first-class, but I'm sure you know that. I enjoyed working with him."

"And he clearly had a lot of respect for you."

"I've no idea."

"I mean for him to telephone you, instead of someone else, to ask for help."

"Oh for Christ's sake, how do I know?" I got out of the

13

chair and went across to the window, and there was the street down there, the lamplight and the first buses, the world waking up for all of us, but not for McCane. I was letting my nerves show, shouldn't have said that, I needed sleep, but couldn't have any. How long would it be, how *long* before this smell was out of my clothes, out of my soul, this smell of burning?

Tilney's voice came from behind me. "Well, I think that'll do it for now." He snapped the recorder off. "Anything else occurs to you, give me a buzz."

I turned round from the window. "All right. Now get me in to see Shatner, will you?"

He looked at me. "Don't you think you ought to crash first?"

"No."

He puckered his lips, then picked up the phone and talked to a couple of people, trying to find Shatner. The controls aren't easy to run to ground in this place: they're either in Signals or briefing or debriefing or holed up with the top brass working out our destinies, where to put which ferret in the field and how soon, how to run him and when to call him in, how much risk to put on his back and how much mercy to show him when it looks like breaking. I was not, on this black winter morning, inclined to think good of anyone.

"He can see you in half an hour," Tilney said, cupping the mouthpiece. "That suit you?"

"Yes."

"Where will you be?"

"They can page me."

"Put your head down somewhere," he said. There are a few rooms here, cubicles really, where we can get some sleep if we need to.

"I'll try."

But when I left him I went along to the signals room to put in time, not eager for the nightmares that sleep would bring.

There were only a few people at the floodlit mission boards—Stacey, Freeman, Holmes, and a couple of new recruits up from training at Norfolk. Only two of the boards were active, with their code names chalked at the top: *Stingray* and *Scimitar*. Croder, Chief of Signals, wasn't in here, so there couldn't be much going on.

I told them I wanted to talk to the ambassador, but it didn't do any good.

"They wouldn't let you into the embassy?" This was Freeman, manning the board for *Scimitar*. He didn't look worried.

They said I could come back tomorrow. Listen, I think . . . then there was some static and all we could hear was his voice behind it, nothing intelligible.

Holmes had looked up when I'd come in, and now he was wandering across, a cup of coffee in his hand.

. . . but I'd say what's happened is that he's caught some of the fallout from the palace coup and he's lying low, can't see me or anyone else. This whole scene's a mess—they've sacked God knows how many diplomats but they can't even get a plane out.

Holmes was standing beside me. "What sort of night?"

"Bloody."

He was watching me steadily in the backwash from the floodlit mission boards. "Flaying yourself, I assume."

"Why don't you bugger off?"

He meant well, but that wasn't the point. I didn't want to talk about it.

That was an hour ago, and she hasn't shown up.

At the board for *Stingray* one of the new people was looking edgy, leaning forward over the console. "Do you think it's a trap?"

In a moment: *I don't know.* Yes, by his tone, he thought it was a trap, but didn't want to say so, didn't want to make it real. The name on the board was Flecke, shadow executive in the field, and in a way I wasn't surprised: he was a world-class womanizer and therefore a target for any kind of honey trap the opposition wanted to set up. He'd been warned more than once about this, and Ferris had refused to work with

15

him on *Pagoda* in Bangkok, said he could endanger the mission.

"If it's a trap, what are your options? Have you got any support out?"

No. The voice coming from the speaker sounded a little tight now. *I came here alone.*

Holmes left me and went over to the central console and picked up one of the phones, presumably to ask the Chief of Signals to get here. With a new man at the board and Flecke out there in Thailand caught in a trap, they'd need Croder to take over.

"Are you under surveillance at the moment?"

I can't tell. This is the market area, with people milling about.

Holmes came back from the phone and looked at me and said, "Come on, I need a break," and we went down to the Caff together, because he needed to do this and if I didn't let him he'd be miserable.

"Tilney phoned me," he said, "just after you left him. I know you don't want to talk about it but at least you can listen." Daisy came limping over with some tea for us and wiped the table down and left wet streaks and went away again and Holmes turned his dark serious eyes on me and said, "From what I gather, you couldn't have done anything. If you'd blocked off the Mercedes when it came up in the mirror it could have gone off the road and you could have found out it was a perfectly innocent citizen out for a joy ride and going a bit too fast and you could have got him killed. When you realized what that car was going to do you had about half a second to get in its way and you were something like a hundred yards behind, not terribly easy." He sipped his tea reflectively. "So what we finish up with is a perfectly competent shadow executive sitting here flaying himself alive in front of his old friend Holmes without the slightest justification, and said Holmes finds it thoroughly distasteful."

I didn't say anything. He didn't want me to.

The first of the winter daylight was coming through the

small high windows. It would be creeping among the trees out there, touching the blackened wreck, giving it highlights.

"It isn't," Holmes said, "that I don't know how you feel. I just want you to stop feeling it. If you like, we could go along to a funfair tonight and bash the bumpers off the Dodg'em cars and get some of that lovely adrenaline out of the bloodstream. Would that be nice?"

He watched me from under his thick black brows, trying to size up exactly how bad things were with me. He would have a rough idea. Holmes is the most sentient being in the whole of this bloody building.

In a moment I said, "It'll pass."

He said quietly, "Not with you, it won't. Not so soon."

"Take a bit of time, yes. There's no hurry."

Most of the really shitty situations in life don't have an immediate answer; they have to work themselves out. The problem with this one was that they were absolutely right, Tilney and Holmes: *nobody* could have stopped McCane getting killed last night, given the setup obtaining. But in a bleak shadowed corner of my mind the excoriating monologue kept up its whispering . . . *He asked you to protect him, and what happened? He was killed.*

"What bothers me," Holmes said, "a bit is that Tilney says you're suddenly very keen to see Mr. Shatner. I don't like that. I don't like that at all." Watching me steadily.

He'd made the quantum leap, and it jarred me, because Shatner might do the same, and refuse me the mission. My only chance was that Holmes knew me very well and was exceptionally sensitive, even intuitive, whereas I'd never seen much of Shatner: we were almost strangers. He might not see what I was after.

"Would you like a nice buttered bun, old horse?"

"You go ahead," I said. Even if I could have eaten anything, the buns in here were like bits off a boulder, and for butter read margarine.

"I don't think I will." He stirred the scum on the surface of his tea. "On the other hand, if you can get away with it,

I realize a thing like that would deal with quite a lot of the angst going on in your soul, and that of course would please me. The eye-for-an-eye principle really does do the job, despite the fact that in my opinion it's morally indefensible. But then again, you're not passionately concerned with my opinion on the moral indefensibility of anything in the world, are you?"

"Not really."

I took another go at the tea. It tasted like sewage but it was hot and there was enough caffeine in it to keep sleep away for a bit and give me the edge I'd need for my meeting with Shatner.

"But in the final analysis," Holmes said, and I began listening carefully because his voice had gone very quiet, "what really worries me is that if they decide to put a mission on the board to deal with the McCane incident, and if they give it to you—since you're obviously going to ask for it—you might easily, somewhere along the line, blow everything up." His eyes watched mine. "Blow everything up," he said, "just because you're a man of too much overweening pride and you can't stand the idea that you've failed someone. Tell me," he said gently, "if I'm talking absolute rubbish."

In a moment I said, "No. You're not." Because there was a risk, yes, if I let personal considerations get in the way of the mission. It's one of the really critical dangers we face when we're out there in the field, because it doesn't come from the opposition: it comes from inside ourselves. Pull up the drawbridge and drop the portcullis, but the enemy within the citadel will undo you.

Holmes lowered his head an inch, his eyes watching me from the deepened shadow of his brows. "I know, of course, that there's nothing I can do to stop you. All I ask is that before you take a risk as big as that, you'll give it some thought before you see Mr. Shatner. And if you still decide to see him, be very, very careful."

Chapter 2

Shatner

I was on the third floor when they paged me and I saw Shatner coming out of Clearance and waited for him while he ducked his head back through the doorway for a moment.

"Tell him that if he can't get here in time, I'll send someone along to clear him on the plane." He came into the corridor again and saw me and gave me a direct look, taking in the nerves and the fatigue. "Oh yes, you want to talk to me, don't you?" He led me along to his room on the other side of Codes and Ciphers, dropping into one of the big leather chairs with the torn hide, stuffing coming out of them in places—they'd furnished this whole building from a discount junk shop, typical of them, won't spend a bloody penny if they can help it, you try fiddling your expense sheet and they'll go for the throat.

"Tilney's spoken to me."

I took the other chair and got a whiff of ancient horsehair as I sat down. I didn't say anything.

"You've nothing you want to add?" He watched me with no particular expression, a man with dark untidy hair and bags under his eyes and a flat night-shift pallor, leaning forward, attentive. "Nothing you want to tell me, I mean, as McCane's control, that you might not have wanted to confide to Tilney."

"No."

When you're debriefed, you're debriefed; I never keep anything back unless it's to protect someone. Perhaps that was

19

what Shatner meant. I'd never thought McCane was especially good on security, for instance, talked a bit too much
when there were people around, didn't take overmuch care
to check his environment for ticks, peeps, bugs. It could have
got him killed last night: he might have talked to someone
about where he was going, and then realized it had been
dangerous; that could have been his reason for phoning me,
to cover himself.

Shatner said, "Then I don't know why you want to
see me."

"You were McCane's control. I was there when they got
him. There might be questions you want to ask. I might not
have covered everything with Tilney. Another thing is, I'd
like to take over."

He moved his head up a fraction. "From McCane?"

"Yes."

"Why?"

I'd got it ready. "I haven't been in the field for nearly two
months, and McCane was on my level, so it must be something I'd be able to handle."

Then one of his phones rang and he reached across to the
desk. "Yes?" Stretched out like that, he'd got one foot half
out of his shoe, a hole in his sock. "Then tell them to route
him through Paris. And Phyllis—no more calls." He dropped
the phone and sat back and looked at me and said, "It's not
your style to ask for a mission. You tend to play hard to get."

"Two months is a long time. I'm getting bored." I tried to
make light of it, but his eyes were on me and I knew what
I looked like, cold with shock still and the nerves flickering.
There was nothing you could have done. Bullshit. There's always
something you can do. So I knew what I looked like, not
quite your eager beaver just dying to see his name on the
board again.

"How do you feel, Quiller"—and here it came—"about
what happened last night? How do you feel personally?"

Tread carefully. "It was a shock."

"Of course. What else?"

I looked away. "I suppose I feel a bit responsible, or at least I did, for a while. But Tilney pointed out that I shouldn't blame myself, and Holmes agreed."

"I see." He waited until I was looking back at him. "So you don't feel any lingering sense of guilt."

"Not really."

"Or anger?" Watching me carefully.

"Oh, I think I've got over that sort of thing by now. He's not the first man I've seen killed."

Shatner waited, in case I made the silly mistake of adding something, of protesting too much. I didn't.

The phone rang again and the sound brought the sweat out on me, because that had been tricky going. "You couldn't have been listening," Shatner was saying on the phone. "I asked for no more calls." He dropped it and sat back again and I saw a look of sudden fatigue on his face. I suppose he'd been up most of the night too, because Signals would have passed on my message about McCane. This man had also had his executive wiped out on home ground and without any warning, and he must have had a lot to do in the last few hours.

"I don't know you," he said, "all that well. I'm not keen on running people I don't know."

I didn't say anything. If I begged for this job I'd never get it.

Pressing the bridge of his nose, his eyes squeezed shut, "You've got a reputation for giving your controls a bad time. I'm not keen on that either."

I got out of the chair, and a spring twanged. "Well, there's only a couple of boards active, so you've got plenty of people to choose from."

I was at the door when he said, "I rather think this is a time for tolerance, don't you, on both sides."

"I was trying to make it easy for you."

He got up too and moved around, not looking at me now, needing to think: that was my impression. I stayed by the door. "I've called Westerby in from Bucharest," he said.

"To take over?"

"Yes."

"How's his German?"

Shatner swung me a look. "Had McCane talked about Germany, when he phoned you last night?"

"No."

He went on moving around the small untidy room. I'd got Holmes to fill me in on McCane before we left the Caff, and he'd told me McCane had come back from Berlin the night before, so I assumed that was where Shatner had been running him. I'd also asked Holmes about Shatner, and it was interesting. Apart from a few other things he'd run Tewson in Budapest earlier this year and flown there himself to direct the end-phase when things had got sticky, and not many of them will do that, only Croder, Loman, Childs, nobody else I can think of, because it's so dangerous at that stage. Shatner had also brought Farrow in from Sri Lanka with a broken thigh and a bullet in him, not personally that time, but he'd organized a last-ditch rescue operation through Signals with a dozen people in support and orders to use deadly force if they had to, no big deal in a place like Sri Lanka but the Bureau is terribly touchy about that sort of thing. I might not be in bad hands if Shatner agreed to run me in Berlin, give or take a stray shot or a blown cover.

"Westerby's German is adequate," Shatner said at last, "but yours is rather better, from what I hear. You've worked there, haven't you?"

"Two or three times. I can pass for a native Berliner."

"Can you now." I was still standing by the door, and he said, "For God's sake, come and sit down again."

I compromised and perched on the arm of the chair, ready to get up and get out of here if he looked like arguing the toss for much longer. If he didn't give me the mission I'd do the thing I wanted to do some other way; I was ready to drop by now, and past the point where I'd lie staring at nightmares on the ceiling.

"You're more conversant, then," Shatner said, "with Berlin than Westerby is. That makes a difference."

"I'm a bit surprised you didn't send for me in the first place." He'd known my background; he must have. All the controls have got to do in this place is press a button and the computers throw you on the screen like an X ray.

He stood still for a moment and looked at me. "As I've told you, you're not my favorite executive."

"That's a bloody shame."

I was getting fed up with him.

"Now that we've got *that* over," he said, "let's remember that we've both had a rather trying night, and make mutual allowances. When can you take over from McCane?"

"The focus of this operation," Shatner said, "is on a man named Maitland. Or rather, on his death."

We were already into preliminary briefing and the little room was full of smoke. He'd asked me if I'd mind his having a cigarette, which I thought was civil of him.

"Maitland was a cultural attaché at our embassy in Berlin, fond of the city, active in his job, though for some reason not particularly well liked among his colleagues. A week ago he was murdered, and his body taken away. His flat had been broken into with some violence, and the police found evidence of massive blood loss. There were marks on the floor indicating that his body had been dragged out of the flat to the lift. The telephone was hanging by its cable—he'd been talking to a woman friend, who came forward, when the flat was entered. She reported sounds of the door being smashed in, an outbreak of voices and finally a cry. Maitland's car was also broken into and rigorously searched, the upholstery slashed open and the carpets dragged up."

Shatner reached for the dented chromium ashtray on his desk. "The Foreign Office suspected that the new generation of the Red Army Faction was involved, and asked us to make inquiries. I sent McCane out there."

"The FO approached us, instead of DI6?"

"We are able to do things, as you know, that DI6 cannot."

23

"But I mean it's that sensitive?"

He flicked ash. "I've been in signals most of the night with some of our agents-in-place out there. They couldn't give me much more than a certain amount of raw intelligence, but the vibrations I'm getting are that there may be more to Maitland's death than some kind of crude wet affair."

Yes indeed. They'd tagged McCane back to London and wiped him out as soon as they found him exposed. "You didn't get anything useful from McCane when you debriefed him?"

"Surprisingly little. He ran into a lot of resistance when he started asking questions. His feeling was that people either didn't want to answer them, or were afraid to. That's not unusual, of course, when there's a strong terrorist faction at large and active."

"Why did you call McCane in? For debriefing?"

"Partly." He got up and went over to a window, freeing the fastener and thumping at the frame until it jerked open an inch, sending down flakes of paint. "And partly because his inquiries led him to think that the person who might know more about what was going on is Maitland's wife. Widow." He brushed bits of paint off his jacket and sat down again.

"And she lives in Reigate."

"Yes. McCane was going there last night, to put up at a hotel and see her this morning."

"That's where I start?"

"That is where you start." He crushed out his cigarette. "I don't think I need to point out that you may well attract the attention of these people simply by showing up in Reigate. You don't normally like support, do you?"

"Only when I ask for it."

"That's a pity. It could finish you off, one fine day. I just hope it doesn't happen while I'm running you."

I went back to my flat in Sloane Square and showered and slept for three hours. When I got up I put the clothes I'd worn last night into a plastic bag and phoned Harry and asked him to take them to the cleaners as soon as he could; the smell of burning was pervasive, lingering. Then I phoned the stage door at the St. James's, but Thea was in the middle of rehearsal and I left a message saying I couldn't make it this evening, and phoned The Conservatory and asked them to send flowers for the opening night tomorrow.

It was eleven o'clock when I checked in again at the Bureau. They told me they'd arranged for me to have tea with Helen Maitland in Reigate at four, and that gave me time to look over the documented briefing that Shatner had given Mc-Cane and go over the present situation in Berlin regarding the Red Army Faction's activities. Shatner said there was no need for me to go through Clearance at this stage; a lot was going to depend on how much Helen Maitland was prepared to help us and whether she could give us any positive information to work on.

When I left Whitehall just after three in the afternoon and drove south along Millbank by the Thames I didn't have any sense of professional engagement. Shatner had officially started running me but there was no actual mission on the board and the truth was, after all, that the reason that was driving me south from London on this cold November afternoon was purely personal. I owed a man a death.

Chapter 3

Helen

She was standing in the middle of the lawn behind the house, perfectly still, her back to me. There was frost on the grass, and dead leaves, their edges silvered in the last of the winter daylight. A birdbath stood on a stone pedestal with ice in it, and something else, a small rounded object, perhaps a dead bird: I couldn't quite see from here. I'd rung the doorbell at the front of the house but couldn't hear any sound. I'd knocked, but not too hard; this was a house of grief. Then I'd come along the narrow redbrick path and through the gate by the hedge and seen her there on the lawn, a thin figure hunched in a sheepskin coat, facing away from the house. I couldn't see that she was watching anything in particular; there was a tennis court and a summerhouse and, farther away, a shed with some gardening tools leaning against it and the door half open. It was intensely quiet here, but in the distance there was traffic, its sounds muted, it seemed, by the cold and the lowering dark.

She turned round and saw me.

I hadn't gone close, not wanting to startle her. We stood facing each other for a time in silence. Then she spoke.

"Who are you?"

"Victor Locke. I'm sorry to disturb you." I meant her reverie. She'd known I was coming; it was just four.

She seemed not to connect, then said, "Oh yes. You're coming to tea." She still didn't move. At this distance she looked insubstantial, a small cold face above the coat, her hands tucked into the sleeves, her feet together in their fleece-lined boots. There was a toy railway engine not far from where she stood, lying on its side among the frosted leaves. I hadn't been briefed that the Maitlands had any children.

I went toward her. "That's right. I'm sorry about your husband."

There was no expression in her cool gray eyes, though she looked at me without blinking. Not at me, perhaps, but at all the things I meant, because I was here, all the things she was going to have to do now that she was a widow. That was my impression. I was breaking into the small confusing world that was taking its place between the old one, where her husband had been, and the new one, where he would not be.

"Oh," she said at last, not having heard what I'd said, perhaps, or not knowing how to answer. "Are you in the Foreign Office?"

"I'm in one of their lesser-known departments." Not true, but the "lesser-known" bit should give her the idea that she shouldn't ask for specifics. She thought about that. She was pretty, in an ethereal way, pale and cool and still. I couldn't see her playing tennis, but of course she might have looked quite different a week ago, before it had happened.

"We'd better go in," she said, but it had the sound of a question.

"Not unless you want to." She might not feel like being in the house now that it was empty. Perhaps that was why she'd come out here.

"But you'd like some tea."

"Not really."

"Oh." She watched me quietly for a moment, then looked around and said, "We could sit down, I suppose." There were some rustic-looking chairs at the edge of the lawn, where the tennis court began, their white paint beginning to peel. "Am I being terribly unwelcoming?" She said it without a smile, dipping her head, so that her long fair hair swung a little.

"Look," I said, "this isn't a social visit, and I want to make it as painless for you as I can."

In a moment: "Painless?"

That was the first clue. "I need to ask you about Berlin. They told you, didn't they?"

"Yes. But that's all right." She moved at last, walking across to one of the garden chairs, her suede boots leaving streaks on the frost; she walked with a slight sway, as if through water. "I don't mind talking about Berlin. I expect I seem a little distrait. Everything was rather sudden. And of course beastly."

She perched on the arm of the chair, throwing her hair back and looking at me a little defensively, I thought. No one likes questions about something they'd rather forget. I said, "We want to know what happened over there. Your husband was—"

"His name is George. Was George. You can call him that."

"All right. He was well into the scene in Berlin, knew a lot of people. He did a good job at the embassy, so I imagine he was pretty popular there."

"Not very."

"People tend to envy success, don't they?" I dragged a chair over and hitched myself onto the arm.

"I don't think it was that, quite. He was rather cocky, you see."

"He wasn't too well liked outside the embassy, either? Would you say?"

"Not enormously."

There was a face over there in the hedge, in a gap in the hedge. "But not so unpopular," I said, "that people would want to ... harm him?"

"Oh no. He was just—I mean he was just George. Rather supercilious. No, I think it was the Red Army Faction that killed him. The police think so."

29

"Do you?"

She seemed surprised. "I've never thought otherwise."
Then she said, "He was provoking them, I believe."

"Oh really. How?"

"Asking too many questions, I'd say."

"Why was he interested in the Faction?"

She swung her head a little, perhaps trying to clear her
mind; or it was just a mannerism; some women do it to show
off their long hair, without thinking.

"Are you feeling better now?"

The voice came from the hedge, from the small round face
in the gap in the hedge.

"Yes," Helen called. "Yes thank you, darling."

"Who's that man?"

"He's just a friend." She threw me a quick little smile, the
first one I'd seen. It changed her completely.

"What's his name?"

Then there was another voice, from the garden next door.
"Billy! Come in at once!"

"There's a man there," Billy called.

"Oh for goodness' sake, come in *at once*! I'm awfully sorry,
Helen!"

"Don't worry. He just wanted to know I was all right."

There was the sound of scuffling among dead leaves, and
a final cry as the battle was lost. "Can I have my engine
back?"

"*Billy*, you little *brat*!" More scuffling. "I'll give you a ring
this evening, Helen!"

"All right."

A door slammed over there. Helen looked around her,
then down at her hands. "I'm sorry. Where were we exactly?"

"We were talking about the Red Army Faction," I said,
"but let's cut a few corners. There must be someone in Berlin
who could give me some clues about your—about George.
I mean someone among his friends. My department wants

30

me to go over there and see what I can find out. We want to know who killed him."

In a moment she looked up. "So do I. It was such a beastly thing to do to a man. Even to him."

That was the second clue. I wasn't sure that she was really aware of what she'd said, of how it sounded. I left it.

"It's probably occurred to you that if you decided to help us in Berlin, you might be running a risk."

She looked surprised. "A risk of what?"

"George was murdered. You were his wife."

"But I never had anything to do with . . . whatever he was doing. He didn't take me into his confidence about anything. I was just his—" She looked away, and said in a moment, "I don't think I'd be risking anything. It doesn't worry me. The thing is, I really don't see how I can help."

"You knew his friends?"

She looked down. She did it quite often. "He didn't actually have any friends. Not real ones. There were lots of acquaintances—he was the first cultural attaché, as you probably know. Lots of parties, picnics with what he called 'cultivatable people,' always something going on. But no real friends."

In the silence we heard the starlings and robins rustling among the frosted leaves, a vehicle in the distance with its exhaust pipe blown, a man coughing in one of the gardens along the street, where smoke rose from a bonfire through the trees.

"Did you go to Berlin often?"

"Quite often, yes. Whenever he sent for me. I mean . . . whenever he needed me."

"You didn't want to stay over there in Berlin, instead of making all those trips?"

"I don't like Berlin. It's too fast, too frenetic, after somewhere like Reigate." A shy smile. "I like quiet places. Old places."

So what I was going to do was leave her here in peace and

tell Shatner it wasn't on, she couldn't help us, didn't know any of Maitland's friends because he'd never had any. I would go to Berlin under cover and start from scratch. She'd had quite enough of that place, and her last memory of it had been "beastly," the brutal end of a man she'd known, not loved, but known quite well. Or had she loved him, "even a man like him"?

"There was," she said suddenly, "now that I think of it, someone you could call a friend of his. They had a lot of meetings. George often said, 'I've got a meeting with Willi.'"

Perhaps a breakthrough. "Can you give me his address?"

She looked at me quickly. "He wouldn't see you. He doesn't trust anyone now, because of what happened."

"Did you go to any of these 'meetings' with him?"

"No. But I saw quite a lot of him at the parties, and"— she shrugged—"around."

So we'd got to go through with it after all. "Would he see me if you took me to him personally?"

She thought about it. "Yes. Is that what you want me to do?"

One of the hardest things in this trade is to keep some kind of liking for yourself, some self-respect, while you're doing the things you've got to do. "Yes," I said. And as a sop, I suppose, to my conscience, "But don't underestimate the risks."

With a nice smile, "I expect you're being oversolicitous."

"Not really. Do you know, for instance, that your house is being watched?"

She swung her head to look at me. "This house?"

"Yes."

"Why would anyone do that?"

She didn't know what had happened to McCane. "They might be waiting for you to leave, so that they can make a search. George could have left something here, or concealed something. They searched his car in Berlin, and his flat." Or of course the man out there in the black Vauxhall could be waiting for me. I was here in a dead man's shoes.

I believe she shivered slightly under the heavy coat; I wasn't sure. She looked cold, despite the sheepskin. Cold or afraid, or both. "Don't worry," I told her, "about the man out there. We'll take care of him, and you won't see him again." I blew into my hands. "On second thoughts some tea might be rather nice, warm us up, what do you think?"

She stood up at once. "I'm sorry, yes, I'm not doing terribly well, am I, as a hostess." As we went across the lawn she asked, "But what will you do, about the man out there?" Then immediately—"I shouldn't ask, I expect."

"He won't bother you, that's all that matters." I picked up the battered red railway engine. "You'd better look after this, or you'll be in trouble."

The smile came again, like a flash of soft light. "Poor Billy— he's got asthma. Or at least that's what they think it is."

She led me through a small conservatory at the back of the house, with some galoshes in a row and straw for tying plants, a big amaryllis in a pot, the smell of earth and damp-ness. "If you're still willing," I said, "to go to Berlin, how soon could you make it?"

She stopped and turned and we were suddenly close and I caught her perfume and looked into the cool gray eyes and wondered what in fact she had been to George Maitland, *I was just his*—and she'd looked away.

"I haven't any plans," she said. "I could go whenever you wanted me to."

"Tonight?"

"Tonight, yes."

"I'll check with my department, see if they can get tickets."

"Whatever you say." She took me into a large low-ceilinged room with beams and a brick fireplace and a small grand piano, framed photographs on a cabinet, copies of *Connoisseur* on a wicker stool, a glove lying on them, its mate on the floor just below, a man's—his?—and some road maps. The room was in perfect order, but as she went past the stool she didn't pick up the glove, though she saw it and I think hesitated before she went through into the kitchen. "Sit down, won't you?" she said over her shoulder. "What sort of tea do you like? I've got Earl Grey, Lapsang Souchong—"

"Whatever you're having. Can I use the phone?"

"But please. It's over there."

I went across to it. There was an answering machine, switched off. I dialed a random number and heard the solenoid trip in and waited for the voice on the tape to tell me I'd dialed a number that wasn't in service, then I rang off. I could see Helen Maitland through the hatchway into the kitchen; she was putting some water into a kettle.

I switched on the answering machine. "I'm just going out to the car," I told her. "If the phone rings, do you mind not picking it up? Let the machine take it?"

In a moment, watching me through the hatchway, "All right."

I went out to the Jaguar and got on the phone to Signals and asked for Shatner. A car was going past the end of the driveway and I slid low in the seat until it had gone. Some starlings were lined up along the telephone wires, nagging and preening; there was no other sound; this was a peaceful part of the world, and I was sorry we were asking this young widow to go to Berlin and into possible danger; it seemed like gratuitous abuse. But some of the things she'd said on the lawn had been interesting. *It was such a beastly thing to do to a man. Even to him . . . I never had anything to do with . . . whatever he was doing. . . . I was just his . . .* Wife? Chattel? There was something subservient about her, unquestioning. *I haven't any plans. I could go whenever you wanted me to. . . . Whatever you say . . .*

"Yes?"

Shatner. I said, "I'm there now. The house is being watched and the phone's bugged. She's ready to go over there with me. How soon can you take care of things here?"

"Stand by."

There was a voice calling, Billy's, I think, not calling to

anyone in particular, chanting some rhyme or other; he was banging at something, keeping time.

"I can put some people in there in thirty minutes," Shatner said, "or not much more. What do you need?"

"I need to get her away from the house unseen, and then we should put a watch on the place round the clock. They may try to break in and make a search. And the phone needs clearing."

He didn't answer right away. He might be making notes. I didn't know whether he was a man to make notes of things; I hoped not; I wanted a control with instant memory to run me in the field.

"You'll get a call," he said. "About half an hour."

I went back into the house.

"Do you take milk?"

"No." Pleasant smell of Lapsang, dry and smoky.

"Sugar?"

"No." Silver tray, white linen, sugar tongs. No one had phoned: the machine wasn't blinking. "Look, I don't want to rush you," I said, "but how long would it take you to pack?"

Her head swung up. "How long for?"

"A day or two. I can't say exactly."

She gave me my tea. "If it's any more than that I can buy things." She'd taken her coat and boots off while I'd gone to the car; she was slighter than she'd seemed. "I've been trained to pack quickly. He never gave me any warning when he wanted me out there." She conjured a faint smile to mean she hadn't minded. She had. "Give me twenty minutes? All I need is makeup and some undies and things." She was leaning forward over the tea tray, small stockinged feet together, hands on the front of her thighs, a lock of fair hair hanging across her cheek. "Would that be quick enough?"

"Just right. I'd like to leave here in about half an hour. Do you use a security service?"

"No."

35

"Alarm system?"

"Yes. But I never switch it on."

"Really. George never asked you to, when you left the place empty?"

"No. Or I would have."

"Never mind. We don't need to set it today, either. My department's going to look after this house with a twenty-four-hour guard, so you don't have to worry about a thing."

Her eyes widened a little. "I see. All right." She straightened up. "I'll take mine up with me, shall I?" She was actually waiting for me, I thought, to approve.

"Of course. I'm sorry it's not quite the leisurely tea party you were thinking of."

"That isn't why you came."

"No. Are there phones upstairs?"

"Yes. There's one in the bedroom."

"Don't answer it if it rings."

"All right."

I looked round the room while she was upstairs. There was just an ordinary lock on the door to the conservatory, no dead bolt, and nothing on the windows, just the usual fastener. The alarm system wasn't wired; it went through a master control from sensors; there was only one of them here, and it was a big room. And Maitland never asked her to set the alarm system anyway, even though she was apparently away in Berlin with him fairly often—*I've been trained to pack quickly.* Perhaps his flat over there was the same, with no real security. I thought it was odd that anyone should have rifled his car and smashed their way into his flat and killed him so viciously, when he didn't seem to have expected any kind of trouble at all.

"Was I quick enough?"

She stood with her feet together at the bottom of the stairs, looking very young in a cashmere sweater and slacks and soft flat shoes, holding a Lufthansa bag. She'd put more scent on, but it seemed almost precocious.

"Yes," I said. "And you look very nice."

"I was hoping you might say that."

"Have some more tea," I said. "We don't have to go just yet."

"All right." She never questioned anything, hadn't said, "Then I needn't have hurried." Her slight breasts moved under the cashmere as she leaned over the tea tray. "Would you like some more too?"

"Thank you, no." I wondered for the first time whether I should have put my trust in Shatner, because in the next ten minutes or so we'd be in a red sector. Last night they'd killed McCane and it looked as if they'd killed him because he'd been coming here to see Maitland's widow. I'd come farther than he had: I was here with her now.

"Will they—" she began, and then the telephone rang and she jumped slightly and looked at me and I shook my head. The answering machine cut in.

This is George Maitland. I can't come to the telephone now, but if you'll leave your name, number, and any message, I'll phone you back as soon as I can.

We were listening to a dead man's voice but she didn't react in any way. She was sitting on the floor with her legs to one side, cupping her tea in both hands. The beep sounded.

"Er, yes, this is Jim, down at the garage. We can pick up your car any time you say, and have the oil changed and everything before seven tonight. Give us a buzz if you want us to fetch it, will you? Number's 483–2230. Thank you."

Another beep. I said, "Is it all right if we have someone sleep here while you're in Berlin?" A place like this would have a guest room.

She seemed surprised. "If you think it's necessary." She hadn't got the message yet. A lot of things were going to be necessary now.

"Yes."

"All right," she said. "There's always a bed made up in the guest room."

"We'll need the keys." I went over and picked up her bag.

The initials G.K.M on the leather in brass. She didn't have luggage of her own?

"All the keys?"

"Just the front door."

She got them from her worn suede bag. She liked old places; perhaps old things, too. "I'd better lock up all round," she said.

"Don't worry. They'll move in the minute we've left." It took her a moment to accept that, too. She didn't ask where they were coming from or how long it would take them. The only clue she had was that she hadn't asked her garage to do an oil change and there probably wasn't a man working there called Jim. She was learning not to ask questions if she could help it, and that was going to be very convenient. I said, "We'll be on our way, then, shall we?"

It was nearly dark when we went outside again. "When you're away for any length of time, you leave the answering machine on, do you?"

"Yes."

I dropped her bag into the trunk of my car and shut the lid quietly. "They'll monitor every message and send the daily take to you in Berlin. Will that be all right?"

"It's not important, really. They'll only be from, you know, the tradespeople or Marjorie next door, or my mother. They need to—"

"There won't be any calls for George? From people who haven't heard?"

"He never had many calls. He was in Berlin most of the time."

I opened the passenger door for her and she got in, her fair hair swinging. I shut the door without slamming it and went round to the other side. The streetlights had come on, but they weren't very high, or very bright; this was a quiet street on the edge of the town. A cat was loping across the pavement opposite, its eyes trapping the light for an instant as it turned to look at us.

"Would you like to slide down a bit," I asked Helen, "on the seat?"

She turned to look at me. "All right."

I picked up the phone and dialed 483–2230 and waited.

The head of the cat moved like a hunter's; its shoulders flexed rhythmically under the dark fur. There'd be a small gift of some sort on the mat by morning, an offering to its patrons, perhaps the bloodied entrails of a rat.

"Jim here."

I said, "The house is open, and I've left the key of the front door on the tea tray in the sitting room. That all right?"

"Sure. We'll be there."

"What's your setup?" I asked him.

"I'll give you a countdown, then you can move. Okay?"

"All right. Listen, if a boy called Billy from next door comes and asks for his railway engine back, give it to him. It's in the little conservatory, next to the amaryllis pot."

"Will do."

I started the engine. "Ready when you are." I put the phone back and looked at Helen and said, "Seat belt."

"I'm always forgetting," she said.

Jim's voice started sounding over the speaker. "All right—ten—nine—eight—"

"A bit lower," I said to Helen, "can you?" She slid down some more, easing her thin hips under the lap strap. "Just for a minute," I told her, "then you can sit up again." I didn't want her silhouette presenting a target against the street-lights.

"Five—four—three—"

I shifted into gear.

"Two—one—zero."

I took it gently at first because I didn't want any squeal from the tires but as soon as we were out of the driveway I gunned up a little and then a lot as we straightened, a bit of a whimper from the treads but it didn't matter now because Jim was going into the routine in the street up there and we heard a crash of metal and then glass smashing as I hit second and gave her the gun and then there was quite a lot of tire scream from behind us as the Vauxhall tried backing up and swinging clear but Jim would have been waiting for that and got in its way again with a lot of noise as we reached the corner and I took the side street and said, "You can sit up now."

Chapter 4

Solitaire

Shatner lit another cigarette, screwing up his eyes against the smoke.

"What's she like?"

I don't think he'd slept, as I had, since I'd seen him last. I would say he'd been in signals with Berlin again, exhaustively.

"Shy," I said, "quiet, nervy, guileless, subservient."

It was just gone six. He'd told me we were putting her up at the Holiday Inn at Heathrow until the plane left; they'd had a car waiting for her when we'd reached Whitehall.

"Subservient?" Shatner said. "Dominated by Maitland, do you think?"

"Yes. But I'd say she was like that when he married her." We were trying to get a bearing on Maitland's character: it could be important. "I mean, women don't usually let a man dominate them unless they've been set up by their fathers first."

Shatner dropped ash. "What was their relationship, would you say?"

I told him how she'd spoken of her husband. Not lovingly. "Look," I said, "she's got to come with me to persuade Willi Hartman to talk to me, and he's our only access for the moment. But as soon as I can, I want to send her back home. She's appallingly vulnerable."

Shatner watched me through the smoke, the light yellowing his dry pale face, the bags under his eyes making shadows. "Is she attractive?"

"Yes. But I want to get her out of Berlin anyway, the minute Hartman's accepted me. It doesn't matter a damn what she looks like."

"I take your point." In a moment—"Now tell me how this Maitland affair strikes you."

I thought about it. "I'd say his death wouldn't have looked very important, as an isolated incident taken out of context. But the opposition cell—presumably the Red Army Faction—sent some people over here from Berlin to monitor McCane, and when they knew he was going to see Maitland's widow they thought it was worth killing him to prevent it. They put a peep on Maitland's house in Reigate and they bugged the telephone and when your support group got me away from there the opposition went crazy—I heard them. So I believe Maitland's death is now looking *very* important and I'd say he was killed because he had something on the Faction and it was something quite big. Big enough for us to take an interest in."

The telephone rang and Shatner took the receiver off and dropped it into a drawer. "I happen to have reached the same conclusion. I think we should give it mission status and send you in as the executive. You're still ready to offer your services?"

"Yes."

I thought it was a rather elegant way to put it, and it pleased me. If at some time in the future I fetched up in a wrecked car or a smashed telephone box or a cell running with rats it was going to help a little, just a little, to know that Control was running things with a certain degree of elegance and that I might, because of it, survive.

"I've set a few things up," he said, and opened the drawer and put the phone back, "and if you've had enough sleep we can get you cleared right away. I've called in Thrower from Pakistan to direct you in the field. Has he handled you before?"

"No."

"I think you'll like his style. He's worked mostly in Europe before now, has good German and a lot of experience. You'll go in with the cover of a medium-weight arms dealer—objections?"

"No." It was perfect logic. If there's one thing a terrorist faction loves it's an arms dealer.

"From your records," Shatner said, "you're quite well versed in that area, but I'll send someone along to update the scene for you." He got out of his swivel chair and moved around, hands stuck in his pockets, a shoelace undone. "I don't know what time your flight is for Berlin tonight, but I've asked Travel to make it as late as possible because I want you to see a man at the National Temperance Hospital before you leave London. He's had some experience with the Red Army Faction, and quite recently, so he might be able to fill you in a little. I'm not sure"—he looked at me sharply—"I'm not sure of that, but it's to be seen."

He went to the door, shoelace trailing, and opened it for me, standing there hunched with fatigue in his leather-patched jacket. "You'll be making any direct signals to the board through the crew on duty but you'll be able to call on Mr. Croder if you need to, and I shall be within reach. Bureau One is in London and we can bring him in if things get difficult." He offered me a dry, nicotine-stained hand. "Let's hope they won't."

"Mary?" She gave me my card back. "Can you come down?"

I didn't say I'd go on up, and save Mary the trouble. I'd been here before and knew the rules. You don't get onto the second floor of the National Temperance Hospital unless you're a close relative of a patient or unless you've got first-class credentials and an introduction, usually from a department of H.M. Government.

"Right-o," the woman said. "At the front desk, then."

On the second floor is the clinic of the Medical Foundation

for the Care of Victims of Torture, and it offers treatment with a guarantee of the closest possible secrecy.

Mary was middle-aged, quiet in her speech, and had the otherworld calm of a nun. "You can see him for a few minutes," she told me in the lift, "just a few minutes, that's all."

He was in a private room, the man. I didn't know his name, and nobody here knew mine: it wasn't on the card I'd shown the woman downstairs. He was in a wheelchair, a book on his lap, *Quantum Healing*, one of his hands—his right hand—buried under the plaid rug, a bandage covering half his face, some of his thin dry hair sticking up at the side.

I said hello. He turned his head to look up at me, a touch of fear in his eyes, I thought, and that would be natural: if things have been taken too far, usually in some kind of interrogation cell, we fear strangers, afterward, as I had, once, for a time.

"He's a friend," Mary told him.

"Oh. What have you come for?"

You don't, in this place, say things like, "To ask a few questions." He'd had enough of questions, and he was here because he'd refused to answer them.

"They said you've had a brush with the Red Army Faction," I told him, and sat down on the edge of his bed so that he didn't have to look up at me anymore. "I'm going to Berlin tonight, and I'll probably run across them. I thought you might feel like giving me a few tips, so I can keep out of trouble."

He watched me for a bit, his eyes full of intelligence: they hadn't pulled his brains out and thrown them away. They sometimes do; not physically, of course, but it comes to the same thing: you can't do any more thinking. "I see," he said.

There was a drip of mucus under his nose, and Mary got a Kleenex.

"Oh shit," he said. "I couldn't feel it." He blew his nose, still watching me, as if he daren't look away in case I did something. I understood that too. "The Faction," he said in a minute, "yes. Well, contrary to popular belief, they're still alive and well. Not the old ones, the new ones. Not Baader and Meinhof, of course."

"No." The story put out was that they'd committed suicide in their cells in Stammheim Prison, but we've never taken that seriously. The main thing was, they were dead. "There's a third generation now, isn't there?"

"Third or fourth. They keep a low profile; you can't easily infiltrate; it was a piece of cake, once, but that's over. The man at the top now is Dieter Klaus, and I hope to Christ you never run into him. Mary," he said, "tell me if I start dripping again, will you? I hate that." He sat clutching the box of Kleenex. They'd worked on his face over there, and it was still numbed, could even stay like that. "Dieter Klaus, yes. He's inhuman."

I put him down now as Department of Information 6, by his idiom—"low profile," "infiltrate." Again I avoided a question. "He shouldn't be too hard to find."

He'd begun shaking now, setting up a vibration in the springs of the wheelchair. We listened to it, Mary and I. Then the man said, "He'll be extremely difficult to find. After the wall came down there were all kinds of rats running all over the place, because Stasi's Division XXII was broken up and their terrorist guests had to find some other kind of shelter, and there isn't any, not now, not in the new Germany." The spring in the wheelchair had started a definite rhythm now as the whole of his thin body began shaking under the blanket. I thought I might not have much longer here so I interrupted him.

"Some people say they've based themselves in Frankfurt."

"Frankfurt? Oh, yes, some of them are there. Don't confuse Dieter *Klaus* with Dieter *Lenz*, though. The police got Lenz for blowing up Herrhausen's Mercedes, remember? Dieter Klaus has never been arrested for anything, because he's a cut above your usual terrorist. He was with Monika Helbing and Werner Lotz when they got picked up—Christine Duemlein was there too and got copped—but Klaus simply vanished in a puff of smoke. He's very agile, very clever, and a real shit, I should keep away from him if I were you, I mean at the moment you're just a *visitor* here, aren't you," the shaking getting worse every minute because I was bringing it all back and I'd asked Mary about that in the lift but she'd said it would be good for him to talk, they were all trying to get him to "bring it out," as she called it. All well and good, but the sweat was starting to come out on his face, giving it a bright sheen.

"Willi told me much the same thing," I said. "Willi Hartman."

"Did he?" He clawed another tissue out of the box and kept it pressed to his nose. "Well there you are." The sweat was running into his eyes, and Mary went to the box too. "Who's Willi Hartman?" the man asked me, not looking at me anymore, looking down, then letting his eyes close as Mary pressed the lids gently with the tissue.

"I thought you might know him," I said.

"Not an uncommon name, not uncommon." His tone had a deadness to it suddenly; he spoke like an old man weary of talking anymore. "Keep away, I would," he said, "keep away from those bastards, if you know—if you know what's good for you, they're not—they're not the original angels of—of mercy, you understand, they're just—they're just a bunch of fucking terrorists, you see, just—just a bunch"— his voice changing to a spasm of coughing that went on and on with some words in it—"some stuff, Mary . . . need more stuff, please—" but she was already at the little white table by the bed, filling a syringe as the coughing went on and on and I took his hand and held it for a while, the wheelchair shaking as if it had an engine running in it, the needle going in while I crouched lower so as not to get in her way as she said quietly, "I'm afraid time's up now."

I said yes and thanked her and squeezed his cold emaciated hand and left them, going out and past the lift and down the stairs and into the lamplit street.

* * *

When I got back to Whitehall a man came across the little square at the back of the building and said through the window, "You can leave your car here and they'll run it over to your place. My name's Bloom and I'm driving you to the airport, all right?"

"Are we cutting it fine?"

"Not too bad, but we don't want to—"

"I'm not cleared yet."

"You'll do it on the way."

He took me across to the dark green Rover parked by the railings and I got in and the man in the back asked me, "Is there anything you need from the office?"

"Is there a bag on board?"

He was Loder. He'd cleared me before.

"Yes, in the trunk."

Bloom shut the rear door and went round and got behind the wheel. "Your flight's leaving at 21:06, so there's plenty of time, but—you know—you can always get a puncture."

Loder put a thin briefcase onto my lap. "Have a look through it, see if it's all there."

Bloom took us into the evening traffic, south through Parliament Square.

I signed the medical form and the codicil and the active-service waiver and checked the maps, two of Berlin with different scales, one of the whole country. Hotel reservation, expense sheet, embassy contacts, signals grid. Signed for the bag though I hadn't checked it, but they knew my sizes by now. No next of kin, money to the battered-wives home.

"Take this bloody thing," I said, and gave Loder the expense sheet. My director in the field would have one and he could look after it for me; one of the really trying chores of a mission was having to deal with those arthritic old harpies in Accounts when you got back, and I'm often tempted to charge them for a bag of cocaine or a tart or a Stealth bomber just to get the dust out of their bustles.

47

"Looking good," Loder said.

"What?" He'd been watching me, I suppose, in the pale shifting light of the street lamps as we turned west along Victoria Street. "I'm feeling fine," I said, "yes." There's never been anything official about it in the book of rules, but the people in Clearance make a point of catching your mood if they can, because they're the last people we see before we leave the building and the mission starts running, and what they're looking for is an abnormal show of nerves. They'd pulled one of the new recruits off a courier job last week because they'd noticed his hands weren't all that steady when he was signing the forms. "Have they got a code name for this one yet?"

"*Solitaire*," Loder said. "It's gone up on the board."

"Who's the crew?"

"Cary and Matthews."

They'd be manning the board in shifts around the clock. I hadn't worked with Cary but I knew Matthews, one of the old hands, a retired sleeper from Marseilles. And if I needed the Chief of Signals he'd be there, Croder, with his basilisk eyes and his hook of a hand and his cold-blooded expertise. And if I needed total support at the signals board there'd be Shepley, Bureau One, host of hosts, with a direct line to the Prime Minister and enough clout to call every agent-in-place out of his foxhole and bring in enough firepower to sink a destroyer, an exaggeration, but you get my drift.

Smell of burning.

"Has she been told," I asked Loder, "not to recognize me when she sees me at the departure gate?"

"But of course."

I shouldn't have asked. It sounded as if I didn't trust Shatner to look after even the basics.

I almost said to Loder, do you smell burning? But of course he didn't. It wasn't on my clothes anymore or in my hair. It was in my head. For all the very good reasons the Bureau had for sending me to Berlin—to infiltrate the Red Army Faction, perhaps prevent some kind of coup—my own reason for going out there still contained an element that was primitive, brutish, and urgent.

They had drawn blood.

Chapter 5

Berlin

She picked up the phone, swinging her head to look at me.

"Do you want to talk to him?"

"Yes," I said, "if he's willing."

There was nothing I wanted to say to Hartman over a telephone: all we needed to do was make the rendezvous; but it would give my voice an identity for him.

Helen dialed.

This was her room, 506. The Bureau had chosen the Steglitz. I was in 402 on the floor below: they knew I would want space and distance so that I could check on any tags when she left her room. There wouldn't be any, at least not tonight. Only the Bureau knew where we were. There'd been no message for me. Shatner had said that Thrower, my director in the field, would reach Berlin sometime tomorrow. There was no hurry; I didn't need him yet.

"Willi," she said on the phone, "this is Helen, and it's just gone ten. I thought you'd be there. I'm in Room 506 at the Steglitz. Will you ring me when you come in? Anytime tonight."

She put the phone down and turned and looked at me, puzzled. "I rang him from Heathrow before we took off. From my hotel there. He said he'd wait in."

"He wouldn't have gone to bed?"

"He never sleeps. That's why he loves Berlin."

She came slowly across the room, watching me, worried.

51

A jet lowered across the window, the lights of the city coloring its wings as it made its way into the airport.

"When you phoned him," I said, "from Heathrow, how did he sound?"

"He said he was glad I was coming to Berlin, and—"

"I mean did he sound nervous? Nervous about meeting me?"

She thought about it. "A little, I think, yes. He said I mustn't tell you where he lives. He's going to meet us somewhere else."

That made sense. His friend Maitland had been dead less than a week, and Hartman knew that any inquiry would risk exposing him to the Faction.

"When he phones," I told Helen, "if he doesn't want to talk to me, try and reassure him. I guarantee his absolute protection—tell him that."

"All right. Would you like something to drink? I can ask them to send us—"

"Nothing for me. You go ahead."

"I don't think so. Although I should be celebrating, in a way. This is probably the last time I'll be in Berlin, apart from the odd trip." She let her eyes wander across the brilliantly lighted streets. "But it's also nice to be here for the first time alone. Without George." She swung her head to look at me. "The way he died was so beastly, and I've only just realized how much I hated him." With a small wry smile—"Do you mind if I unpack?"

"Not a bit." There was a copy of *Stern* on the small round table and I went over and picked it up.

"Things get so creased," she said from behind me, and I heard her pulling the zips of the bag open. "At least mine do—I wear cotton when I can."

I took it that the small talk was to cover the last thing she'd told me, about hating George. I didn't think she wanted any kind of answer. But it was interesting, and I wondered whether she was feeling a sense of relief that he was dead, and had even, perhaps, seen it coming.

"It was probably the last thing," I said, "you'd been expecting."

She was pulling drawers open. "I'm not absolutely sure. He was a rather mysterious person, rather secretive. In fact he was *very* secretive." Her voice had become louder and when I looked up I saw she'd swung round from the chest of drawers, a pair of white cotton briefs in her hand. "Do you think he could have been a spy?"

"It sounds possible."

"Berlin's almost a beautiful city again, and look what they're planning for the Potsdamer Platz and everything, but there are still some very strong undercurrents here, aren't there? You must know about them. And George—" She broke off as the phone rang. "That's Willi." She dropped the briefs onto the bed and picked up the telephone. "Hello?"

I went across to her, in case Hartman let me talk to him.

"Oh, Gerda, how are you?"

I covered the mouthpiece and said, "Tell her you'll call her back."

"Gerda," she said, "do you mind if I call you back? I'm just out of the shower and dripping all over the floor."

I wondered if she'd thought the easy lie was necessary, or if it was just social habit. When she'd hung up I said, "She's a friend of yours?"

"Yes. Gerda Schilling. I've known her for—"

"I want to keep the line clear for Willi, so if anyone else rings, tell them the same thing. You'll call them back." And then I asked her—"How did Gerda know you were here?"

She looked contrite. "I rang her from Heathrow, before I left. I shouldn't have, should I?"

"Did you ring anyone else?"

"No. Only Willi."

She watched me with something close to fear in her wide gray eyes, the fear of authority. It told me a little more about George Maitland.

"You didn't tell anyone at all that you were staying at the Steglitz, or that you were coming to Berlin?"

"No." She didn't look away. "Nobody else."

"Then don't worry. Don't talk to anyone until we've met Willi."

"Whatever you say." In a moment: "You probably think I'm a bit—I don't know—naïve, don't you?"

"You're just not used to subterfuge, that's all."

"Oh," she said, looking down, "I don't know about that. I tell lies easily, don't I?" She looked up again and the shimmering smile came. "I think it's just that I'm not terribly bright. I was a model, that was all, before I met George. I've never had to use my brain." A soft laugh—"It makes life awkward for me."

"A touch of innocence," I said, "is refreshing in this day and age."

"You're very—" and she was looking for the right word when the phone rang again, and I picked it up and gave it to her.

"Hallo?" She turned to me and nodded slightly. "Yes, Willi. Don't worry, it's still not late. Would you like to have a word with Mr. Locke?" She listened for a moment. "All right. But he wants you to know that he guarantees your"— looking at me—"safety, was it?"

"His absolute protection."

"He guarantees your absolute protection, Willi. So everything's all right."

She listened for another minute and then said good-bye and put the phone back. "We're to meet him at the Café Brahms in twenty minutes."

"Do you know where it is?"

"Oh yes. Ten minutes from here."

"Have you been there before?"

"Yes. I—"

"How often?"

She began looking anxious again, as if she'd done something wrong. "Oh, just a few times, when—"

"With Willi?"

"Yes."

"And with George?"

"Yes."

Then Hartman wasn't terribly bright either. I said, "I just need to know things like that. Don't worry."

In a moment—"You'll be rather glad to be rid of me, won't you, when I leave Berlin?"

"Not really. But I've guaranteed your absolute protection, too, so we've got to take a few little precautions."

But yes, in point of fact, I would be very glad indeed when I could put Helen Maitland onto a plane for London. In Reigate I'd thought she was vulnerable, and she was; but here in Berlin I realized she was also a distinct risk to security—her own, mine, and the Bureau's. *Solitaire* was running close to exposure.

There was a cold drizzle in the air when we walked out of the lobby at the Steglitz and got a cab and drove through the late-evening traffic.

"How big," I asked Helen, "is the Café Brahms?"

"Not very." She sat close to me, her thigh against mine. Her face looked cold and pinched in the colored light from the street; she was sitting close because she wanted to touch someone who knew much more about what was going on than she did; she needed to feel the protection I'd told her about. This was my impression. "It's a basement," she said. The Café Brahms.

"I'm going to drop you off there," I said. "I want you to sit as close as you can to the bar, where I can find you easily."

"Why aren't you coming in with me?"

"I've got a chore to do. I'll be there as soon as Willi is, don't worry. What does he look like?"

She was picking at her nails, looking out of the window at the street. "Willi? Oh, he's short, thirty or so." With a nervous smile "He usually wears a rather rakish trilby."

"Face?"

She thought about it. "He's got blue eyes—he's German-looking in that way, blond hair, thinning a bit—he's self-conscious about it."

We were going east along Steglitzerdamm, crossing Bismarck; the pavements were shining under the drizzle. "What kind of nose?"

"I can't really say I've noticed."

"Pale skin? Red? A heavy face?"

"Oh no. Pale, and sort of soft."

"Mouth?" I kept on at her until I'd got all I could. It was going to be a situation where I could make a mistake if I weren't careful.

"Will he be coming by car, do you think, or by taxi?"

"I don't think he's got a car. If he leaves the city, he flies."

"I see. How far is it now?"

"We're almost there. The next block." Her elbow was resting on my thigh; I could feel its warmth. "Everything's all right, is it?"

"Of course. As I told you, we're just taking precautions. Don't worry. By this time tomorrow you'll be back in Reigate. Are your people there?"

"Mummy is. They're separated."

"You see your father much?"

Nervous smile. "I haven't seen him for ages. He's all right, I suppose, but he likes playing the patriarch. Mummy finally couldn't stand it." The taxi began slowing. "I'd like to see Gerda, before I leave Berlin, and some other friends." Her head was turned to watch me.

"I'd forget it for now. Wait till things have blown over. And please don't leave the hotel, or even phone anyone, unless you check with me first. Do that for me?"

In a moment, "Whatever you say."

"And I'm not being patriarchal."

A soft laugh—"I know."

"Café Brahms."

"*Danke.*"

I opened the door for her but stayed where I was. "I'll see you in a few minutes."

As she crossed the pavement her long fair hair caught the

light from the marquee; she didn't look back. I had a moment of doubt, which I'd expected, because she looked so alone as she opened the door of the café and vanished.

"Fahren Sie und lassen Sie mich an der Ecke aussteigen."

"Sehr gut."

I got out at the next corner and paid the driver and walked back toward the Café Brahms on the other side of the street and then crossed over, looking at the jade and ivory chess sets in the window of a store, putting in time. Hartman was a German and would be punctual, and that made it easier.

There were canopies over most of the stores here and I stayed under them; the rain hit their canvas with the sound of distant drums. People came by, some of them stopping to take shelter, looking along the street for a taxi. A police car slowed at the traffic lights and went through as they changed to green.

A BMW stopped at the curb and two people got out, going across the pavement and into the Café Brahms; the chauffeur drove away. A bus pulled in at the stop on the other side of the street, its massive tires hissing on the wet tarmac. A taxi drew in to the curb on this side and a man got out and paid the driver and turned across the pavement and I checked him against Helen's description and he matched it but I didn't move. I was working on the assumption that Hartman was under surveillance, just as Helen Maitland had been in Reigate; she was the widow of the dead man and Hartman had been his close friend. It made sense, and as the small black Mercedes slid to a stop behind the taxi and a man got out I started off and opened the heavy wooden door of the Café Brahms and let it swing shut behind me.

There was a tiny hallway and then stairs and I began going down them as the door opened again and I heard someone coming across the hall and then down the stairs behind me. A door marked *Damen* was on the right and a door marked *Herren* was just beyond it and then there were three telephones on the other side of the passage, and I stopped and turned and looked at the man and said in German: "You're to phone Dieter Klaus right away. Tell him that Hartman has just got here."

He said, "Very well. But who are you?"

There was no one else in the passage so I dropped him with a sword hand to the carotid artery and dragged him into the men's room and pulled out his wallet and searched him for weapons and left him propped in a cubicle.

Helen was three tables from the bar and Hartman had joined her and I went over there and said, "We're leaving here now and we'll take the rear exit, it'll be through that archway past the end of the bar, you first, Helen, then you, Hartman, and I'll be right behind, don't move too fast and don't attract attention but start *now*."

Helen threw me a glance and left the table but Hartman was slower.

"I don't understand. We—"

"There's a *Rote Armee Faktion* hit man in here and you are the target."

Not strictly true but the color left his face and he moved at once for the archway and I closed up. There was a man playing a violin and quite a few people dancing and I don't think anyone noticed us going out. It worried me a little that I'd got these two people on my hands because I knew now that they were going to need a lot of protection, but at least I had that man's wallet in my pocket and could send a signal to London later tonight: *Have made contact and gained access to the opposition.*

Chapter 6

Willi

*I*t was almost dark in here.

"Shall I check your coat?" Willi asked.

"I'll keep it on," Helen said. She was looking paler than usual; perhaps it was the lighting, or she hadn't realized it would be quite like this when she came back to Berlin; she'd thought there was just going to be a quiet talk with Willi. He was lighting a cigarette, black with a gold tip. His hands were quick, nervous.

"A *hit* man," he said. "How did you know?"

We hadn't talked much in the taxi on our way here; we'd been looking for somewhere quiet, and there aren't too many places like that in Berlin. "I'm not sure he was there in order to make a hit," I said. "He was just the type, that was all. He'd followed you there."

"But how do you *know*?"

"Willi, it's my job to know things like that. You've got to trust me."

He flicked his cigarette but there was no ash on it yet; it was just a nervous gesture.

"What happened to him? Where did he go?"

"He went into the men's room," I said, "with a bad headache. He didn't follow us here. I had to get you out of the Café Brahms because he'd been dropped off by a Mercedes, and that would have stayed in the area. They're waiting for you to come out of the Café Brahms and here you are in this

59

place and you're absolutely in the clear, so cheer up, all is well."

"Guten Abend. Was möchten Sie trinken?"

The girl stood looking down at us, holding her tray, pale and skinny and wearing a black satin slip, rouge and red lipstick and short bobbed hair: this place was called *Die Zwanziger*—The Twenties—and there were girls at the bar and dancing with some pale-looking men on the miniature spotlit stage. Some of them were flourishing long cigarette holders; the place was thick with smoke.

"Helen?"

Willi was attentive, considered himself the host.

"Oh, whatever you're having."

"Mr. Locke?"

"Tonic. My name's Victor."

"Zwei Schnäpse und ein Tonic."

I waited until the girl had left us. "Have you been here before, Willi?"

"No."

"Good. For a while, keep to unfamiliar places. Change your daily routine. Don't phone friends. Take a private mailbox at the post office. Watch for people you've seen before somewhere, in the street, in the shops. Take a good look at people who stand with you in a taxi rank or sit near you in a restaurant, so that you'll recognize them easily if you see them again. Just until things get themselves straightened out."

"But I have an apartment. Must I move?"

"I would just get the things you need from there, say for a week or two, and lock it. Are there security guards in the building?"

"Yes."

"Slip them something to look after things, the newspaper and deliveries."

"But if they were following me," he said, "they'll watch my apartment, won't they?"

"Yes."

"Then I can't go there to pick up my things."

"You can if I help you. It depends on how much you're ready to tell me."

He looked down. "About George Maitland, you mean."

"About why he was killed, who did it, where I can find them, things like that."

"Yes. But there are personal things."

"I don't need personal things."

Another girl came and stood looking down at us. She'd come through the black velvet curtains at the back of the little stage: her slip was white and diaphanous; her nipples were rouged, and thick black pubic hair showed under the silk. She smiled, the tip of her tongue between her teeth.

"Möchtest Du ein Spiel spielen?"

Would we like to play games?

No, Willi told her. Perhaps later. She went back through the curtains and he looked at Helen. "I'm sorry, I didn't know it was that kind of place. Shall we go somewhere else?"

"It doesn't matter. They won't bother us, will they?"

"No. I shall see that they don't." He turned to look at me. "So what can I tell you, Victor?"

"Do you think it was the *Faktion* that killed Maitland?"

"Yes."

"Why?"

"He was getting too interested in them."

"What started him off in that direction?"

He looked down for a moment. "I think perhaps I did."

"How?"

"It wasn't deliberate. I had a girlfriend, Inge Stoph. She was very attractive." To Helen—"You met her, several times. She—"

"Yes. I thought she was terribly good-looking."

Willi shrugged. "Thank you." To me—"But I found out she was involved with the *Rote Armee Faktion*. I was seeing quite a bit of George, at that time, and Helen, when she was over here from England. Just—parties and that sort of thing. Good friends. Good friends?"

"Of course, Willi." Her beautiful smile came. "Of course."

He drew in smoke. "I mentioned my girlfriend to George, just casually. I told him I thought she was too thick with those people."

The girl came with our drinks. *"Zwei Schnäpse, ein Tonic."* She left the tab.

I leaned forward. "What did George say about that?"

"He was interested, which surprised me."

"Interested," I said, "in the *Rote Armee Faktion.*"

"Yes. He began asking me questions about them. Then later I realized he was—how will we put it?—playing a kind of game with himself. He had a master plan, he told me once, about how to assassinate Muammar Qaddafi."

"A counterterrorist game, then? He fancied himself as an armchair counterterrorist?"

"I think, yes." Willi slipped another black cigarette from the pack. "George was a very . . . unusual man. Very intense."

"He carried a gun," Helen said.

"Always?"

"I don't know. I just saw it sometimes when he was taking off his jacket. It wasn't a very big one."

"But it's illegal," Willi said, "in Berlin."

I asked Helen, "Did he know you'd seen it?"

"Oh, yes. It didn't worry him. I think he was rather proud of it." She played with her glass of schnapps; she hadn't drunk any. "George was very intense, as Willi says. He had a lot of dynamic energy, a *lot* of energy, all the time." A faint smile—"It was a little wearing."

"But there was a lot more," Willi said, "under the surface. Don't you agree?" He flicked his gold lighter.

"It went down deep," Helen said. "It was rather attractive, in a way, when it didn't get too wearing. It was like being near—I don't know—a small power station."

"He was neurotic," Willi said with sudden force. "May I say that?"

"Oh, of course. Terribly so, terribly neurotic, yes. He fascinated me." She gave a short laugh, embarrassed.

Hate, and fascination. *I've only just realized,* she'd said in the hotel, *how much I hated him.*

"He was also very secretive," Willi said, "despite his energy. Sometimes he would be very quiet for a while, and"—his hand brushed the air—"and you didn't want to ask what he was thinking." He looked round for the waitress.

"I know that part of him," Helen said, "rather well. George hated being asked what he was thinking about. He'd shut you up at once, and go very cold. But then it's a silly thing to ask people, isn't it? It's an invitation to a lie."

I watched the man over there.

"I never knew," Willi said, "that he carried a gun. It surprises me."

The girl came to the table and he asked for another schnapps; Helen and I passed. The man had come in alone and was talking to someone near the stage. "Willi," I said, "did George ever meet your girlfriend, Inge?"

"Yes."

"Did he show any interest in infiltrating the *Faktion?*"

"Infiltrating . . ."

"In getting closer to them."

"He was—how will we put it?—like a moth at a flame. And I thought that was not good for him, as a member of the British embassy and everything. He had an official position, and I thought he might be in danger of—of compromising himself. So I stopped telling him anything about the *Faktion.*"

The man was asking for a girl, I saw now, and one of them slipped off the high stool at the bar and went across to him.

"You stopped telling George about the *Faktion,*" I said to Willi. "So what had you told him already?"

He drew on his cigarette immediately, looking down, squinting against the smoke. "Oh, various things. Things that Inge had told me." With a slight shrug—"I miss her, you know. She was . . . good-looking, yes. You have seen Mai Britt? She is—"

"Important things, Willi?"

"What?"

"Had you been telling George Maitland important things about the *Faktion?*"

Cigarette. In a moment, "I do not think so."

The girl was taking the man through the black velvet curtains. There was only the slightest chance in any case that we'd been followed here. I'd checked the environment with *extreme* care when we'd got into the cab outside the Café Brahms; the black Mercedes hadn't been in sight: not that one, with the three-pronged antenna on the trunk.

The waitress brought Willi's drink.

"*Schnaps,* darling."

"*Danke.*"

He raised his glass, and I nodded. Helen wasn't looking. She was watching the girls perched at the bar, their white spindly arms angled, hands on hips, their long legs reaching from their brief silk slips. Two of them had bruises on them. As Helen watched them she stroked her cheek against the soft lamb's-wool collar of her coat.

I leaned nearer Willi. "You see, I'll be glad to help you fetch your things from your flat, as I said, as long as you do your bit. What, for instance, was the *most* important thing you told Maitland about the *Rote Armee Faktion?*"

He shifted on his chair. "I stopped telling him anything at all," he said with a trace of impatience. "I even stopped seeing my girlfriend. I tried to wean her away from those people, but she was too involved. It excited her, you understand. So I stopped seeing her. It's all . . . finished with now." He brought his eyes back to mine at last, but it wasn't easy.

I spoke quietly. I didn't think Helen was listening anymore; she was watching the velvet curtains now, stroking her cheek against her collar. "Willi," I said, "I'm afraid it's not all finished with now. Since George was murdered, 'those people' mounted surveillance—put a watch on the house where our gentle friend here is living, and they put a watch on your flat, as you know, and when you left there tonight they had two men tracking you—at least two, possibly more. And you're now cut off from your home and your normal life and I have to tell you, Willi, that unless you earn my protection you may well follow your friend George Maitland in a matter of days, even a matter of hours. I would've thought this much would be clear to you, and I'm sorry to have to spell it out, but it could in fact save your life."

I sat back and drank some tonic; it was getting warm in this place, but that wasn't why there were drops of sweat forming on Willi's forehead. I glanced at Helen; she was still absorbed by the girls. One of them had noticed it, and was returning her gaze steadily, her long thin fingers playing with her cigarette holder.

I looked back at Willi. "It's getting late," I said. "I've come a long way to see you, and for your own sake I want it to be worthwhile."

"It is difficult," he said, and crushed his cigarette out in the black onyx bowl and took another one from the packet, his hands moving with the speed of a conjuror's, the sweat giving his forehead a sheen below the blond thinning hair. "Already I am being followed, and I have done very little. What will happen if I reveal things to you, and they find out?"

"They won't find out."

"But you cannot guarantee that." Flicking his lighter, his pale face bright suddenly, his eyes strained—"They may capture you."

"I've never talked yet."

"They are vicious," he said urgently, "those people. I know this."

"Of course. They're terrorists." I leaned close to him again across the little table. "You'll be much safer, Willi, if you trust me and let me help you, than if you walk out of here on your own tonight. Where can you go? I'm used to this kind of thing, Willi. It's my job, and I know how to handle it. For you it's very different. We're sitting here tonight talking about George Maitland. I don't want to be sitting with Helen somewhere in a couple of days' time, talking about Willi Hartman."

Pulling on his black cigarette, his hands on the move the whole time, his eyes darting everywhere, seeing nothing. I was sorry for him. He'd taken up with a very good-looking girl and suddenly he'd found himself on the fringe of a very nasty set and before he could pull out they were on to him. If I hadn't felt sorry for him I would have given him the message a lot less gently than I had—either talk or get out and duck when you hear the shots, so forth.

"The *Faktion*," he said at last, "has set up an operation, and they call it Nemesis." He'd got the message all right, and I began listening carefully. "The object of this operation is to place a bomb on board an international flight scheduled by one of the major U.S. airlines. I do not know which airline, or which flight."

Oh my God. In a moment I asked him, "Have they got a mule lined up?"

"I don't know. There is never any problem with that; they will be using a Semtex bomb, obviously, and they can persuade almost any passenger to take it on board concealed in a suitcase or something like that; it's what they did with Pan Am Flight 103; they just got a girl to take it on board with her." The sweat was bright on his forehead and he got out his handkerchief.

"You know more than that, Willi."

His eyes widened. "But I swear to you—"

"What's their timing for this? Were they—was Inge talking about days, weeks, when you last spoke to her?"

"She said nothing about—"

"You must have got an idea, Willi. Did it sound as if they were getting near the deadline? Did Inge sound excited about it?"

"Yes, yes, she did, but that was the way she always sounded when she talked about the *Faktion*. She—"

"But I'll bet she was as high as a kite about *this* one, Willi, I mean she wasn't talking about just another financier in a Mercedes, like Herrhausen, or just another judge in a restaurant, like Soderheim, she was talking about another Lockerbie, wasn't she, Willi? You'll find you can remember more than you think you do, so keep on trying."

If he was telling the truth, and if Inge hadn't been selling him a line to make herself look big I was going to have to send a signal to London tonight that I didn't want to, that I very much didn't want to. The ghost of Lockerbie had started walking again.

Willi was sitting with his eyes squeezed shut, pinching the bridge of his nose. "I remember Inge said something about waiting for a passenger list, a certain passenger list."

"With important people on it?"

"Yes, I think. She—"

"Or just one important person?"

"No." He looked up at me. "There was no name mentioned."

"Did she talk about a day operation, a night operation, the weather conditions—"

"I don't remember—"

"The plane's destination, the distance involved?"

"I don't remember," shaking his head all the time.

"She talk about warning a particular airline, a particular nation?"

"America. An American airline."

I gave it another ten minutes, another twenty or thirty questions, and got a little bit more but not much: this was Dieter Klaus's personal pride and joy, something he'd set his heart on, he had a lot of rage in him because they'd been making so many arrests within the *Faktion*, he needed a really important coup to reestablish the group as a major organization, things like that.

Willi got himself another schnapps and put it away in one go. "I'm glad," he said in a moment, "I'm very glad you obliged me to tell you about this, about Nemesis, and what they want to do. Perhaps you can stop them. That would be good. Very good."

"There's a chance."

A girl came through the velvet curtains and dropped a short black whip onto one of the little tables and laughed to someone, another girl at the bar, her lipstick bright and her teeth flashing. The man hadn't followed her out, the man who'd gone in there with her.

Then Helen said, "I think I'd like a drink now, Willi."

"Of course."

"Cognac." She pulled her coat closer as Willi looked round for the waitress. "Did George know all this, about Nemesis? Did you tell him?"

She'd been listening more than I'd thought.

"Yes. I told him." Tilting his head, "If I had known..."

"If we all knew the future, Willi. Don't have it on your mind." She turned to look at me. "Do you think you'll be able to do something to stop this awful thing from happening?"

"It'll be a question of how much time we've got."

"And it's so very difficult," Willi said. "I telephoned all the major U.S. airlines, do you know that? But they all said the same thing—thank you very much, we'll certainly take this seriously, but we get these threats every day, and we're operating with the best security we can."

"Was möchten Sie trinken, darling?"

Willi looked at me, but I shook my head.

"Ein Cognac."

When the girl had gone, Helen said, "They had people watching my *house*, do you know that, Willi? It's not only you."

"Then you must be careful."

"Yes. And Victor's looking after me."

"He came from East Germany," Willi said. "I've just remembered. Dieter Klaus. He came across just after unification. He's a rabid Communist, of course."

"Then he would have trained there." It wasn't anything new. When the East German secret police had started to do their laundry it had brought a whole army of villains into the open and running for cover.

"*Cognac Schwenker.*"

"*Danke.*"

Helen cupped her hands round the balloon glass. "Do you think he killed George, this man Dieter Klaus? I mean personally?"

"Does it make any difference?" Willi said. "Maybe we shouldn't be morbid."

"It'd be interesting to know," she said, "that's all." I think she shivered, under the thick coat.

I gave her time to finish the cognac.

"Willi," I said "can I do this?"

"No, thank you." He got the girl over. "We are going?"

"Yes. And I need your address." He hesitated, and I said, "They know it already. You're not giving anything away. And where do I find Inge?"

"She's moved. She's met someone else, and she lives with him. I don't know where."

I let it go. Perhaps he was trying to protect her, from a belated sense of chivalry. I'd find her anyway.

"Willi, we're going to leave here first, Helen and I. Then you wait five minutes and go outside and get a taxi. You'll be perfectly safe. Go and buy a toothbrush at an all-night pharmacy and then book in at one of the big hotels, make it the Ambassador or the Kempinski, take a room on the top floor and use room service for whatever you need." I wrote a number for him on the back of his receipt. "Call this number at ten tomorrow morning; be as punctual as you can. By that time I'll have arranged for you to go and take whatever you need from your flat. No one from the *Rote Armee Faktion* will see you there—*no one*, do you understand?"

There was fear in his eyes but he said, "Very well."

69

"Then do the other things I told you about, give the security guard a very good tip, then go and hole up somewhere quiet."

"For how long?"

"I can't tell you. Phone the security guard every week, in case I've left a message for you. And watch the newspapers. Now wait here for five minutes, and trust me: there'll be no trouble."

The rain had almost stopped when Helen and I went out to the street, and the air was cool and fresh after the smoke we'd been breathing. We walked half a block and crossed the street and came back on the far side and I saw Willi come out of *Die Zwanziger* and flag a taxi down and he was absolutely clear when it drove away. Then I found one for ourselves.

"Hotel Steglitz."

"*Jawohl.*"

She sat close to me again, Helen, huddled in her coat, the scent of the cognac on her breath. "Poor Willi," she said. "I think he feels responsible for what happened to George."

We turned into Birkbusch Strasse. The wet streets shimmered under the lights. "I think George was going to hell in his own handcart anyway, wasn't he?"

"That could be. He wanted so desperately to make an impression, on himself more than other people. He was quite a short man, did you know? Almost as short as Willi, but not quite. I think that was partly why he liked him—in Willi's company he looked a little taller, or thought he did." I felt her shiver against me. "It's suddenly begun to hit me, all this. In England the shock was distanced for me, but now I'm back here it's come into sort of close focus. And there's this terrible thing about what they're planning to do, those people."

Along Sedan Strasse the leaves were spilled across the pavement from the park, yellow and red and gold in the lamplight. I didn't say anything. I didn't think she wanted me to. I had something to ask her but it could wait.

70

"I have a friend," she said, "who lost her husband in the Lockerbie crash. I mean they loved each other; he wasn't just her husband. She cried for days. It was all that stuff in the papers, all the beastly details they love to put in, bodies strewn all over the place. She still doesn't read a paper; she canceled it." In a moment, "Is there something you can do to stop those people?"

She'd asked me that before. I said I could only try. And then I asked her, "Who was the man in the nightclub?"

I was watching her reflection in the glass of the division. She looked at me and then away. "What man?"

"The one you recognized. The one who recognized you."

"Oh," with a soft laugh. She hadn't hesitated, or at least not for very long. "It was rather embarrassing. He was just someone I knew, a friend of George's at the embassy. I met him a few times at parties."

A BMW cut across our bows, swung in too soon, and our driver got the window down and shouted something, *Schweinhund*, I think. "What is his name?"

Helen turned her head against my shoulder. "Kurt. He's—"

"What's his surname?"

"Oh. Muller, I think. I'm not sure. I mean it was embarrassing because neither of us expected to see the other one in a place like that."

I let it go. We'd come away absolutely clean from the nightclub. The taxi turned east along Steglitzerdamm and I said, "You'll be home by this time tomorrow, and you can leave Berlin behind."

In a moment she said, "You still don't want me to see Gerda, or any of my friends?"

"No. It'd be too dangerous."

She shivered again but I wasn't sorry I'd said it; she had to get the message: she was too exposed here, and I wanted to think of her safely back in Reigate taking Billy for long walks, kicking up the leaves.

Things had moved very fast since I'd got here: only this

morning Holmes had said there was no actual mission on the board and already we had *Solitaire* running and I'd got access to the opposition and there was something much bigger on my mind than making a private kill in the name of McCane. At some time tomorrow, unless we could stop it, tomorrow or the next day, anytime at all, there'd be a flight taking off with three or four hundred people on board and it was going to make a sunburst in the sky.

Chapter 7

Samala

*I*t was gone midnight when we got back to the hotel and I saw Helen up to her room.

She was still shivering, and her face was haunted as she looked at me in the low light of the corridor, her thin hands holding the fleece collar of her coat pressed against her cheeks.

"Do you want to come in for a little while?"

I said, "No. You need sleep."

"Just for a few minutes." She leaned her head against me and I held her until the shivering stopped.

"I've got to make some calls."

In a moment she said, "I'm cold, and a bit frightened, that's all. I thought it would be all right to come back to Berlin, but it wasn't, because this is where that beastly thing happened."

The plastic key was clutched in her hand and I pulled it gently from between her fingers and put it into the slot and opened the door. "Didn't you bring any gloves?"

"I forgot them. I'm always forgetting them."

"Phone room service," I said, "for some hot milk, Horlicks if they've got it. Not alcohol, no more brandy." I gave her a final hug. "And call me if you really can't cope."

Going down in the lift I felt a touch of anger. We shouldn't have brought her to Berlin; she was so bloody *young* for all this, not so much in years but in her mind; she wasn't much more than a schoolgirl, got at by the men in her life, by her

73

father, by George Maitland, perhaps by others, until the personality that had been trying to grow had been crushed and thrown away.

Whatever you say.

In my room I called London and found Matthews at the signals board and asked him to get the tape running.

"Are you debriefing?"

"Yes."

Through the window the floodlit spire of St. Johan's stood against the hazy dark; one or two pigeons were still awake, dipping from a parapet and circling and going back, their shadows flitting across the stone.

"All right," Matthews said at last, "we're running."

I wondered what had taken him so long; all you've got to do is push a button on the console. He could have been helping out at one of the other boards, some kind of panic going on.

"Executive debriefing," I said, "00.12 hours, Berlin time, November 7. The subject has been questioned and this is the main content. The Red Army Faction is planning an operation code-named Nemesis, repeat Nemesis, under the direction of a former East German national, Dieter Klaus—will you run a dossier on him for me? You might be able to pick him up from what's left of the Stasi files, maybe get some help from *Grenzschutzgruppe-9*." London would have to notify GSG-9 in any case; they were the official German counterterrorist organization, and if they hadn't got wind of Nemesis and the bomb threat we'd certainly have to brief them.

"The object of the Klaus operation," I said, "is to put a bomb on board a U.S. airliner." I filled it in for them, told them everything that Willi Hartman had given me plus several assumptions, because he'd told me a lot more than he actually knew. It's always like that: you learn to fit bits and pieces of information into the overall picture, stuff that nobody tells us but we know must be there, the way the astronomers discover dark stars. "I have a feeling," I said, "that Klaus might not actually be running the Red Army Faction as such, although that's what I was told. I think that Nemesis could be the code name not for an operation but for a group he's formed, a separate cell, possibly taking some of the Faction people with him. I don't think he's the kind of man who'd take over a third-generation outfit that hasn't done much lately. But this is just my feeling."

There was a police car down there, wailing through the streets; I could see its colored lights reflected in the windows below.

"End of debriefing," I said into the phone. "Questions?"

"You want this to go to Mr. Shatner right away?"

"To Mr. Shatner, Chief of Signals, and Bureau One. They may want to alert the major U.S. airlines: they'll make a bigger impression than the subject over here. They'll also want to keep a close watch on passenger lists for a heavy contingent of VIPs or a single prominent diplomat or financier or army general, someone like that. What we've got to think about is how to protect every next flight of a U.S. airliner taking off from Berlin."

Shatner would alert the U.S. embassy in London in any case and trigger a CIA response in Berlin, long before daylight.

"I've got that," Matthews said. "What else?"

"How soon can you get my DIF here?"

"He's booked out on the noon plane, British Airways."

"Get him here sooner than that. Put him on the first plane in the morning, I don't care which airline. I've made contact with the opposition and I've got access and I need a director. I want him to see the Reigate subject out of Berlin as soon as possible, but she must not, repeat *not* take a U.S. plane. When do I get my briefing on the arms-dealer scene?" Shatner had told me he'd set it up for me, bring me up-to-date.

"I'll call you back on that. How soon do you want it done?"

"As soon as you can make it, because now that I've got

access to Nemesis I'm going right in to the center and it's going to be very tricky and if I'm not fully briefed I could blow my cover."

"Priority," Matthews said.

"Yes." I thought I could hear Croder's voice in the background. Yes, there was some kind of panic going on, or Croder wouldn't be in the Signals room at this hour.

"How's *Stingray?*" I asked Matthews. I wasn't on the tape anymore: I'd finished the actual debriefing a few minutes ago. They'd been having a problem with that one when I'd looked in at Signals this morning; the shadow had got himself holed up in a trap in Thailand.

"Not all that good," Matthews said. "He shut down on us."

The trap must have closed, and I felt a chill along the nerves.

"Mr. Croder's looking after things?"

"Yes."

In a moment I said, "All right, that's all from here. Just—"

"Control," someone said, and I recognized Shatner's voice. "Look, I was listening to your signal, and what I'm going to do is get the RAF to fly your director into the German Air Force base at Werneuchen as soon as I can get the right people out of bed, because no one can go into Tempelhof until morning, because of night-flying regulations. Then we'll ask them to send him into Tempelhof by helicopter, and with any luck he'll be on the ground by something like 04:00 hours, which is going to be much sooner than if we waited to use an airline. Will that suit your purposes?"

"Very well."

"There shouldn't be any problem because we'll do it through Bonn at Foreign Secretary level. I haven't heard the whole tape but it sounds rather encouraging: you've got access, I believe."

"Yes."

"Well done. Anything else I can do for you?"

I told him there was nothing else and he gave the mike back to Matthews and we wound up the signal and I pressed the contact and dialed the first number on the list of local support people they'd given me this morning before I left. There were five on the night shift, ten on the day. The name of this one was Horne.

There were only two rings, and I liked that.

"Wer spricht, bitte?"

"Solitaire."

"Blackjack."

"Executive," I said. "I need a car. What have you got?"

"I've got an Audi GT, couple of Mercs. You need something fast?"

"No." By fast he meant a Lamborghini. "Black, low profile."

"Need a phone?"

"Yes."

"You'd better take the Audi, then."

"All right." I had one of the maps on the bed, and the wallet I'd taken from the man in the Café Brahms. "Make it 04:00 today at the T-section of Einstein Ufer and Abbe Strasse, by the canal. Can you do that?"

"Oh yes."

"I'll be in a taxi. Have you seen me before?"

"No, sir."

"One glove on, one off."

"Got it. But why don't I bring the car to you, if—"

"Because I don't want you to." He wasn't too seasoned, and it worried me. If I'd wanted him to bring the car here I would have asked him, and he should have known that. "What's the number of the Audi?" He gave it to me and I said, "You can take over the taxi, all right? Now listen, who's your senior man?"

"Kleiber."

"Is he there?"

"I'll get him. I just meant—you know—that if you wanted the car there, I would have—"

77

"I appreciate it."

Sat on the bed while I waited. It was going to be good to get some sleep: I'd only had three hours in the last forty. After that I'd need food, find an all-night hamburger stand. There might be—

"Kleiber."

I switched to German. "You know the city?"

"I was born here."

"There's a man named Willi Hartman. Here's his address."

"Got that."

"There'll be some surveillance on the building, possibly more than one man. Hartman will phone your number at 10:00 today. I want you to take care of the surveillance while Hartman goes into his apartment and fetches some things. Tell him he's got thirty minutes. How many people can you use for this?"

"Six, seven."

"It shouldn't take more than three. When Hartman leaves the building I want him tracked, to make sure he gets absolutely clear. I also want to know where he goes and what he does: put him under surveillance for the next twenty-four hours. I've guaranteed him total protection, so make sure no one slips up."

"I understand."

Her scent was on me, Helen's; I kept catching a hint of it when I moved. "I want you to keep a complete record of anyone he meets—get their names. Watch especially for a woman named Inge, described as very attractive."

"I understand."

"Report to the DIF if you feel it's important. I'm taking the Audi and you know the phone number. As soon as I know which room the DIF will be in at the Hotel Steglitz I'll call you. He should arrive in Berlin early this morning. Questions?"

"You want me to report to you, too?"

"No. Only the DIF." He'd screen information for me; that was what he was for; I didn't want to use the phone in the

Audi more than I had to: there could be some tricky driving to do. "Anything else?"

"Nothing."

"Use discreet force if you have to, but I don't want any drama."

"I understand."

It was 12:32 by the TV clock when I rang off, and while I got ready for bed I went over the whole setup and couldn't find anything else that needed doing, but it was a little while before I could sleep. The *Stingray* thing was on my mind, even though it was someone else's mission and nothing to do with me, but then it's like that: no man is an island, so forth, and when the bell tolls for some poor bastard out there with his karma running hot it tolls for all of us. Other thoughts drifted into my head, some things she'd said, Helen, because her scent was still on my coat, things she'd said in the taxi, *Those girls, in the club . . . do you think they were attractive?* Touch anorexic, I think I'd said. And Matthews, at the board for *Solitaire*, it'd been two or three seconds before he'd switched the tape on, was he always going to be slow?

Do you think I'm attractive? I suppose that's the very last thing a woman should ask a man, isn't it? . . . As a matter of fact, I used to be anorexic, once, like those girls in the club, but I got over it.

That man Horne, and the thing about bringing the car here . . . if the shadow executive makes a precise rendezvous ten kilometers away it surely means he does *not* want to be met at his hotel . . . I'd better report it to the DIF, because I wanted totally seasoned people in the field for this one, there were lives in hazard, too many lives . . .

I expect you think I'm just fishing for compliments, but then I am, I suppose . . . it's this awful self-image I'm saddled with . . . it's why I let George do the things he did with me. . . .

How's Stingray?

Not all that good. . . . He shut down on us. . . .

For whom the bell . . . the bell tolling as the dark came down and her scent followed me through the delta waves.

* * *

04:00 and the streets still wet, with fog drifting from the canal and the diesel knocking as the taxi pulled up and I gave the driver twice the fare and told him to wait.

Horne met me on foot—at least he knew that much—and took me round the corner into Abbe Strasse and gave me the keys.

"Recent service, full tank, phone's already switched on, is that all right?"

"Tires?"

"Forty all round." He was a short man in a duffle coat and a woolen hat, his breath clouding on the air. "Normal's thirty-five, I thought you'd like—"

"Yes. Spare keys?"

We'd had a case where the shadow had been tracked back to his car and it was locked and he'd lost the keys and had to smash the window to get in and it had taken him too long and they'd found him reaching inside to unlock the door and taken every vertebra out of his spine with a 9mm Uzi carbine and it went straight into the book at Norfolk: *The importance of providing spare keys.*

"They're under the front bumper, nearside."

I shouldn't have had to ask: he should have told me right away.

"How long have you been working in the field?"

He almost flinched. "Two days, sir."

"When did you graduate?"

"Three days ago."

Oh *Jesus*, those bloody people were out of their minds.

"Then you're doing well," I told him, and got into the Audi and started up and took it as far as the next T-section and turned away from the canal and doubled back and found a bit of wasteground with a few cars and a rubbish dump on it and pulled in between a van and a broken-down pickup truck with a smashed window and the front bumper hanging off. The house was five or six hundred yards distant, the house where Sorgenicht lived: that was the name on the papers in the wallet I'd taken from him, August Sorgenicht.

I'd swung wide at the T-section to let the headlights play across the entrance and pick up the number. The house was at the end of a row, and I could sight it from here between the buildings at the end of the short deserted street. At this angle I could see two of its walls, five of its windows. The windows were dark.

The inside of the Audi smelled of stale smoke and I ran the driving window down and pulled out the ashtray and emptied it. The air was cold and very still. Traffic was moving on the far side of the canal but the wall deadened its sound: for the next three hours I'd be able to hear things clearly in the environment.

I picked up the phone and got the signals board in London direct and gave Matthews my exact position and asked him to inform Kleiber, chief of support here in Berlin. "I'll be in the car for the next few hours," I told him, "and this is the number." I waited until he'd repeated it. This would have been going through my director in the field if I'd had one, and we were wasting a lot of time. "Give my number to the DIF as soon as you can. Where is he now?"

I heard the pitch of his voice alter a fraction as he raised his head to look up at the board. "He landed at Werneuchen Air Force Base at 03:51 local time and left there in a military helicopter at 03:59, so he'll still be airborne. His ETA Berlin is 04:07, a minute from now."

I felt a certain degree of relief. You can sometimes push a lot of the way through a mission on your own if it's low key and there's no hurry, but with this one the deadline was any next flight of a U.S. airliner and the first one of the day was due for takeoff in three hours from now, destination New York via London, I'd checked the schedules in the paper.

"You've put him into the Steglitz?" I asked Matthews.

"Yes."

"Room?"

"510."

On the same floor as Helen Maitland. I felt reassured. "Ask him to phone me as soon as he can."

"Will do."

"Is Control at the board?" Shatner.

"I think he's resting up, but he's in the building. You want me to—"

"No, but listen. Norfolk's sent a support man out here, name of Horne, with absolutely no experience in the field— he's just graduated. He's quite good but he shouldn't be working on a major mission for at least twelve months and they should know that." The sound of a vehicle was coming into the environment, some kind of truck. "This isn't a complaint, as far as he's concerned, it's not his fault, but for God's sake tell Norfolk to watch what they're bloody well doing, they can get people killed like that."

In a moment Matthews said, "This is to go on record?"

"You're dead right. It's for COT Norfolk, Control, COS, and Bureau One."

Chief of Training Norfolk, Shatner, Chief of Signals, and the head of the entire Bureau, host of hosts. Life's cheap in this trade and on our way through the labyrinth of a mission there's often a dead spook left behind in the shadows when it's all over but with *Solitaire* we'd got civilian lives to look after, hundreds of them, and if any one of us made a mistake somewhere along the line then yes indeed, it should go on record.

"I'll see to it," Matthews said, and I shut down and watched the flood of light sweeping across the front of the houses over there as the banging began, garbage truck.

The ashtray still stank so I pulled it away from the dashboard and threw it out of the window. There hadn't been time to eat anything because sleep had been more important, so I was having to take the stink of someone's nicotine fix on an empty stomach.

Bang of the garbage truck—I could see it now, a humped silhouette against the wall that ran the length of the canal.

04:51 on the digital clock.

I was feeling all right at this time, the nerves quiet. They'd start tightening up a bit before long because of what we had to do, but for the moment I felt relaxed, the smell of the hotel's sandalwood soap on my skin; I'd had some sleep and I was clean, and when you feel clean you feel in control again, as I'm sure you've noticed.

At 05:03 faint light began flooding from somewhere behind, and I tilted the mirror and waited, watching the things the light began picking up in the environment as it brightened: a parked baker's van, three bicycles chained together, one with a pedal missing, a wrecked brass bedstead leaning against a shed. Then a black VW came onto the wasteground and made a U-turn and swept its lights across me and straightened up and stopped not far away and the headlamps went off and I watched the man get out, watched him carefully.

He walked slowly across the littered ground, a short fat man, his arms hanging at his sides and held a little way out from his body, the posture recognizably harmless, and when he reached the Audi I ran the window down on the passenger's side.

"*Solitaire*," he said, his face dark, bearded, smiling sweetly as he peered into the car. I could see him better than he could see me, because of the streetlights over there. "Ahmad Samala," he said, garlic on his breath.

I answered the parole. "I'm sorry they got you up so early, Mr. Samala."

"It is of no importance. Here is what you want."

I reached for the cassette, still watching him, not looking at the cassette, because if anyone is going to do anything inconvenient you see it coming in their eyes first, before their hands move. I was virtually sure of him, because the Bureau doesn't often send the wrong people to a night rendezvous with the executive, but in this trade you can't take anything on trust: look what those clods at Norfolk had done.

"Thank you," I said, and put the cassette on the ledge below the windscreen.

"I would have liked to talk to you about it all," Samala said, "but they told me this way was better." He sounded infinitely sad.

He'd wanted, I suppose, to go through the whole thing with me, enjoying the role of tutor, bringing his sweet smile to bear upon the business of trading a consignment of Heckler and Koch HK91s for a dozen bags of cocaine on the dockside in Istanbul, or of buying Semtex by the square yard without blowing up the freighter. It would have been amusing to hole up with him for an hour or two in some kind of safe house; he was obviously an interesting man. I have been bathed in smiles as sweet as his before, sometimes over the muzzle of a gun.

"Perhaps we can meet again," I said, "when it's more convenient."

"I would enjoy that." He offered his hand, not knowing any better, and I broke every rule in the book and shook it politely. "Now I am going back to bed," he said, and backed away and went over to the VW and squeezed himself into it. He made a U-turn again, this time with his lights off.

London had done well: it had been 12:00 this morning when I'd called Signals to debrief and ask for an update on the arms-dealing scene to secure my cover, and they must have got on to Samala in Berlin not long afterward and asked him to get it onto a cassette for me, and then they'd had to phone him soon after 04:10 to give him my precise location for the rendezvous. Even without my DIF in the field, signals and support services were running efficiently, and it calmed the nerves.

The windows of the house beyond the end of the street were still dark. One of them, or more than one of them, would show a light when August Sorgenicht got up and began his day. Then I would move in a bit closer.

Calmed the nerves, but only a little: they were starting to tighten now as the minutes went by, because the opposition knew what had happened to him at the bottom of the flight of stairs at the Café Brahms last night. It had looked like a simple mugging, with the wallet gone; I hadn't taken his keys because he would have had all his locks changed right away, and in any case it would have been less interesting to look around his house than to track him to whatever contacts he would make during the day, because one of them could lead me to Nemesis, right to the center. When I'd signaled London that I'd secured access, this is what I had meant.

But Nemesis would know it hadn't been a simple mugging, because Sorgenicht would have told them what I'd said to him: *You're to phone Dieter Klaus right away. Tell him that Hartman has just got here.* He'd assumed I was one of them, a new recruit he hadn't seen before, but when he'd come to in the men's room he had known better.

The five distant windows were still dark. Traffic on the far side of the canal was on the move now as the city's longitude swung toward morning.

He would have known better, yes, Sorgenicht, he would have known that the opposition cell from London had now got his address, and this was why the nerves were starting to tighten a little as the minutes went by, because Dieter Klaus was a professional and he wouldn't leave me free to track Sorgenicht through the city today. It had been good news for London that I had access to Nemesis. The bad news was that when I began tracking Sorgenicht, Nemesis would have access to me.

Chapter 8

Krenz

Despite the proliferation of sources of supply, mainland China still remains important, and I would place it about eighth on the list of the major world suppliers.

05:43.

The five windows in the house over there were still dark. August Sorgenicht was not an early riser.

You should know that there are still over 200,000 Soviet troops stationed in former East Germany waiting to be sent home, and many of them are busy pilfering their arsenals and selling whatever they can get hold of to whoever will buy it.

A sweet smile: you could hear it in his voice. Mr. Samala was showing me over his toyshop. I kept the volume low, barely audible, because I needed to hear sounds from the greater environment. Both windows were down.

Bang of a metal can somewhere, bringing a frisson along the nerves. There was a dog, I thought, rooting among the rubbish that had dropped from the truck along the edge of the wasteground.

I am speaking of AK-47 assault rifles, antitank weaponry, small arms, and mines. The Red Army Faction is known to have purchased a consignment of bombs and grenades. Another development in—

The phone was ringing and I picked it up and shut off the tape.

"Hallo?"

"DIF."

Thrower.

I've called in Thrower from Pakistan, Shatner had told me, *to direct you in the field. I think you'll like his style.*

I gave him *Blackjack.*

"What can I do for you?" he asked me.

"Get Helen Maitland back to the UK."

In a moment he said, "Of course. I was told you're concerned about her."

"She's at risk. Just get her home." Perhaps the implication wasn't really there—that for some reason I shouldn't be concerned. I'd been the only one in the field until now, the only one who knew the risk she was running. I didn't want it disputed.

"Of course," he said again. I didn't want humoring either. "I've got the ticket for her in my pocket, according to your request to Control."

"What airline?"

"Alitalia is the first flight out."

"What time?"

"09:34."

Faint light began flooding from behind the Audi.

"I want her escorted onto the plane."

"Of course, since you say she's at risk. I've laid that on."

His tone was soft, a degree smooth. He didn't sound like an experienced director in the field; he sounded like a lawyer.

"That's all I need," I told him.

The light was spreading across the wasteground; then it vanished.

"What is your situation?"

"I'll have to call you back," I told him, and shut down.

The light hadn't been switched off: it had moved behind the buildings. I heard a car turning and stopping. This time the lights were cut dead.

I waited two minutes, three. No one got out of the car. It was in the next street, facing the house where Sorgenicht lived: the lights had been shining in that direction.

Five. Five minutes. No one got out of the car: I would have heard the door slam.

So I took the cassette out of the slot and slipped it into my pocket and got out of the Audi and left the door open and walked across the wasteground to the street at the top and turned right and kept on going and then turned right again, and right again, coming back on the street where the car had pulled up and cut its lights. It was cold, outside the Audi. I felt very cold.

He was there, sitting in the car, in the black Mercedes 300E, sitting at the wheel. He wasn't reading anything; there was no light inside the car. His face was pale, square-looking in the light from the distant street lamps. His head was against the padded rest; I couldn't see where his hands were; they weren't on the steering wheel. He was watching the house, the house where Sorgenicht lived. It's always dangerous to assume things on simple appearances, but this man's aspect and behavior were a model of the archetypal surveillant, and I decided to go to work accordingly.

He was here, then, as I had expected, not to watch the house, but to watch for anyone who set out to track Sorgenicht when he left there. He would then keep station in the traffic stream and use his phone and call in mobile support to cut off Sorgenicht's tracker and deal with him, as they had dealt with George Maitland, and soon afterward, McCane. That was what this man was doing here: he was watching, in effect, for me.

There was deep shadow where I stood, at the end of an alleyway joining the two adjacent streets. I was perhaps fifty feet from him, but if he turned his head he wouldn't see me. He was a quiet man, well in control of himself; he didn't fidget; he'd got up early but he didn't yawn. He wasn't smoking. He hadn't got the radio on: I would have heard it. He was a good surveillant, first-class, the kind they try to turn out of Norfolk when they're thinking straight. If I hadn't seen him here, and began tracking Sorgenicht, this man in his Mercedes would become the equivalent of a shark fin in the water, and I would be the swimmer.

I leaned my head back to rub the nape of my neck against

the rough collar of my coat to ease the chill of the nerves. He wasn't a young man—I would have said close to fifty; but his head was square and massive and he was thick in the shoulder. He would not, then, be very fast, but quite strong—even, if he were trained, dangerously strong. But soon it would be getting light and there would be people about, and I didn't want to attract attention. It could also be that Sorgenicht would leave his house before dawn, though the windows were still dark. I had better do what I had to do as soon as I could.

There were soft echoes from the brick walls in the alleyway and I stepped lightly and broke the rhythm, because the regularity of footsteps is extraordinarily perceptible, the brain stem recognizing the sound of another animal in the environment. I turned right when I reached the street, and right again at the T-section, and as I turned I saw a light come on in a window of the house, on the second floor. It wasn't necessarily Sorgenicht getting up: it could be his wife or his girlfriend or someone else there; but I would have to assume it was Sorgenicht himself. His car would be one of those parked in a line along the wall by the canal: there were no garages here.

I turned again and began walking up the street where the Mercedes was standing. The distance from here was a hundred yards or so, and it was facing me. I didn't walk quietly anymore; I walked quite fast toward the Mercedes, because I'd overslept and was late and had to hurry. I blew into my hands: it was a cold raw morning and I didn't relish it. There was another dog over there toward the wasteground, or perhaps the one I'd seen before, scratching for scraps among some rubbish; I gave it a whistle—I was fond of dogs. My breath clouded in front of me as I passed under a street lamp, and I blew into my hands again, quickening my step; but there was a big notice in the window of an ironmonger's shop and I slowed for a moment, reading it as I went by: there was a sale on, with a 20 percent discount on tools, well worth remembering. I noticed the Mercedes but paid no attention; you see cars parked everywhere.

I looked at my watch, then dug my hands into my coat pockets again, leaning forward a little, my head down as I breasted my way into the rat race of another workaday morning. The Mercedes was quite close now and I gave it another glance, and it was then that I noticed something wrong. I stopped when I reached the car, and tapped on the window, pointing.

The man inside swung his massive head and looked at me, taking his time. I pointed to the rear of the car again, and he opened the door. "You've got a flat tire," I told him, and would have walked on, but he had a gun in his right hand and his finger was in the trigger guard and it was pointing at me. I was alarmed. "No—please don't shoot," backing away, my hands spreading open, "I just wanted to tell you the tire was flat—please don't shoot me!"

He watched me with a dead stare. It hadn't looked good enough, then, natural enough, whistling to the dog and reading the sale notice, not a good enough act, too late to clean it up now, just kept my hands raised, fingers open, and then he moved.

The front tire wouldn't have worked, because I'd had to assume he was right-handed: the chances of that were very high. So it had to be the rear tire, and as he leaned out of the car to look at it he kept the gun trained on me and the nearest part of his body was his gun hand and I had something like two seconds while he looked at the tire and I used enough force to paralyze the arm through the median nerve and deaden the trigger finger because if I'd used more it would have caused a great deal of pain and I didn't want him vomiting, I can't stand that. It was a sword-hand strike and its force brought the top part of his body down and left his neck exposed and I used the left hand before he could do anything and he sagged suddenly and I caught the Mauser before it could hit the pavement.

There was no one in the street so I snapped the doorlocks open and pulled him out and dragged him round to the passenger's side and got the door open and heaved him into the car and sat him with his head back against the rest and his hands on his lap. They were cold to the touch and his face had lost color but I didn't think I'd overdone the strike to the occipital area: you're not going to kill anyone there unless you use enough force to break into the skull or snap the vertebrae: he'd be out for a while, that was all, and I used the ignition keys and got some jump cables from the boot—I was hoping for some rope but there wasn't any. I lashed his wrists to his legs and shut the door and went round and got behind the wheel and saw two more lights come on in the house down there, one of them on the ground floor: I was worried now because it was possible I'd missed something—Sorgenicht's bedroom and bathroom could be at the back of the house and I wouldn't have seen the windows light up; it could have happened half an hour ago, an hour; he could be close to leaving.

I picked up the phone and touched the numbers.

It was very quiet inside the car, but I couldn't hear the man's breathing; that would be normal: I'd pushed his blood pressure right down and his brain had shifted into a mode that in certain creatures would be hibernative. I reached for his throat and found the pulse slow but still there. That too was normal. He was—

"*Bitte?*"

"*Solitaire.*"

"*Blackjack.*"

"How soon," I asked Thrower, "can you get support here? Only need one man."

"Same location?"

"Close. The next street to the west of the wasteground."

"I'll contact Kleiber and take it from there. I'd say thirty minutes if they're coming from his place."

The light in one of the windows had gone out.

"All right. But I might have to be mobile before then."

"We can tail you."

"Yes." I told him the car I was in now, gave him the

number. "Relay that to the support, will you, and get someone to pick up the Audi that Horne delivered to me. It's in
the wasteground and the keys are in the ignition."

"Shall be done."

"I'll keep in touch." I put the phone back. Thirty minutes
was going to be too long by the look of things but there was
nothing I could do about it: I could have called in a whole
support unit, five or six people, when I'd first come here,
but it wasn't a red sector and I didn't want a lot of movement
going on.

I checked the man beside me. His pulse was still slow and
there was a sheen of sweat on his face. His eyelids were
parted slightly and I could see the glint of the conjunctiva.
I found his wallet and checked one of his credit cards, a
Berliner Bank Visa. His name was Stefan Krenz. His business
card said he was an electronics engineer, but that could be
his cover: an electronics engineer would be wasting his time
working as a tracker dog. I made a note of his address and
put the wallet back.

This was at 06:11, and three minutes later I saw the front
door of Sorgenicht's house open and a figure show up against
the light inside. I had the engine running by the time he'd
shut the door and I was rolling the Mercedes with the headlights on as he walked out of sight beyond the building at
the end of the street. When I reached the corner he was fifty
feet away and still walking but now he was digging into his
pocket and as I closed the distance he found his keys and
stopped by a dark blue Volvo 242 and glanced up when I
went past but my lights would have dazzled him and he
didn't take any notice: in the mirror I saw him getting into
the Volvo and slamming the door. I made four fast turns and
found him a block ahead of me going west along Einstein
Ufer.

I'd recognized him and that was the main thing but we'd
got problems now because this man Krenz was in the car
with me and he'd surface before long and try to give trouble.
It would have been no good putting him in the trunk of the

car because at any time Sorgenicht could park the Volvo and I'd have to follow him on foot: I was after contacts, people he'd be talking to, and I wouldn't find them unless I kept close, and if I left this man in the trunk he'd come to and start yelling and banging and someone would let him out and he'd get straight on the phone and give his location and there'd be a swarm of Nemesis agents moving into the area before I'd had time to get results.

But I couldn't leave him sitting here on the front seat either.

I picked up the phone and got Thrower.

"Where's my support coming from?"

"Kleistpark."

"Then it's not going to work. I'm mobile now and I need someone right away."

"Where are you?"

"Moving southwest in Cauer Strasse."

"You don't know your destination?"

"No."

"I'll get back to you," he said and we shut down.

I could have given him a lot more information but it wasn't necessary because when the shadow asks his DIF to do something for him right away it's understood that he doesn't want to delay things by protracting the signal. We don't chat when we're tracking.

Traffic lights came up and I stopped between a VW and a delivery van. I wasn't happy about the van because the cab was high and the driver could look down into the Mercedes and might notice the jump cables round Krenz's wrists. I angled my head and watched the driver's face but he was looking in front of him at the long blond hair in the BMW.

"Krenz," I said in German, "how are you feeling?"

He didn't answer, so I slotted the cassette in and turned the radio on.

As an example of how very dangerous the present-day arms market is becoming, rumors have been circulating well below media level that the U.S. Army has either miscounted its stockpile of tactical nuclear missiles or has had one stolen from an unnamed military base. *The weapon is said to be the NK-9 Miniver, a missile capable of being launched by one designated officer of high rank in the field at his personal discretion. The NK-9 has the capacity to knock out an entire division. If these rumors have any substance—*

The phone was ringing and I picked it up and touched for receive.

"DIF."

"Hear you."

"Location?"

I gave it to him.

"Then we're doing better: I've got someone starting out from the Siemensdamm U-Bahn area, not far from you. His name is Roach and he's in a black SAAB with Frankfurt plates." He gave me their number and the number of the phone. "You can call him direct at this stage."

I said I'd do that.

"*Wasser.*"

Krenz.

"Shut up," I told him, and got on to the support man, Roach. The line was scratchy but his voice was clear enough. I told him where I was and he said he'd try to intercept me somewhere near the autobahn.

"*Wasser!*"

Krenz, thirsty, not surprising, and fidgeting with the jump cables. "Shut up and sit still," I told him in German, "or I'll blow the brains out of your bloody head." On the phone I told Roach: "The situation is that I'm tracking someone and I've got a prisoner on board and what I want you to do is take him over when there's a chance and put him underground somewhere for the duration. Check with the DIF and ask for his instructions. His name is Stefan Krenz. You'll also take over his gun. Questions?"

"Is he for interrogation, sir?"

"Ask the DIF."

We sometimes take prisoners during a mission but it's usually forced on us as the only alternative to the extreme sanction thing, and we do it when they've got enough information about us to cause damage if we let them go, and this man knew enough about me to bring me down.

"Do you know what I'm driving?" Roach asked me.

"Yes."

"Where are you now?"

"Northbound in Tegelerweg, just going under the S-Bahn and coming up on the autobahn."

"Ten minutes, then."

Sorgenicht was three vehicles ahead of me in the same lane. He didn't know he was being tracked. If he'd suspected it he would have put the Volvo through a series of turns to find out. He hadn't done that.

The lights of a train crossed the morning sky as we passed under the S-Bahn. It was between there and the autobahn that Krenz heaved his weight off the passenger seat and hurled it against me and I took it on the right shoulder and the car swerved and I got it straight in time but the Lexus on our left had swerved too and the driver hit the brakes and shouted something. We were in a traffic flow of something like thirty miles an hour and I was in the middle lane and couldn't pull over and stop. Krenz had bounced back onto the seat and now he was coming at me again, hands still tied to his thighs but with his massive head free to smash against mine if he could get it right, so I swung a backfist to his forehead to stun the pineal gland and he lurched back onto the seat and sat with his bulk against the passenger door, shaking his head like a boxer on the ropes, animal sounds coming from him, not quite words, I think, but just grunts of rage, and I left him like that and touched the numbers for Roach and spoke through the remote microphone.

"Still in Tegelerweg, approaching the autobahn from the south at fifty yards, middle lane. The dark green Volvo 242 is three vehicles ahead and that's the one I'm tracking."

"Got you. Five minutes."

I took the cassette out of the slot and put it into my pocket. The Volvo was changing lanes and I looked for a gap but there wasn't one. The traffic on both sides was moving ahead: I was in a slow lane and perhaps that was why the Volvo had used a chance and changed to the lane on the right. It was now four vehicles ahead and I'd have to do something because he could go through the next traffic lights just before they changed and leave me stuck: I couldn't afford to crash a red because I could hit something and in any case there could be a patrol car in the area and that wouldn't do any good, show me your license please while the Volvo pulled away into the distance, and is this man sick and why are his wrists tied to his legs, so forth.

Krenz had gone quiet and I took a look at him. His head was lolling but he wasn't out: the gland was still in shock and he felt giddy, that was all. I couldn't be sure that he wasn't faking it, or some of it, while he got enough energy back to come at me again.

The pickup truck on my left was hanging back a little and I pressed into the gap and he used the horn but I stood a better chance now of pulling up on the Volvo. I called Roach.

"Under the autobahn and going into Jakob Kaiser Platz."

"Okay. Two minutes."

But the traffic was heavier now as the rush hour got under way, and it was getting more difficult to keep the Volvo in sight. Aggressive driving could give me what I wanted but I'd got this man beside me waiting to go off like a bomb and I couldn't concentrate.

"Krenz," I said. "You try that again and I'm going to kill you. Do you understand?"

Some kind of grunt.

"Krenz. You're in our hands anyway and you know that. We're going to take you to our base and we're going to fry your brains and if you come out of it alive you'll finish up in a funny farm. But I can make things a bit easier for you, Krenz. Just give me the airline and the flight number."

I didn't know if he was able to take it in but it was worth trying. "What's the flight number, Krenz, where the bomb's going to be?"

The Volvo was rounding the Kaiser Platz, now heading west, and I called Roach.

"Entering Siemensdamm."

"Got you. I'm in the Kaiser Platz and coming up on you."

Then a flashy red Porsche cut across my bows and I had to brake and it put me back in fourth place behind the Volvo and I looked for a gap and there wasn't one.

"Krenz. What *flight* is it?"

Because if I was going to lose the Volvo we'd have to work this bastard over just as I'd told him. He might not know the flight number because they might not have chosen it yet, might be waiting for a really impressive passenger list, but if Krenz in fact had a number in his head then we were going to try getting it out of him and that meant contravening the Bureau's strict interdiction covering what is known in the trade as implemented interrogation, but we'd have to do it anyway because there was a planeload of people moving in their daily lives toward an airport with their travel agents' envelopes in their pockets with the tickets inside, the tickets and the flight number, on their way to the big bright sunburst in the sky.

"Krenz. *What is the flight number?*"

He didn't say anything. I couldn't tell what state of consciousness he was in: I'd worked on the occipital area and he probably couldn't focus very well and I'd worked on the pineal gland and he'd be feeling disoriented but to what degree I didn't know: I'd used more force than I would have used with a smaller man but it might not have been enough to get him below the beta waves where he couldn't do any constructive thinking.

The phone rang and I touched for receive.

"Listening."

"I'm three cars behind," Roach said. "You want me to stay there?"

"No. Come right up on my tail."

"Will do."

There was a gap on my right and I moved in, got some protest, but I was in the same lane as the Volvo now and three behind.

"Krenz, you tell me the flight number and we shan't have to do it to you. Are you listening, Krenz? You know what I'm talking about, we shan't have to leave you outside a hospital with your brain gone, you know the things we can do, you've seen them done, Krenz, so *give me the flight number.*"

He'd keeled over now with his head resting on the top of the dashboard and it wouldn't look very good from outside so I pulled him back and he came off the seat and smashed into me and I swerved and got straight again and he bounced back onto the seat and used the rebound and came at me again and the front tires screamed as I corrected and used my left hand for a strike in the killing area because it was the only thing that would stop him. He slumped back onto the seat and I dragged him upright and he fell against the door and stayed there. I'd made the strike in the killing area but I hadn't used lethal force, hadn't gone out to break through the cartilage, but he was losing color and I felt for the carotid pulse and couldn't detect any.

There was a sudden roar as a jet flew over, a TWA flight lowering into Tegel Airport, leaving the air hazed with its exhaust. Lights flashed once in the mirror and I saw a black SAAB sitting there and raised my hand to acknowledge. There wasn't anything I could do about the man sitting beside me so I stopped thinking about him and we kept heading west and then turned north and crossed Saaltwinklerdamm and the canal and came up on the outskirts of the airport with a jet gunning up on the runway and the first light of the day breaking beyond the control tower.

The Volvo was peeling off and taking a down ramp into an underground car park and I held back to let a Mazda 323 move in between us and then followed it through the gate. Roach sized things up and chose a different lane as the Volvo found a slot and Sorgenicht got out and gave a brief look around him and slammed the door and started walking to the B exit, steadily, not hurrying.

Roach came across from the SAAB and I got out of the Mercedes and opened the passenger door and heaved Krenz upright and felt for a pulse and still didn't get anything. Roach stood looking down at him, no expression, hands by his sides, head tilted.

"He gone?"

"I don't know."

"Give him mouth-to-mouth?" He had cool eyes, Roach, voice was a flat monotone.

"If you want to," I said. "Not in public. Get him out of sight."

"No hospital?"

I looked down at the heavy face. "No. No hospital."

"If he's gone?"

"Dig a hole."

And chalk it up for McCane.

Roach gave me the keys of the SAAB and I followed Sorgenicht through B Exit into the terminal.

Chapter 9

Inge

This place was a trap.

He was sitting over there by the wall, Sorgenicht, the man I'd tracked here, Karl Sorgenicht. There were two women with him. One of them had been sitting by herself when I'd come into the cafeteria; I'd noticed her because she was striking, in the Nordic way: ice-blue eyes and ash-blond hair, a wide, sensual mouth. She wore a crimson leather ski jacket and crimson calf-length boots; her bag matched and had steel studs as a decoration. The whole outfit was Berlin-style bisexual chic.

Sorgenicht had got himself a coffee at the service counter, and he'd been taking it across to the corner when the blond had called out to him. He'd hesitated and then joined her. The other girl at the table was dark, slim, elegant in Pan Am uniform. She had joined the blonde just before Sorgenicht; the two women were friends or acquaintances and they'd arranged to meet here: that was my impression.

I had a girlfriend, Inge, Willi Hartman had told me in the nightclub. *She was very attractive.* Helen had agreed: *Yes. I thought she was terribly good-looking.*

The girl over there wasn't necessarily Inge; there were a lot of good-looking women in Berlin, and she could be cabin crew out of uniform. But she'd called Sorgenicht over to her table, and he was a Nemesis agent.

I poked at my eggs on toast, eating very little although I was hungry. This place was a trap and I might have to use muscle to get out of it and I didn't want the digestive process slowing the organism down.

It was a trap because that man Krenz would normally have kept in touch with his cell by telephone from the Mercedes. Nemesis had thought it important enough to send him to watch Sorgenicht's house to see if anyone tried to track him when he left, and it would therefore be important for him to report on events. He hadn't done that. In terms of signals, he'd been missing ever since I'd taken over the Mercedes, and they wouldn't just assume the phone wasn't working: they would check up. They would know where Sorgenicht was going and they'd send some people here to look for Krenz and when anyone came in I paid attention.

Flight 147 to Frankfurt will be leaving from Gate 6 in ten minutes. Passengers for Flight 147 to Frankfurt should report to Gate 6 and board immediately.

There were four tables between my own and the table where Sorgenicht sat with the two young women, and the people in between provided reasonable but not perfect cover. As some of them moved in their chairs, leaning forward, leaning back, I moved my head so that I could keep observation and have time to cover my image if Sorgenicht looked in this direction. If he did, he would recognize me. The lighting at the bottom of the stairs at the Café Brahms last night had been subdued but we'd been facing each other, and unless the strike had left him with any degree of retrogressive amnesia he would remember me if he saw me now.

They were speaking in English over there. I haven't been trained in lip-reading but the difference between *Yes* and *Ja* is quite distinct, and you can pick up the affirmative in most languages by watching for a nod of the head. It's the same with *No* and *Nein*, and the shaking of the head is often more emphatic than the nod. The girl in the Pan Am uniform didn't speak German, perhaps, or not too well; or the others were simply showing courtesy to a foreigner.

Passengers for Flight 232 for London should go to Gate 17 im-

mediately. Flight 232 for London will be leaving in fifteen minutes.

It worried me, the voice on the loudspeaker. This is what it had sounded like in Frankfurt that day: *Flight 103 will be leaving in ten minutes. Passengers for London on Flight 103 should report to Gate 10 immediately.* It was said later that few of them, perhaps none of them, had even heard of the remote Scottish village with the name of Lockerbie.

If that man Krenz was dead, that man with the massive skull in the Mercedes, if I'd gone too far, put too much force into the strike, I would have no conscience. None. I would have no conscience if, in the urgent process of the mission, others also died, and at my hands.

Three men came in and I watched them. Two were pilots.

I felt a resonance along the nerves; it was not unpleasant. If they found me here, the people of Nemesis, if Sorgenicht recognized me, I would have a fair chance of getting clear. It's very difficult to attack and subdue and seize or kill a man in a place as public as a major airport without bringing security or the police on the scene. The resonance along the nerves was due to excitement, not fear, because I had made access to Nemesis and I would stay with the opposition now wherever they moved, and if I got things right, if I didn't lose them, didn't slip, didn't fall, I would reach this man Dieter Klaus, and reach him in time, and bring him down before there was another hideous sunburst in the sky.

The man at the top now is Dieter Klaus, and I hope to Christ you never run into him. He's inhuman. His body shaking, setting up a vibration in the wheelchair.

It would be well, then, if Klaus were to follow Krenz.

One of the pilots who had just come in had parted from the other two men, moving between the tables until he came to the one where Sorgenicht was sitting with the girls. Sorgenicht and the blonde knew him; they shook hands perfunctorily. Then the blonde introduced the pilot to the Pan Am stewardess, and he gave a slight bow. I'd seen the winged flash on his uniform when he'd passed closer to my table. He flew for Iran Air.

It was twenty minutes before anyone at the table made a move. During that time I picked up what I could of the conversation, but it was difficult because I had to allow for German and Iranian accents. I gleaned more from their body language: Sorgenicht sat stolidly and said little, listened a lot, especially to the blonde, who sometimes leaned toward the Pan Am stewardess, touching her hand for emphasis. The two women smiled now and then; the men did not. The Iranian pilot said almost nothing. I thought the name of the stewardess was probably Debbie: the lingual combination of *d* and *b* was often formed when the blonde spoke to her.

The Iranian was the first to move. The pilot he'd come in with passed close to the table, looking at his watch, and the Iranian nodded and got up, shaking hands with the blonde, nodding to the others as they began leaving, too. As Sorgenicht turned away from the table I picked up my cup of coffee and held it in both hands like a bowl as I drank, masking the lower half of my face and keeping my eyes down, but I think he hesitated as he passed my table, not far away. I couldn't be sure, couldn't look up, but the feeling was there: that he'd recognized me but had kept on going.

I waited long enough for him to leave the cafeteria and then took what would probably be the biggest calculated risk of the whole mission and put the cup down and got up and turned and went out. Sorgenicht was in the main hall, going toward the telephones, his back to me. The two women were near the elevators, shaking hands. Debbie, if that was her name, began crossing the hall as the blonde took the down elevator and I followed, keeping distance between us.

He could be telephoning, Sorgenicht, calling for support. He could be tracking me as I crossed the lower floor and followed the blonde out to the car park, and I used reflective surfaces where I could find them, but didn't see him. It didn't mean he wasn't there, standing off at a distance: there was good cover to be had as cars and shuttles pulled in to the departure hall.

There was a different vibration now along the nerves as I walked through the cold morning light.

She moved athletically, the blonde, the metal-studded bag slung at the shoulder, the crimson calf-length boots tapping the tarmac as she passed between the cars.

"*Inge!*" I called, and she turned.

"*Ja?*"

I caught up with her and asked in German, "How are you?"

She studied me. "I'm very well. Do I know you?"

"I'm sorry—Hans Mittag. I'm a friend of Willi's."

"Willi Hartman's?"

"Yes." I held out my hand and she took it, but briefly. "He sends you his good wishes," I said. "He misses you."

Her eyes were cool. "Really. But I still don't remember you."

"We met at one of his little parties. But look, I don't want to hold you up." I stood back. "Should I return his good wishes?"

"I think he's out of town."

"Oh really? Well, it was good to see you. My car's over there." I moved past her and then turned to face her again, bringing the airport terminal into the background. "I'll remember you to Willi, when I see him. He was telling me so many interesting things."

She watched me with the stillness of a cat. "About what?"

"About you." I brought my voice down. "And your exciting plans."

People moved in the background, against the façade of the terminal. Others were standing still, but I could only see them in the outer vision field; my eyes were on hers.

She said, "What kind of plans?"

"Perhaps I can help you with them." The people standing at the shuttle station would be unrecognizable at this distance, even if I could look at them directly. Any one of them could be Sorgenicht. He would be the spotter, if he were there at all. He would show them where I was, tell them to get Inge away from me before I could do her any harm. "But perhaps you don't need any help."

She didn't move. "Did you follow me here?"

"Yes, when I saw you leaving the terminal. I called out to you, but a taxi got in the way."

In a moment she said, "I think I'd like to hear what Willi's been saying about me."

"He was very discreet. I want you to understand that. We'd better talk in your car." I needed cover; my skin itched for it: I was too exposed here in the open. "Where is it?"

She stood watching me, her eyes luminous in the cold morning light. Then she said, "It's over there," and I followed her.

It was a crimson Porsche 911, recognizable ten blocks away in thick traffic. She didn't make any concession to security, didn't want to, wanted to be seen, to make an impression, didn't know how appallingly dangerous it was in the game she was playing.

She sat behind the wheel, her arm across it, her body half-turned to me, a heavy gold chain across the neck of her white polo sweater, a gold bracelet on her wrist, blond hairs on her fingers catching the light, one knee in a black stocking crooked against the gear lever. "So what did Willi say?"

"That you were in Dieter Klaus's organization."

"What organization?"

"Nemesis."

The pulse beat in her throat. In a moment she said, "Willi tends to fantasize, as you probably know."

Someone was getting into a car not far away and when the door slammed I used the excuse and looked through the windscreen and checked the background and saw two men standing there a hundred yards away, talking.

I said, "Willi wasn't fantasizing this time, and you know that."

She took a deep breath to deal with the tension, looking away, looking back. "Do you live in Berlin?" It sounded as if she were changing the subject. She wasn't.

"Yes," I said, "but I don't see much of it. I travel a lot. I've just got back from a meeting with the Secretary of the General People's Committee of Libya, Muhammad az-Zarruqu Rajab, second in command to Colonel Muammar Qaddafi. The deal was for two million U.S. dollars."

Her pupils grew larger for a moment. "Are you talking about arms?"

"I don't always deal in arms. I deal in information, military and paramilitary services, mercenary personnel, presidential security, things like that. My last actual arms deal, which I made two weeks ago, was with the IRA. It wasn't big money but I support people who make a genuine attempt to bring down the capitalistic and democratic establishments, in particular those in London and Washington."

She expressed very little with her eyes, Inge Stoph; they were liquid blue crystal set above the finely wrought cheekbones and under the thick blond eyebrows, a perfectly matched pair of gemstones, beautiful to contemplate but devoid of any real interest; one would get bored with them, I would think, after a time. I looked for other signs of reaction to what I was saying: she looked wonderfully fit and I would have thought her heart rate would be something less than seventy-two but the gold bracelet was swinging against the squat black knob of the gear lever with a rhythm significantly faster than that.

In a moment she said, "You lead an exciting life."

I gave a shrug. "Business of any sort is still only business, but sometimes I make up little jokes to keep the boredom away."

The two men were still talking over there but I didn't think they were anything to worry about: they wore coats with astrakhan collars and homburg hats, and this wasn't a situation where the opposition would need to falsify the image; if Sorgenicht and his people wanted me, they would simply close in.

"You make up little jokes?"

She was delightfully attentive, Inge Stoph.

"Oh," I said, "not often. But this summer I was in Africa, in a state that shall be nameless, and my assignment was to see that the Minister of Defence should be rendered incapable of launching an armed insurrection, which was thought to be in his mind. I was present at a state banquet three days after my arrival, and the cuisine was French: *Faisan rôti à la bergère, Boeuf Stroganov* and for dessert a *compote* of fresh strawberries in a sauce of *Crème de papaya*. But the *pièce de resistance* was carried in on a silver platter, and when the cover was lifted, there was the head of the Minister of Defence on a bed of vine leaves with a glazed passion fruit in his mouth." I touched her arm quickly. "I knew the President well, of course, and his particular sense of humor. I've never been accused of questionable taste."

I caught a spark of interest in her eyes at last, or possibly it was a trick of the light. "Did you kill the man yourself?"

"Some questions are more delicate than others, aren't they?" I looked at my watch. "Let me leave you with this, Inge. I realize that Dieter Klaus has substantial backing from Colonel Qaddafi—the Secretary of the General People's Committee happened to mention it when I was with him yesterday—and this is why I was particularly glad to see you this morning. Klaus is a difficult man to reach, and I respect that, so you might like to suggest that I meet him, as soon as convenient." There was a microrecorder lying in the well between the seats. "May I use this?"

"If you wish."

I spoke a telephone number into it and put it back. "You can leave a message for me there at any time: it's an answering service. Tell Klaus that I can offer him a missile with a nuclear warhead, the American-made Miniver NK-9, in case he feels like spelling out a really spectacular statement for the prime-time news." The increase in her saliva was triggered immediately, and I saw her swallow. "I'm talking," I said, "of taking out an entire international sports stadium during a world-class match or a major airport on Christmas Eve or the Houses of Parliament in London, with subsequent fallout megadeaths and mass evacuation and the closing down of the relevant city for the next hundred years—a lasting monument, if you like, to Nemesis." I opened the door and got out of the car. "You know how to find me, but you must tell Klaus that time is of the essence. If he'd like a rendezvous, I can only give him till midnight."

The sun had cleared the airport buildings and floated in the haze, a pale membrane speared by the black antennae at the top of the control tower. Shadows had begun to form on the tarmac as I walked across the slip road to the underground car park where Roach had left his SAAB.

I could see no one, had seen no one since I'd left Inge, but the skin was crawling at the nape of the neck and the scrotum was tight because in the last hour I had taken appalling risks, however calculated, and if I were going to survive long enough to debrief to my director in the field he was going to blow my head off and send a report to London.

The roar of a jet came like a soft explosion as British Airways C-10 cleared the buildings and tilted into the haze. Something was moving at the rim of the vision field and I turned my head; it was a radar scanner. Echoes began coming from the underground garage, echoes of footsteps, and I stopped, listening; I'd been making them myself. I don't like the nerves pulling tight when there's no reason, but I never ignore them. There are vibrations in human affairs that have nothing to do with speech or contact; they are there because the primitive brain stem still protects us in a world of technological sophistication, analyzing the environment, interpreting data that the senses have picked up even without our knowing, and on that level we don't understand the signals; we just feel uneasy, on edge.

The black SAAB was standing where Roach had left it; the Mercedes had been too hot for me to use again, and he would

have dumped Krenz somewhere in the field for support people to look after and then driven the car to the east section
of the city and left it there.

The windows of the SAAB were up and the doors were
locked; he'd given me the keys, but I handled them gingerly,
slipping the door-key in and waiting before I turned it. There
were other people down here, and I listened to their footsteps, and the echoes they made, expecting a rush, a closing
in. There was nothing of that sort, and I opened the door
and got in and sat behind the wheel and took a look at the
instrument panel and waited again, listening, hearing the
roar of another jet that was taking off, the sound setting up
a metallic hum in the lid of the ashtray.

Then I put the ignition key in and sweat sprang instantly
on my skin but I turned the key because there hadn't been
time for them to rig a bang, it was just nerves, that was all,
and the engine started right away and I shifted the gears in
and got rolling and the BMW that was parked three cars
away in the same line started up too and the tires whimpered
a little as it pulled ahead of me and swerved inward and the
380SL on the other side went into the same maneuver and
I gave the SAAB the gun and the tires shrilled and the left
fender hit the Mercedes and was ripped away as I kept going
and felt a shudder from the rear as the BMW moved right
in and tried to close the trap as a Volkswagen came in from
the next line and swung across my bows in a curve and I
rammed it and broke through.

Another car was moving past one of the concrete pillars
and it braked hard and I saw a woman with a white face
behind the windscreen and then the Mercedes pulled alongside the SAAB its tires yelping under the acceleration and I
swung the wheel and bounced off the pillar and heard the
offside fender tearing away. The windscreen snowed out as
something glanced across it and I thought I heard the pop
of a silenced gun and then it came again and the driving
mirror shattered and I kept low on the seat and swung the
SAAB full circle across the dry concrete and looked for a gap

and found one and went for it but the VW blocked me and I swung the other way, ramming the front end of the Mercedes and bringing a burst of water from the radiator and a lot of clatter from the fan.

They were shooting and they were using silencers and the clock on the dashboard took a ricochet and the bullet dropped into my lap and I left it there. Something moved in from the left side and the SAAB rocked and I dragged it straight and saw another gap and took it and hit a pillar and broke free but the Mercedes was close and we rocked again and righted and then rolled over with the roof metal screaming on the concrete and I hit the belt buckle and got the door open and found the Mercedes alongside with the driver slumped at the wheel with blood on his face so I smashed the window and found his gun and saw the BMW moving in and fired twice and rolled clear as it lost control and hit the Mercedes and bounced back with the driver's foot still on the throttle and the engine screaming.

The Volkswagen was coming in and I dropped the gun and waited and saw the driving window coming down and a muzzle poking out and I dropped flat as he fired and fired again and I came up from under the window and hit the gun and felt the shock as it went off and then I found the man's throat and smashed the larynx and dragged him out of the car and got in and gunned up for the exit and went through with the man in the box there shouting because I hadn't paid and he wanted to ask me about all the noise he'd heard. I merged with the main traffic from the terminal and kept going until I found a telephone and got out and called Thrower and he picked up on the second ring.

Chapter 10

Thrower

"**I** need all the information you can get me," I told Thrower, "on the NK-9 Miniver tactical nuclear missile. Ahmed Samala should have all I want, but ask London too, tell them to fax it to you."

"How soon?"

"Now."

I felt blood creeping on the side of my face and got out my handkerchief; my head was throbbing, just over the right temple, and the cold air was sharp on the wound. The shoulder on that side was burning but I could use my arm all right. It had happened when the SAAB had rolled.

"I'll see to that," Thrower said. "Where are you?"

"Tegel Airport. I need to debrief."

"All right. I've moved you nearer there, in point of fact. You're at the Hotel Klinghof in the Haselhorst district. You're booked in and your things are on their way. You can go there now."

He must have his reasons but I wanted to keep the call short. I needed the information on the NK-9 as soon as I could get it: Inge could phone Kleiber's number at any time to make a rendezvous and if I were going to talk to Dieter Klaus I'd have to be *absolutely* sure of what I was saying.

"All right," I told Thrower. "What street?"

"Eider Strasse. I shall be moving to the Prinzen, nearby."

"When?"

"I'll be leaving here in a few minutes; I was hanging on

in case you signaled." There was something about his voice that was different, I thought. It was just as smooth, but there was a note of frustration coming through. It wasn't because of what had happened in the underground garage; I hadn't told him about it yet because I didn't want to waste time.

I said, "I'll wait for your call. How long?"

"We should be able to debrief in about an hour."

"Where?"

"I'll tell you when I phone."

"All right." On a thought—"Have they got Helen Maitland to the airport yet?"

In a moment he said, "In point of fact, no. She's missing."

The place smelled of leather and coconut matting and sweat.

"Come on in," he said.

He was a big man with thick black hair on his bare arms and a round pink head with tiny blue eyes in it that looked as though they could bore through the steel door of a strong room. Thrower had told me his name was Jim, and that was all. The battered sign outside said JIM'S GYM. Someone was bashing at a punching bag.

"Thank you," I said, and he stood back for me. We'd exchanged paroles.

They were mostly boys in here, some with black eyes.

I couldn't have shown anything on my face but Jim said, "They didn't get them here. They got beaten up by their fathers. My job's to stop it happening again." His eyes shifted a little. "He's waiting for you up there," he said.

He led me across to some stairs in the corner.

Thrower was on the first floor in a room used for storing things, mostly half-broken furniture and a few car seats with the stuffing coming out. It was freezing in here.

"Come along in," Thrower said.

"Is there any water around?" I was thirsty.

"I don't think so. Downstairs, perhaps."

"And no bloody heating?"

"I didn't ask."

He looked as smooth as he sounded, Thrower, what you'd call well groomed, almost as bad as that bastard Loman, although this man's shoes weren't polished: he was wearing fur-lined boots. A long face, pale eyes, a tight mouth, fresh cuts from shaving, a short man, thin, hands in the pockets of his elegant black coat, nothing I could see to like about him, but then I wasn't in the mood.

"What happened," I asked him, "to Helen Maitland?"

"We'll get to that," he said.

I was warned. It sounded as though he was used to calling the shots.

"What exactly do you mean," I asked him, "she's 'missing'?"

He turned away—impatiently, I think. He would have to improve, this man Thrower, he would have to improve a great deal. My hands were in my coat pockets too but it wasn't just to keep them warm; they were still shaking from the reaction: those bastards had come very close indeed to writing me off and it had been noisy down there and I hate loud noises.

"I began calling her room," Thrower said carefully, "at seven o'clock this morning, to give her comfortable time to catch the plane. There was no answer. I called her twice more at intervals of ten minutes, then I phoned security and told them I thought there could be something wrong. They let me into her room. She wasn't there and she hadn't packed, not even her toilet things."

"She leave any kind of note?"

"I couldn't find one. I—"

"What about—" and he waited for me. "All right," I said, "go on."

"I talked to the doorman, who said that Mrs. Maitland had left the hotel at about six-thirty, saying that she didn't want a taxi, she wanted to take some air. She had a coat on. That is all I can tell you."

My fists were clenched in my pockets, to stop the shaking.

I said, "Have you phoned the Steglitz since you left there?"

"Ten minutes ago, from my hotel."

"And she's not back?"

"No."

Do you want to come in for a little while?

She'd been shivering, standing there outside her door, her hands pressing the collar of her coat against her cheeks. I'd said no, she needed sleep.

Just for a few minutes.

She'd leaned her head against me, and I'd held her until the shivering had stopped. I had to make some calls, I'd told her.

I'm cold, and a bit frightened, that's all.

And I'd told her to call room service, ask for some hot milk and Horlicks. *That is what I had told her.*

Thrower was watching me.

She'd asked me to come in for a few minutes because she was cold and frightened. Jesus *Christ*, it wasn't much to ask, was it?

"I've informed London."

"What?"

Thrower, saying he'd informed London.

"I'd hope so," I told him, "I would very much hope so."

Something hooted, down there outside the building, a barge, I suppose, on the river. Fog still clung to the water, but the sun was throwing a clear cold light across the buildings on the other side.

"Why don't we sit down?" Thrower said, and I looked at him.

"And what did London say they'd do?"

"All that's necessary."

"*We* brought her out here, you know that? The *Bureau* brought her out here, on *my* recommendation. So they'd better bloody well find her again, hadn't they?"

He turned away, turned back, and I didn't like the way he did that; he wanted me to see how very patient he was being with me. "Look, Thrower, if they don't find—" and I stopped. In the silence I could hear the thumping of the punch bag downstairs. It was freezing cold in here and I'd just come out of an action phase and I'd have to get some control back, especially if this man Thrower was going to run me in the field. I'd need some patience, too.

"You don't have to feel any guilt," he said, "about this."

"I *don't*?"

"The recommendation to bring her out here was yours, but the decision was London's. You—"

"Split hairs if you like."

"You also blamed yourself, I'm told, for what happened to McCane." He took a step toward me, perhaps because I'd been raising my voice and he wanted to keep things quiet. "Didn't you?"

"Is this place all right? Is it a safe house?"

"The safest in Berlin."

"McCane? Yes, that was my—" and I stopped again. I wasn't under control, didn't sound under control.

He came closer still and touched my arm. "We're going to sit down," he said. "I've been on my feet a lot."

Bloody lie—he'd been in bed all night and then got into a taxi. I said, "There wasn't any sign of—you know—any kind of disturbance? In her room?"

"None at all. I was careful to look for that."

With George Maitland they'd found blood all over the floor, and I didn't want to think about it. They'd have to find her. London would have to find her. I went over to one of the car seats, he was right, I suppose, I looked as if it'd do me a bit of good to sit down. He took the other one, brushing the dust away. "Tell me what's been happening," he said.

"What?"

"To you."

"Oh. I was got at. You want to record?" We were suddenly into debriefing.

"I don't use a recorder. Just tell me."

It didn't take long; it was just an attack, that was all. But he wanted to know the casualty figures: London's fussy about that. "I'm not sure," I told him. "One of them had knocked his head against the windscreen, I think, blood all over his face. The man I shot at was certainly hit but he could be still alive. The one I pulled out of the car is dead. I went for the larynx."

He was looking at the floor, Thrower.

"One down," he said, "for certain."

"Yes. What happened to that man Krenz?"

"The same thing."

"That was an accident. I went for the throat because he was trying to send the car off the road and we were in traffic, but I didn't go deep, I pulled it. I just needed to incapacitate."

In a moment Thrower said, "Possible heart failure."

"Whatever. I mean I'm not trying to get out of it, if I killed him I killed him. Whatever Records want to put it down as." I could hear a jet gunning up at the end of the runway—we were only two miles or so from the airport. "I've remembered something," I said. "There was a man in the nightclub where I talked to Willi Hartman, a man who recognized Helen. She knew him. She told me his name was Kurt Muller."

Thrower turned his head to look at me. I suppose he thought I wasn't taking it seriously enough, the fact that I'd killed at least two people since I'd got out of bed this morning, shouldn't be thinking about Helen.

"Look," I said, "my job is to bring this mission home and prevent a couple of hundred perfectly innocent people from getting blown out of the sky at thirty thousand feet and if you want me to weep over any graves I dig as I go along you're clean out of luck." *Punch* bag thumping down there, *punch* bag thumping, I wouldn't mind having a go at that bloody thing myself, *punch* the bloody stuffing out of it. "All I want," I told Thrower, "is a director in the field who understands these things."

Of *course* I took it seriously, taking human life, I always have, I've spent the dark hours huddled in the keening wind where the ghosts walk, gone sleepless through the night often enough, I'm not a *clod*, I'm not made of bloody *stone*.

But I hadn't got time now to rake over the ashes of what I'd done today, I wasn't finished with it yet, and there's another thing—it's a minefield, this trade we're in, a whole complex of booby traps set up in the dark, and I know—I've always known—that somewhere out there there's one with my name on it, too.

He was still watching me, Thrower.

"Relax," he said.

"What?"

"Relax. You've had a busy time." He pulled out a notebook. "Kurt Muller, was it?"

"Yes." I couldn't sit still, got up, went across the bare splintered floor to look at the river, the Havel, barges on it, small boats, a hulk rusting near the bank opposite, the cold winter sunlight setting the scene in amber. "But God knows how many Kurt Mullers there are in the telephone book." He hadn't followed us away from the nightclub, no one had, I knew that. But he might have phoned her, later, or she might have phoned him.

"Description?" Thrower had a gold pen ready, a *gold* pen, withal.

"Thirties, pale face, black hair, five-ten, on the thin side, a bit round-shouldered."

"Eyes?"

"I don't remember, but black or brown, dark, not blue."

Thrower put his notebook away. "Let's do some more debriefing."

"Yes. I suppose," I said, "you changed my hotel because of Helen, did you?"

"Of course."

In case she talked, in case she was made to talk. "Why did you put me into the Klinghof?"

"We know it. We've used it before: it's small, tucked away, and the woman who runs it is discreet."

"I saw a couple of tarts there."

"That's why she's discreet. I need Krenz's address, don't I?"

119

I gave it to him. "He carries a *Berliner Bank* Visa card, and his cover's an electronics engineer—or he could even be one. What did London say when you told them Helen was missing?"

In a moment Thrower said, "They're very concerned. They feel responsible. I'd like you to feel reassured."

There was a Pan Am plane coming into the approach path, settling nose up through the haze, the strobes flashing. I turned away from the window. "As long as they're doing something to find her," I said. He didn't answer. He sat with his pen ready, watching me. "All right, that man Sorgenicht went straight to the cafeteria when he reached the airport. There were two girls at one of the tables, and he sat down with them." We were into the major phase of the debriefing and Thrower made notes sometimes, the gold pen flashing in the light from the window, the only thing of beauty in this beleaguered hole. "The name of the German girl is Inge Stoph. Were you actually at the signals board when I debriefed to London last night?"

"I was."

"You keep a lot in your head."

"I used a recorder then. I don't use one in the field."

Some of the DIFs do—Ferris does, Pepperidge does—but others wouldn't be seen dead with one: halfway through a mission or even before then a tape has got a lot of hot information on it and when Crenshaw was running Jayson through the field in Cyprus a few years ago he got exposed and the opposition got hold of his tape and blew the whole mission and Jayson was found with his head off in the back of a garbage truck because he'd had to write off three of their cell and they hadn't liked that. A tape recorder doesn't carry a capsule.

"My impression," I told Thrower, "was that Inge Stoph was trying to persuade the Pan Am stewardess to do something, or agree to something." I told him about the Iranian, and Thrower looked up sharply.

"A pilot?"

"Yes." He made a note and I said, "I think Inge Stoph and the Pan Am girl are friends. Sorgenicht and Stoph are both in Nemesis. I couldn't fit the Iranian in: he listened a lot but didn't say much, and I didn't pick up anything of a relationship between him and either Stoph or the stewardess."

"Iran Air," Thrower said, "doesn't normally fly into Berlin. They go into Frankfurt. But the Iranians have an extensive network of sleepers and agents-in-place in Europe. What happened when you left the cafeteria?"

"I followed Inge Stoph." I gave him a complete picture of the scene with her in the car park and then we wrapped it up and he put away his notebook and got off the car seat and looked at the river with his hands dug into his pockets and his eyes nowhere and I didn't disturb him.

When he was ready he asked me: "You think Stoph went for your approach?"

"I got a lot of reaction when I mentioned the nuclear missile."

"Did you get any idea of her standing with Dieter Klaus?"

"No."

"She could be a girlfriend?"

"Possibly. She could get any man into bed."

"You?"

"No. Most men, then."

"She doesn't appeal to you?"

"Her type doesn't."

"She's a lesbian?"

"I'd say a bi."

"Is she, do you think, a Venus trap for Nemesis?"

"If she's not, she could be."

"Did you give her the impression she didn't appeal to you?"

"I'm not *stupid*, Thrower."

He looked down, tilting on his toes and heels for a moment.

"Sorry," I said. It had sounded as if he wasn't sure whether I knew the value of a Venus trap: no experienced agent will ever give a Venus the impression she doesn't appeal to him, in case he wants to use her and walk into the trap and get out again with information.

"That's all right," Thrower said. "We're getting to understand each other, that's all." For the first time I wondered whether I should signal London and change him as my DIF, have him replaced by someone who'd run me before. But that would blow the board and *Solitaire* was running flat out and I didn't want to slow it down.

I had to keep this one thing in my mind the whole time, above all others: *It could be any next flight.*

"What I need to know," Thrower went on, "is whether you feel that if Inge Stoph comes through with a proposed rendezvous it will be in order to trap you."

"I can't say, because I don't know Dieter Klaus or the way his mind works. If she comes through with a rendezvous it'll be on his instructions, either because he can't resist the temptation of blowing up the Houses of Parliament and getting his face on the front cover of the *Terrorist's Gazette* or because he wants to find out who I am and what I'm doing in Berlin."

Thrower stood looking out of the window, and he didn't turn round when he said, "Of course you realize how very dangerous it is for you to agree to such a rendezvous. For you to meet Dieter Klaus."

"Yes."

"You know his reputation."

"Yes."

"Suppose you meet him, and of course it will be on his own ground and in the presence of his bodyguards, what will you rely on to get you away again, still alive?"

"My cover."

I was getting impatient but he'd got a right to ask me what my plans were: he was my director in the field and his job was to support them.

"Your *cover*," he said, and turned round from the window now and looked at me. "Is that all?"

"It's all I've got."

122

"It won't be enough. If they suspect you're using a cover they'll try and break it and they'll succeed. You know that—you talked to that poor devil in the hospital in London. They turned him into a—"

"I'm not saying it's going to be easy."

"I'm glad you appreciate that. What would you hope to achieve, in any case, by meeting Dieter Klaus?"

"Access to information. Which plane, which flight. That's all I want, and he's got it."

"What if you failed to get information? Would you try to take him out?"

Kill him, he meant kill him. "Of course. It'd blow Nemesis."

In a moment he said, "If I let you do this, I shall need time to call in as much support as I can. It may take—"

"No support."

"I realize"—showing much patience now, much patience—"that you normally prefer working without support, and I understand that, but if you mean to walk right into the center of an opposition network with a man like Dieter Klaus running it, I'd have to insist on support. I'm here to direct you in the field, not stand by and see you take this mission deliberately into hazard and destroy it."

"That isn't my plan." A crack in one of the windows buzzed as a jet gunned up on takeoff and lifted across the skyline, the Pan Am insignia on the tail, and the last of my patience broke. "My plan is to stop those bastards putting a bomb on a plane full of people and I know the best way to do it and if I hang around waiting for you to call the bloody troops in and clutter up the rendezvous with enough people to start a bloody war then I won't get anywhere, I won't get into the center of Nemesis and they'll rig that bomb and blow all those people out of the sky, for Christ's sake, don't you *understand*, Thrower, don't you understand that it could be *any next flight?*"

He watched me steadily with his pale expressionless eyes, not saying anything yet, letting me listen again in my mind to what I'd just said, to how I'd just said it, too forcefully, too emotionally. Then he said, "You've just come through some action that almost cost you your life, and your nerves are going to take their time to settle down. When you've got your control back, we'll talk again. Now let me drive you to your hotel."

He didn't understand. He wasn't thinking.

"Thrower, I'm going in to the center of the opposition and I've got to do it alone because they'll have people deployed in the environment, and if you put people in as well I shan't know one from the other if it's a night action and I could easily kill one of them, one of ours—but more important than that, you can't put support in close enough to help me without exposing them, and an arms dealer doesn't move around with a crowd of peons, he's a businessman and he behaves like one, so if you put support on the scene when I go in you'll blow my cover before I've got a chance in a thousand to make it work, can you hear what I'm saying, *you'll blow my cover*. Do you think that's what I want from my director in the field?"

He turned away, turned back, hands in the pockets of his dark elegant coat, his head tilted slightly, his voice smooth, placating. "We'll talk about it later. I have my arguments too, but I don't feel that at the present moment you're sufficiently receptive."

I took a step toward him. My head was throbbing because of the wound, and because of what was happening to the mission, to *Solitaire*, just when I'd got access, just when I was ready to move in on the opposition and destroy it if I could, and if I couldn't, get clear and try again, try again until I found the way, and went in for the kill.

"Thrower," I said, "I want you to tell me something. If there's no time to talk, if I don't have time to listen to your arguments, if I have to go in to this rendezvous at a moment's notice, will you send in support anyway, despite all I've said?"

He didn't hesitate. "Yes. I would have to."

So I turned away and went down the stairs and found Jim showing one of his kids a *gedan kosa-uke* and asked him if I could make a call and he showed me his little office in the corner of the gym and I picked up the phone and dialed the number and the code extension and blew the board for *Solitaire* all over the signals room in London.

Chapter 11

Showdown

"Executive. Get me Control."

Smell of sweat in this place, Jim's office, not much bigger than a cupboard.

"Control."

Shatner.

I said, "I want a new director in the field."

There was a short silence and I wasn't surprised.

"What is the problem?" he asked me.

"Incompatibility."

Grounds for divorce. The relationship between the DIF and the executive is very much like a marriage: trust is involved, and above all else, understanding.

Shatner said, "I need to know more than that."

I think I heard quiet anger in his tone. *As I've told you,* he'd said to me in his office yesterday, *you're not my favorite executive.*

"There isn't much time," I said. "I'm going into a strictly red sector and he's insisting on sending in support."

Shatner thought about that. Then he said, "I imagine he thinks you need it."

"It could kill me."

There was another silence. I could only wait, only keep what patience I had, because this was thin ice and I could crack it if I didn't take care how I walked.

"Is he there?" Shatner asked.

"Yes."

"I'll talk to him."

Shatner didn't understand, any more than Thrower understood. I'd only come into the field last night and I'd secured access to the opposition and at any time the call could come through from Inge Stoph arranging the rendezvous and I was in a position to go right into the center of Nemesis and blow it apart and these two hidebound bloody bureaucrats were trying to stop me dead in my tracks.

"You can't talk to him," I told Shatner. "You don't understand the situation. The executive in the field is in a fully active phase of the mission and he's urgently requesting a change of the DIF and he's got every right to do that, and his control is expected to bear in mind that in these circumstances the executive makes the decisions, not his DIF."

In the silence I could hear the ice cracking. The thing is that Control picks the director in the field very carefully from those available, making sure he's the right choice for the mission: Thrower knew Berlin and was fluent in German, so forth. But what Shatner hadn't done was make the right choice for the specific executive and that's even more critical. But I was taking an appalling risk in asking for a new DIF in the first twenty-four hours of the mission because those bloody people in London can come back at you like a boomerang and leave the director in the field and call the executive in and send a new one out in his place and you won't work for the Bureau again and for me that would be the end of things, *finis*, *finito*.

"I rather think I understand," Shatner said, "my responsibilities as your control. I am asking you to put your DIF on the line."

There was a mug, a ceramic mug on Jim's desk, in the middle of a mess of papers and bottles of ink and hand-grips and rubber bands and paper clips and curled photographs of Japanese martial artists, and in the mug were some pens and pencils, and one of them was vibrating as another jet was cleared for takeoff and thundered into the sky, and I was glad to hear the small intimate sound of the pencil sending its message to me, if I wanted to hear it. In the complex chemistry of life there are always messages for us, if we make time to listen, and this one was perfectly clear: *Any next flight.*

I had to get the words exactly right. "I request the immediate attention of Chief of Signals."

The ice cracked again and I heard it. I've talked to a lot of my own kind in the Caff and other places, but I've never heard of anyone telling Control to his face that they wanted higher rank to talk to. Least of all when the control was *Shatner.*

In the silence I could hear things going on in the underground signals room: voices, beepers, the sharp clink of a teacup. They were there under the floodlit signal boards, hunched over the mikes or leaning back to check the progress of a mission, reaching for the bit of chalk, *Executive requires backup, Rendezvous established, Courier down, red sector.* As the data went in, the decisions would be made, and—

"Chief of Signals."

Croder. We'd never got on well, but I respected him above most others. He wasn't a bureaucrat.

"I'm asking for a new DIF." I told him why.

He was standing there at the board for *Solitaire*—he roves the room, Croder, from board to board, taking over in a crisis, keeping the heat down, bringing people back sometimes from the edge of a certain grave.

"Thrower is a very good man," he told me. "He is very experienced." Standing there under the floodlight with his black reptilian eyes scanning the board, his steel hand hanging like a hook. "I know your style," he said, "and you're quite possibly misjudging things after going through a difficult action phase. Am I correct?"

I felt a shiver. It sounded like clairvoyance: Thrower hadn't had time to send my debriefing to the board, the stuff on the underground garage. Croder was inside my mind.

I had to cut corners, save time, because of the pencil. "Do you know Thrower's style?"

I waited. In a moment: "Yes."

"Then you'll know that he and I can't work together."

It meant a lot more than it sounded: it meant that if a wheel came off we wouldn't be able to agree on a decision and the mission would crash; it meant that if I went into a hot rendezvous with support I hadn't asked for, people could get killed.

"I need more information," Croder said.

"There isn't time."

"You will have to make time."

So I went in blind, didn't think about it, otherwise I couldn't have done it. "I request the immediate attention of Bureau One."

Shepley, king of kings, host of hosts, head of London.

It was all I could have done and I'd had to do it. Some people would have called it professional suicide, and I would have agreed.

"Bureau One is in Washington."

His voice hadn't changed, Croder's, but he was now in what amounted to a towering rage. That's one of the things I like about him: he's a complete master of control. But it can be deadly.

I said, "I need his immediate attention."

There were some voices in the background, louder than before; one of them could be coming over a speaker at the console, some beleaguered shadow *in extremis*, calling for help. They would want Croder at the board.

His voice came again. "Give me your number."

I read it to him off the base of the telephone.

"Be available," Croder said, and shut down the line on me.

I stood there with a sense of being in limbo, cut off from the day and its affairs, lost, isolated, disenfranchised. The throbbing went on in my head with the rhythm of a slow drumbeat. I would have liked to sit down somewhere, rest a little and then wash my face, feel civilized for a few minutes before I went into the rendezvous with Nemesis, because once I was there it could turn out to be difficult, not civilized at all, it could turn out to be bloody murder.

There was a grimy bit of glass here next to the door, call it a window, and through it I could see Thrower out there in the gym, standing on the other side of the punch bag, not watching anything that was going on, watching the wall.

I opened the door and stood just outside it, waiting for the phone to ring. In Washington it was three in the morning and Shepley would almost certainly be in bed, but they'd wake him. The signals room in London can reach him within seconds wherever he is, by calling direct to his pager, and his pager is never switched off: it's the equivalent of a presidential hotline. And Croder wouldn't fail to signal him: when the executive is in the field he's considered to be in hazard, whether he's in a red sector or not, and London undertakes to keep Bureau One in constant touch with him: it's in our contract.

Thrower was coming across the gym, walking carefully; his footprints on a sandy beach would make a straight line— and this was my problem with him; you can tell a lot about people by the way they walk, and this man's mind, like his footprints in the sand, was unwilling to deviate.

When he reached me he asked, "You were signaling London?"

He'd seen me through the window, known what I must be doing.

"Washington."

His expressionless eyes rested on me. "Bureau One is in Washington, I believe."

"Yes."

"You're signaling Bureau One?"

"Yes."

He looked away, watching two of the kids struggling on the mat, one of them trying to get out of a choke hold, pulling and tugging. I felt his frustration.

"I've always heard," Thrower said, "that you are intractable."

"I expect you have."

"It is in my mind," he said smoothly, with no rancor, no rancor at all in his tone, "to ask that you are replaced. I assume that doesn't surprise you."

"No."

I didn't want to talk to him; we didn't speak the same language, and it was so bloody *cold* in this place that my mouth felt clamped by it, by the cold, my jaws felt frozen, but it was a consolation that with a bit of luck I would shortly be on my way to a hot rendezvous, joke, my good friend, that is a little joke, we must do what we can to keep cheerful, must we not.

"Perhaps you would give him my respects," Thrower was saying.

"What?"

"Bureau One."

"Of course."

The kid on the mat got free suddenly, and I felt a bit better. *Yes?*

We've just got a signal, sir, from the executive for Solitaire. *He requests your attention.*

It's the correct term, you see, straight out of the book, requests your attention, means the poor bastard stuck out there in the field wants to talk to you, for Christ's sake, can't they speak the Queen's English?

Cold. I wanted to move my feet to get some warmth in them but I didn't because this bastard was here, Thrower, sign of weakness, cold feet, wouldn't do.

Is he in a red sector?

Sitting up in bed in his pajamas, Bureau One, host of hosts, just a touch difficult to imagine the godhead in pajamas.

No, sir, but there's a problem with his DIF.

Shatner, in the floodlit signals room, standing there at the board with his arms folded, looking at his shoes, his cracked and rather ancient suede shoes, the hole still in his sock, standing there looking down at them because he didn't want to look at Croder, because Control's responsibility had been passed on by the executive to the Chief of Signals and that was a little embarrassing.

He's in Berlin?

Yes, sir.

Croder, in the signals room, walking up and down like a bloody vulture with its wings folded behind it, he looks like that, actually, Croder, he's got a thin neck and it tends to disappear into his collar, and that hook he's got for a hand is so very like a claw, walking up and down and looking at nobody because the Chief of Signals' responsibility for the mission had been passed on by the executive to Bureau One, and that too was embarrassing.

He's talked to Mr Croder?

Yes, sir.

Head throbbing, my head was throbbing, the pulse rate would be a degree elevated, say 73, 74, because epiphany was setting in and I was beginning to wonder whether it was a terribly good idea to bring the mission to a dead stop and risk crashing it over a difference of opinion, there were so many lives in the balance, all those people in the plane.

No, I refuse that. Their lives would be at a greater risk if I let this dictatorial bureaucrat get in my way, because *I knew what to do*, in the deep reaches of the psyche where everything is known *I knew what to do*.

Then I'll talk to him myself.

He'd got to. He was party to my contract.

But it was a long shot, Christ it was a long shot despite all the wonders of technology and telephones because it might not be like that at all in the signals room—Croder could have taken Shatner outside to work out some kind of decision, rather than disturb Bureau One at three in the morning five thousand miles away, they could very well be agreeing to hold things off, wait until this infamously intractable executive had cooled down a little, seen some sense, because—

Phone ringing.

Jim looked up from the mat and I said I thought it was for

me and he said go ahead and I went into the cluttered little office and picked up the phone.

"Yes?"

"Bureau One. What is the problem?"

"Incompatibility."

"In what way?"

I couldn't say there wasn't time to tell him: he was as high up as I could go and if I couldn't make him understand that the mission was jeopardized I'd have to play the last card I'd got, and I didn't want to do that, it would make things infinitely more difficult, more dangerous. So I told him about the impasse we'd reached, Thrower and I, on the subject of sending in support when I went in to the rendezvous, and told him also that my DIF didn't seem to understand the way I worked, the way I had to work if I was to bring the mission home. Then I waited.

Play the last card, yes, if I had to. If Shepley called me in or if he told me I'd have to work out my differences with my DIF, I would go to ground, cut myself off from the DIF and from London and go it alone, let them chalk it up on the board in Signals, *Executive withdraws,* a graceful way to put it, typically euphemistic, because what it would really mean was that I would have to find myself a burrow in the bowels of Berlin and operate from there, surface from there and do what I could to infiltrate Nemesis, penetrate to the center, blow it up on my own without any help, without signals, without franchise, without authority.

Infinitely more difficult, more dangerous, but I would do it if I had to.

I've done it before.

"Do you feel," Shepley was asking me, "that your DIF has a case? That he's thinking of your protection, rather than of imposing his own will?"

"Possibly."

"You concede that?"

"Yes. But he doesn't understand what's involved. I'm going to be on sensitive ground, ultrasensitive, and I don't want the opposition to pick up the vibrations. It could be fatal."

I waited. In the ceramic mug the pencil was buzzing again as a plane got airborne. Hold fast, yes, I must hold fast. And if necessary, go to ground. They hate it, in London, if you do that. They like to keep their puppets on the string, they don't like to think they've got a rogue shadow loose in the field, you can see their point.

"You realize," Shepley said, "that I might feel it best to have you recalled?"

He had a calm voice, Bureau One, calm, measured, and contemplative.

"Yes," I said.

"And you realize that your DIF has a case to make, on your own admission, and that I might feel it best for you to settle your differences and proceed with the mission?"

"Yes," I said.

Thrower had moved away from the door; he was watching the wall again, his feet neatly together. I suppose he'd thought it rather rude if he'd stayed by the door listening. He was a gentleman, give him that. But this is not a trade for gentlemen.

"What would you do," Bureau One asked me from Washington, from his bed five thousand miles away through the night, "if I recalled you, or if I instructed you to work with your present DIF?"

One of them was on the punch bag again, *thump—thump— thump*, and it gave me energy, I think, gave me strength, gave me the feeling that it was my own fist pounding into the leather bag, *thump—thump—thump*, a good feeling, sanguine, confident.

"I'd go to ground," I said.

Australian Airlines came drifting across the skyline, a winged kangaroo on the tail, lowering to the runway with the pale winter sunshine flashing on the windows, the soft scream of the jets pitching up a little as it reached for the surface of the earth.

Shepley hadn't answered me. I didn't mind. I'd said all I wanted to say and he'd have to take it from there. If all went well I had a rendezvous to keep and nothing was going to stop me. But I'd rather do it for the Bureau, stay on the signals board, keep the lifeline open. I'd have a better chance that way.

His voice came, Shepley's. "Who do you want as your director in the field?"

Thump—thump—thump on the bag, come on, bust the bugger.

"Ferris."

"Ferris is directing *Stingray.*"

"Mayhew."

"He is in Morocco."

"Cone."

"You can have Cone. I'll instruct Control."

The line went dead and I put the phone down and tucked the corner of a hundred-deutschemark note underneath it and went out of the office and across to where Thrower was standing.

"You can go home now," I said.

Chapter 12

Cone

*I*t is contended legally that Voest-Alpine of Vienna licensed Gerald Bull's howitzer technology about 1979, sometime before he dismantled his American operation and went to work with Poudrière Réunie Belge, which wanted to produce and market howitzer shells together with Austrian gun sales.

Crumbs dropped from the meat pie as I took bites at it, and I held it over the greaseproof paper. A jet took off, leaving echoes among the buildings.

It was just gone 10:00 hours.

By eleven I had got through the whole cassette, made notes, turned them face down, making up questions, answering them, some of them right, not all of them, not enough.

Terpil and Korkala were convicted in absentia for conspiring to sell 10,000 machine guns and 10 million rounds of ammunition to a small unit of New York undercover police officers posing as South American revolutionaries. Several private people and agencies are now looking for these two in Lebanon, but their hideout is quite difficult to locate.

It was cold in here, in this small oblong room at the top of the building; there was an electric heater but it didn't do much more than warm the air within a few inches of it, where I had my feet. The cold was coming from inside me, some of it. I hoped Cone would get into Berlin before I needed him, before Inge Stoph telephoned, if she were going to telephone, if Klaus had told her he'd see me.

A woman laughed, lower in the building, one of the tarts, I suppose. I didn't think the top-floor rooms were used, or at least not by the girls: when I'd been shown along the passage most of the doors had been open, with nothing in the rooms except for tin trunks, mattresses, a portable bidet, some newspapers, no beds or furniture. But the room was all right because it was on the third floor and the one window wasn't overlooked and there was a metal fire escape and a courtyard with six-foot walls on three sides. When the woman with the huge mole on her neck had left me I'd stood outside on the fire escape and checked on the roof; there wasn't easy access but it could be done if it didn't snow. It surprised me that a man like Thrower had chosen a place like this; it should have offended his sensibilities; perhaps he'd just signaled Kleiber's support group and asked them where he should book me in.

The biggest dealer across the globe is Sarkis Soghanalian, born a Turkish-Armenian Christian and naturalized as a Lebanese. He lives most of the time in the U.S.A. The weaponry he has sold has been used in Lebanon, Nicaragua, Angola, Ghana, Biafra, you name it, even against Britain in the Falklands miniwar, though Soghanalian claims he is friendly to the U.S. and her allies in the West.

He spoke quietly, Ahmad Samala, leaving silences for note taking; sometimes I could hear his smile when he talked about new weapons, the latest and shiniest of his toys... *Terpil was after that particular model but I beat him to it, and he was most upset....*

There was a telephone in here; they'd led an extension cable from the next room, but there was a big enough gap under my door for it to shut. I would be glad when the thing rang: I didn't know the timing for the day. Inge could call Kleiber and make a rendezvous an hour from now and it could take me an hour to reach there. I would also be glad when Cone rang to say he was in Berlin; the executive would have a director in the field and *Solitaire* could start running again and those bloody people controlling the board in London could settle down and try and get things right in future:

Shatner must have been out of his mind to pick someone like Thrower to handle me.

My head was still throbbing, I think because I was feeling under pressure with so much information to take in against the clock.

He deals in everything from Brazilian tanks to helicopters and army uniforms, sometimes legally but not always. There are widespread thefts that go on at military bases all the time.

11:00 hours.

He's rather touchy when people tell him he's a merchant of death. He asks them how the big chemical manufacturers feel, selling the stuff they do—if they don't feel guilty, why should he?

12:00 hours.

He couldn't have been in Europe, then, Cone, when Signals had called him in.

They don't have allegiance to any flag or organization, remember, and they need wars in order to prosper. It makes them different.

I wanted to phone Kleiber and ask him if he'd had instructions from London to mount a search for Helen Maitland, but it would tie up the line and I had to stay open for Cone, for Kleiber.

A TWA jumbo dropped through the sky on its approach path, trailing a skein of exhaust gas through the winter sunshine.

We must remember that because arms dealers meet so many people in government and military circles, they pick up some very sensitive information, and there are those who trade that information for as high a price as they can get, and that is often very high indeed. They—

The phone began ringing and the nerve light flashed behind my right eye, the side where I'd banged my head. I picked up the receiver.

"*Bitte?*"

"Mr. Jones?"

"Yes."

Cone.

"Your place or mine?"

I asked him: "Does Kleiber know you're here?"

"I phoned him from the plane."

"You'd better come to my place," I told him. It was Kleiber's number I'd given to Inge, and this was where he'd call me.

"Bring anything?" Cone asked.

"No."

I shut down and switched on the tape again.

There was another accident in Kansas, U.S.A., during a propellant transfer for a recycling operation. A pipe broke loose from the missile in the silo and there was a release of nitrogen tetroxide.

Samala was talking about the availability of nerve gas from legitimate sources when Cone arrived, his footsteps picking their way across the bare boards of the corridor with deliberation. I opened the door and he came in and took a quick look around.

"Economy class."

"It's good in terms of security."

"Oh yes." He would have noticed the fire escape and the fact that the room was at the other end of the building from the stairs, so that you could hear people coming.

"Sit down," I said, and he looked carefully at the iron bedstead and the two art deco chairs and sat down in one of them and pulled a manila envelope out of his coat and gave it to me.

"Stuff on the Miniver missile. You wanted it, didn't you?"

"Yes."

"They gave it to me in London. It's also been faxed to Thrower's hotel, and I'll have it picked up there. It's nothing classified, just the specifications, mostly from Jane's. Bit of action was there?"

I suppose my eyes were still a bit nervy.

"Yes. Nothing serious. Bump on the head."

"Doesn't show. Anything else?"

"Bruised shoulder."

"Still use it?"

"Yes." I showed him.

"How d'you feel?"

"First-class."

He nodded and stopped talking. He'd been like this in Moscow, fussing about injuries, part of his job. One of the responsibilities of the director in the field is to make sure his executive doesn't go into any kind of action unless he's fit. He sat watching me with his bright, attentive eyes, the window throwing light across his raw, peeled-looking face, the cheekbones sharp under the skin, the ear nearer the window so thin that it was translucent. Cone, wherever he is, even in summer, looks as if he's walking against a blizzard, and more than that, as if he created it for himself, perhaps as a penance.

"Did you get any briefing in London?" I asked him.

"The lot."

"From Shatner?"

"Yes."

"How was he?"

"Pissed off."

"He could've got me killed, giving me that clown. What about debriefing on this side?"

"I was an hour with said clown at the airport—London set it up. He was told to wait for me to come in before he booked out."

I would have expected London to do that, to have Thrower go through the whole of the debriefing he'd given me so that I wouldn't have to do it all over again for Cone.

"Let's hope it was accurate," I said.

"It sounded all right. He's got a good memory. What about timing, then?"

"I'm waiting for a call from Inge Stoph through Kleiber. Whatever time she suggests, I'll have to be there."

"So tell me what's got to be done before you leave."

"As soon as you can, tell Kleiber to send someone along to the taxi rank outside the Steglitz Hotel. Ask them if Helen

141

Maitland got into one of their cabs and if so, where she was taken. The doorman offered to get her one but she said she felt like a walk."

"Description?"

I gave it to him.

"All right. You trust her, do you?"

"We can't. She's naïve and she's totally subservient to men. If anyone told her to walk into a trap, that's what she'd do."

"And that's what you think she's done."

"Possibly."

"And if anyone asked her the wrong questions?"

"That's why Thrower moved me out of the Steglitz right away."

Cone got out of the chair, moving around. "Better not phone Kleiber yet."

"Not until he phones us. You can tell him then."

"Right."

I was going through the documents in the envelope; they were a breakdown on the Miniver, specifications, capability, technical drawings, disposition of all known models, mostly in the U.S.A., some in the U.K., some in Germany.

"That what you wanted?" Cone asked me.

"It's perfect."

"Thank goodness something's perfect, then."

I dropped the documents onto the bed. "I hope you're not worried," I said.

He leaned one shoulder against the window frame, looking down at me, sometimes turning his head as a plane moved through the pale sunshine outside. "Thrower said you're going to try getting into Nemesis on your own and with no support, and you'll be relying on your cover and nothing else, is that right?"

"Yes."

In a moment he said, "You did this to me before, in Berlin."

"Then you should be used to it."

"True."

142

He watched me steadily for a moment and then turned away, and I've seen that look before when the mission's running hot and there's no place for the shadow to go except into a red sector: they wonder if it's the last time they're going to see you. It used to worry me, but it doesn't anymore.

"There's no other way," I told him.

You couldn't stop anyone putting a bomb on a plane by relying on conventional security measures, with forty or fifty thousand commercial flights a day going through the airports worldwide. The high-tech plastic explosive, Semtex, was colorless and odorless and it could be molded into any shape, a shoe or a hairbrush or a teddy bear, and at the moment there was no equipment in Europe that could detect it in a suitcase or a handbag. Cone knew that.

"The only way," I told him, "is to get inside the organization that's planning to plant a bomb and wipe it out in time."

He watched an Air France 727 nosing into the sky. "Oh, I'm not arguing. So are you going to use any kind of base?"

"A car."

"Where?"

"I don't know until I know where the rendezvous is."

He came and sat down again, facing me, his arms across his knees. "You want somebody to watch the car?"

"No."

It could be a night action and I wouldn't be able to identify him. Nemesis could find out that the car was mine and put a watch on it too.

"Are you going in wired?" Cone asked me.

"No."

The idea was tempting, but if they found a mike on me it'd blow my cover, and my cover was all I'd have.

The cold was getting into me, into my bones.

"You don't carry weapons," Cone said, "that right?"

"No."

A successful arms dealer is a businessman and he doesn't carry a gun, and even if I had one on me when I went close enough to Nemesis they'd look for it and find it and take it away.

"You carry a capsule?" Cone asked me.

"No."

I wasn't infiltrating the regime of the host country and the only interest Nemesis would take in the Bureau was personal: they didn't want us to get in their way, that was all. If they put me under implemented interrogation and blew my cover and found I was operating against them they'd simply finish things off and get a body bag.

"You need a courier?"

"No."

I was taking the ultimate risk and it wasn't likely that I could make contact with a courier without exposing him.

"What about a deadline?" Cone asked me.

"I can't give you one. I don't know where I'll be by 18:00 hours or midnight or 06:00 or noon. In any case you can't send in anyone to look for me. But for the board, if you like, call it noon tomorrow. If I haven't been able to make some kind of signal by then, you can tell them to send out a new shadow."

Cone studied his dry, scaly hands. "There's not much," he said, "I can do, then, for the moment."

"Not much, no. But if I can go in and get out you'll have a lot to do." There'd be enough signals to light up the board in London, because if I could blow Nemesis from the center there'd be a lot of fallout and we'd hand things over to the *Bundeskriminalamt* to hunt down the survivors and make arrests.

"Questions?" Cone asked me.

"No." He'd had the London briefing and my own debriefing and he knew as much about the way the mission was running as I did. There was nothing I needed to ask him.

"Then you better get on with your homework."

"Yes."

He got up and stood at the window for a moment, watching a TWA jumbo go sloping into the sky.

"It must give you the willies," he said as he turned round. "All those people."

"Yes."

"You know where to find me," he said, and I opened the door and watched him picking his way along the passage, his thin body angled forward a little against the blizzard in his soul.

14:00 hours.

The statistics relevant to the legitimate sale of AK47 assault rifles are as follows. . . .

15:00 hours.

The U.S. dollar is the standard currency in all arms deals of any importance. . . .

16:00 hours.

And as the late-winter sunshine changed from rose to purple across the roofs of the buildings opposite my window, and the planes moved through the twilight with the stealth of phantoms before their sound came in, I became prey to the feeling that the telephone standing on the lopsided barewood table was never, after all, going to ring, that Dieter Klaus wasn't here in Berlin or that Inge Stoph hadn't been able to contact him.

I couldn't assume that he'd be interested, in any case, in a tactical nuclear missile: his plans to put a bomb on board a Pan Am plane could already be advanced. He might not even have time for a meeting with a strange arms dealer with new toys to sell: he might have all he needed.

Singapore and Israel both possess several high-tech armaments that are not available anywhere else in the world. . . .

At 17:00 hours I sat in the semidarkness of the little room, with the recorder shut off and my mind ranging across the data that I'd been feeding into it since this morning. A big jet reached for altitude across the skyline with its strobes flashing and the thin line of its windows slanting through the dark.

So Dieter Klaus wasn't in Berlin or Inge Stoph hadn't been able to contact him *or she knew about the ambush they'd set for me in the underground garage, knew my cover story was false*, was that why the telephone hadn't rung?

I didn't think so. If Sorgenicht had recognized me in the cafeteria and phoned for support they would have gone for me in the car park while I was talking to Inge: they wouldn't have waited. It hadn't been Sorgenicht who'd got onto me; when they'd started the search for Krenz they must have intercepted some of the calls going out from the Mercedes to the SAAB and traced them and found the SAAB in the garage and set the trap, waiting for me to go back to it.

There was no connection between the unknown man who had taken over the Mercedes from Krenz and the man who had openly approached Inge Stoph in the car park.

She didn't know who I was, or if she knew, and telephoned with a rendezvous, it would be fatal to keep it.

But I wouldn't know.

I walked about, restless, up and down the narrow room, the floorboards creaking and the sound of the girls rising from the rooms below as they laughed for their money at the outset of the long night's parody of love.

A plane thundered into the dark.

And now the appalling idea came to me that I'd been wasting time, trusting the whole of the mission to a hypothetical rendezvous while all those people were busy packing their bags and saying good-bye to friends and filing through the departure gate for their exciting ride with the little teddy bear. I'd have to signal Cone and tell him there was a change of plan, I'd need to find another way in to Nemesis if it wasn't already too late, but the phone began ringing suddenly in the quiet room and I swung round and picked it up and Kleiber told me that Inge Stoph had called to say that if I wanted to talk to Dieter Klaus I must be at the northwest corner of Waldschule Allee and Harbig Strasse at 5:15 this evening and that I must go there alone.

Chapter 13

Klaus

*A*nd *now Johan has the puck and he's leading with it all the
way and he's going as if there just isn't anybody here to stop him.
This is only his second time out since the injury he sustained at
Frankfurt, but that's obviously old history by the way he's moving.*

Floodlights roofed the night.

"Isn't he amazing?" Inge asked me.

I said yes, amazing.

"Would you like one?" Waving a *bratwurst*.

"Thank you." I hadn't eaten since this morning.

*But we didn't expect Tommy Warnke to get across there so fast
and it looks as if Johan's going to have his work cut out unless he
can pile on that extra turn of speed he's so famous for.*

The stadium was packed, the colors of the sweaters and
scarves and woolen hats turning it into a vast flower bed.

"You like ice hockey?" Inge asked me.

"Very much."

I'd reached the northwest corner of Waldschule Allee and
Harbig Strasse at the precise hour for the rendezvous and
paid off the taxi and the crimson Porsche 911 had pulled in
to the curb with a squeal of tires.

"Hans!"

She waved from the car and I went across to it and got in.

"It's so nice to see you again!" Showgirl smile, the eyes
ice-bright and observant. She took the Porsche away with a
dash of expertise, her right hand caressing the gear knob.
She was wearing the same crimson calf-length boots, but

tonight she sported a Russian fur hat with fur gloves to match.

A dark green Jaguar was trailing us: it had pulled up behind the Porsche and started off again, keeping close enough to make sure no one slipped in between. Later it overtook us and the woman at the wheel glanced across at Inge and away; then she held back and began trailing again. Inge knew the Jaguar was with us, but didn't say anything. She drove steadily, playing the lights and the traffic lanes without flash but with effectiveness.

"Dieter said he can only give you a few minutes," she told me as we waited for a green. "But even so, you're lucky."

"So is he," I said. "I assume you told him what I've got for him?"

She looked at me. "You don't understand. It's very difficult to get Dieter to see anyone at all."

"It's very difficult," I said, "to keep me waiting so long for a meeting."

The lights changed to green and she shifted the gear-lever. "So? Then why did you decide to wait?"

I let my eyes move over her face. "For one thing I find you charming."

"Thank you."

She wasn't impressed: she was a knockout and she knew it. But she flashed me the dazzling sharp-toothed feline smile, and I was fairly sure now that Dieter Klaus had instructed her to spring a Venus trap on me, and I was going to walk right into it because I knew how to pick up information that way. It would also be in keeping with my cover: an international arms dealer passing through Berlin wouldn't turn down the chance of a night with a girl like Inge Stoph.

"And for another thing?" she asked me.

"I confess to a certain admiration for Dieter Klaus."

She said rather quickly—"What do you know about him?"

"Not very much, but in my trade the word gets around that he's different from the kind of thugs you find, say, in the *Rote Armee Faktion*."

"That's exactly the word," Inge said. "Dieter Klaus is very different."

It was all she said, and she drove in silence until we reached the stadium.

I'd telephoned Cone before I left the hotel, and told him what time the rendezvous was, and where. He said he already knew: Kleiber had signaled him. I canceled the car: it was a mobile rendezvous with no fixed address and I didn't know the area, didn't know where they could leave a car for me to reach if I needed one. Cone made a last try, asking me if I'd changed my mind about using support. I said I hadn't.

I don't think I've ever seen Braun so quick with the passes—I think the comeback Johan has made is inspiring him, and in fact the whole team.

I glanced sometimes at Dieter Klaus.

"He's over there," Inge had told me when we'd sat down.

There were two men and four women around him: they were three rows down across the aisle in the best seats, the *Ehrentribüne*. My view of him wasn't obstructed but it was at an angle of ten or fifteen degrees from behind, and I only saw his face when he turned to speak to the woman on his left. His head was bare; his hair was dressed in the Prussian style, brush-cut and blond. He wore a black overcoat with a dark sable collar, no gloves, a pair of designer sunglasses.

His entourage was fitted out with the same black padded tracksuit for each of them, except for the woman on his left. She wore a tourmaline mink coat and hat, a flash of gold at her ears, nothing on her wrists unless it was under a sleeve. She was young, dark-skinned, a Latin, and she was giving more of her attention to the game than to Dieter Klaus, even when he turned his head to say something.

Inge watched him with a lot more interest. She was sitting on my right, so that when she moved her head to look across at Klaus I couldn't see her eyes, but the angle of her head and its stillness told me a great deal, and when she turned to look at me for a moment to talk about him, the expression in her eyes was clear enough: Dieter Klaus was the object of her adoration.

"He's here in Berlin tonight," she told me, "for a special reason. Normally he stays in Frankfurt—he flew in an hour ago."

"Quite an *aficionado*."

She looked surprised for an instant. "Yes, but he didn't come to Berlin tonight to watch ice hockey."

"It sounds interesting," I said. "Something, perhaps, I can help him with?"

She gave me a long look. "No. Everything is arranged."

Teddy bear.

And Lange takes the puck but he's not too well placed for a strike if he means to go for a goal at this distance and with those two quarterbacks moving in from the flank. But he's got the speed if he wants to take it closer before he strikes—just look at that!

Teddy bear in the sky.

He was fifty feet away from where I was sitting, Dieter Klaus, and the thought was running through my mind that if I could get close enough to him when we were leaving the stadium I might go for a quick direct kill and take it from there, keep the others off me if I could, use the confusion and the crowd for cover. They wouldn't use guns, even if they had any; it was illegal to carry arms in this city and the sound of shots would bring the police and security much faster than a brawl.

It was simply a thought, running through my head. I was not mad; I knew the risks; but the situation was so obviously attractive: the executive for *Solitaire* was within fifty feet of the target and if he could close that distance to within killing range he could complete the mission in a matter of seconds and two or three hundred people would board their flight and feel nothing worse than a touch of jet lag at the other end, *attractive*, such a *very* attractive situation.

"With legs as long as that," Inge was calling above the

sudden roar of the crowd, "I'm not surprised he can make that kind of speed!"

I said no, it wasn't surprising, something like that.

There was another thought in my mind, less attractive. Inge had been full of suspicion this morning at the airport when I'd told her we'd met at one of Willi's parties, and I couldn't tell how much I'd convinced her that it was true—that she simply didn't remember me. I might not have convinced her at all: she could have brought me here tonight to have me killed.

"Do you smoke?"

She had a packet of Players in her hand.

"I'm trying to quit."

She flashed her smile and lit a cigarette, and the scent of marijuana came on the air.

To have me killed, because I didn't know what she'd said to Dieter Klaus when she'd phoned him in Frankfurt. *I've just met an arms dealer who says he respects you and what you're doing. He supports people who try to bring down the capitalistic establishment, and he says he can sell you a nuclear missile. Are you interested?*

That would be all right. That would be very nice. But she might have said something quite different. *I've just met a man who says that he knows you and your organization—he even knows its name. He says he knows that you have substantial backing from Colonel Qaddafi. He pretended he'd met me before, but I've never seen him in my life, and I think you should have him worked over to find out who he is. If you like, I can bring him to you.*

That would not be all right. It would not be very nice at all. But that is what I thought she'd probably said to Klaus, and those were the terms of the critical risk I was taking. I hadn't walked in here with much hope of getting clear again if I wanted to, if I had to. I was committed now: if I got up and tried to walk out of here I wouldn't get farther than the car park if they didn't want me to, the people in the black tracksuits. I didn't underestimate them because three of them were women: I've trained too many women myself at Norfolk in the lethal use of the hands. The man would only be there in case he was needed.

And as Johan gets through and shapes for the strike he's no more than two feet ahead of Lieberman and he'll need an awful lot of speed to bring this one off.

I was committed, and that had been my intent. From here I could only go in deeper, all the way to the center, and I could only get out by destroying Nemesis first.

"She's one of his girls," Inge said.

"Yes? What's her name?"

"Dolores. I'm one of his girls too, one of his concubines. We share him. It's an honor."

Her eyes were shimmering.

"How nice for him."

She drew on the cigarette, deeply. "We'd do anything for him." She looked at me with her eyes narrowing. "We would kill for him."

I said, "He must have quite a lot of enemies."

"Of course. They are dealt with."

One of the players made a goal and the crowd roared and I tried to think how to bring George Maitland into the conversation, and Helen. This girl might know where Helen was, what had happened to her. *There was an Englishman, I remember, killed in Berlin last week, Mayford, was it, or Mason? Was he one of Dieter's enemies?* But I couldn't risk it; there were too many reasons for murder in a big city, and there didn't have to be any connection with Nemesis.

"I must ask Dieter," I said, "why he flew in to Berlin tonight. You've got me interested."

She looked at me. "He might tell you. He might not."

"I'm a salesman, Inge, and at the moment I'm selling something rather impressive. As I told you, he could take out an entire sports stadium like this one."

She looked around her. "That would be impressive, yes. That would be powerful." Her eyes had darkened, the blue ice gathering shadows. "I like power. That's why I'm with

Dieter Klaus. He's the most powerful man in Europe. It'll be interesting to see what he thinks about you, Hans, but I must tell you something. I have a very good memory, and I've never been to one of Willi Hartman's parties in my life."

Please check to make sure you haven't left any belongings on your seat, and be patient with children and elderly people . . . they may be a little slower than the rest of us.

"Wait," Inge said.

People moved past us, and she slipped between them and went down the steps and spoke to Klaus, and for an instant he looked across at me. Then Inge turned and came back, her eyes bright as she said, "He'll see you for a moment outside the stadium."

She put a hand on my arm, and we waited until Klaus and his bodyguards moved past us to the exit tunnel. He didn't look in our direction; none of them did. It was a huge crowd but we kept up a good pace once we'd started moving.

"Then it must have been somewhere else," I'd told her, and she'd laughed lightly and said yes, it must have been, but I knew now that when she'd phoned Dieter Klaus she might have told him that I was an arms dealer but she'd also told him that I'd pretended we'd met before and seemed suspect, so perhaps he should have me worked over.

"Did you like the game?" she asked me.

"Very much."

Her smile was different now; it had secret amusement in it, and her eyes were cold fire. I didn't think it was the marijuana. I thought that if she could consider the idea of destroying a packed sports stadium and find it "impressive," she'd probably feel turned on by escorting a man to his execution.

We were held back at one of the gates to the car park by an old man with a ruff of silver hair below his black wool hat; he'd dropped something, a glove, I think, and Inge brushed past him with a quick laugh—"Don't you think that when people get to a certain age they should be shot?"

153

They were ahead of us, Klaus and his guards and the woman, Dolores; then they slowed as they neared a black Mercedes limousine with smoked windows and an array of antennae over the boot. A uniformed driver opened a rear door and Dolores got in; then Inge stopped me with her hand as Dieter Klaus swung round.

"What do you want to see me about?"

"I'll tell you in private."

"Why in private?"

"Because I don't talk in the presence of hirelings."

He studied me, his hands in the pockets of his black sable-trimmed coat, his blunt head forward, his mouth tight. I couldn't see his eyes. He spoke in jerks, his whole body moving, energized by his thoughts.

"You've heard of bodyguards. I don't talk to strangers except in the presence of my bodyguards."

"I won't hurt you, Klaus."

I caught a soft sound from Inge. I suppose she thought I was being disrespectful to the *Führer*.

"You say you are an *arms* dealer. An *arms* dealer."

"That's right. If we—"

"Why should that interest me?"

I took a step forward, as if to be closer so that I could lower my voice, and the bodyguards came in very fast indeed and crossed in front of Klaus in a protective shield with their hands coming up into the *Ken-po* defense posture. One of them was Asian, I thought Mongol. They stared at me with the indifference in their eyes of a predator before the kill. I had needed to know how good they were.

I couldn't see Klaus anymore, or at least not much of him, just the left lens of his dark glasses. I waited.

In a moment Klaus said, "Leave him."

They moved slowly backward, lowering their hands.

"Klaus," I said, "you've been told what I've got to offer you. That offer expires at midnight. I've got an appointment tomorrow with the Soviet Foreign Minister in Geneva. My plane—"

"Answer my question. Why have you approached me with this offer?"

"Because you're a professional in your field. I like dealing with professionals. We could—"

"What do you know about me?"

"I can see you in private," I said, "for half an hour. But—"

"What do you know about me?"

I looked at my watch. "I'm afraid you're wasting my time. I'll give you another—"

"Take him."

They wore soft shoes and were with me almost in silence, locking my arms, and then Klaus said, "Take him to the garage. Give him to Geissler. Tell Geissler to find out who he is and what he wants."

I saw Inge, her eyes bright as she called out to Klaus— "Can I be there too?"

He swung to look at her. "Yes."

Chapter 14

Strobe

I was spinning on the wall of the vortex, spinning very fast.

The vortex had been the sea itself, and then the wind had come and the sea drew down in the center and began whirling and I was in it, whirling on the dark wall of the vortex, a thing with its arms and legs flung out and its mouth open, screaming.

But sometimes lucidity came, like a shaft of brilliant light, and I saw myself in the chair, my wrists handcuffed to its arms, my head held back by a strap so that I couldn't lower it, couldn't look away from the light.

It was a strobe light.

Then the vortex took me down again, a huge dark wave leaping and roaring down and sweeping me with it and leaving me spinning on the wall of water, the wall of the vortex, and I began screaming again, but the other sound was louder, drowning my voice. I was in terror of the sound.

It was a piezo electric siren.

It was filling the room, the garage, with such a volume of sound that the walls would belly outward before long and the roof crash down, surely it must happen with this monstrous volume of sound filling the room, the garage. The piezo had a faster beat than the strobe light. The flashes of the strobe were hitting my closed eyes at something like fifty or sixty per minute, but the rhythm of the siren was in the region of five oscillations a second, slicing through my head

157

and pinning me to the wall of dark water.

Whirling and screaming in the huge dark vortex, a black hole, an otherworld, death.

Lucidity again and a degree of self-awareness, enough to know that the sweat was crawling on my face and my pulse racing, the saliva springing into my mouth so fast that I had to keep swallowing: the whole of the nervous system had become galvanized.

Flash—flash—flash.

Any conception of time had been destroyed somewhere in the past. I didn't know if I'd been here for three hours or three days. The thing was to keep the integrity of the organism unbroken, to hack out a pathway through this miasma and maintain orientation, but my brain was in theta waves and it could only surface with an effort of will, and in the theta region access to the will is diminished, dangerously diminished, *flash—flash—flash*—as the mind rocked, as the dark wall of the vortex reared and whirled.

Then they shut off the sound.

Silence exploded and I was left in the debris of the shock, spinning among waves of color, powerless to reach any kind of shore where beta-wave thought could begin again, until over the minutes the colors of the waves of silence drained away, and I thought I heard a voice.

"Who are you?"

My face was wet. The whole organism was vibrating: it felt like a bell, vibrating. "What?" I heard someone say, "What?" But that was me.

"Who are you?"

Flash—flash—flash.

"Turn off that light," I said.

"Who are you?"

"Turn off that *fucking* light."

Flash—flash—flash.

"I'm going to ask you some questions. When you've answered them, I'll turn off the light."

Rage was beginning now as the natural reaction to shock, and if I hadn't been handcuffed to the chair I might have got up and killed him, killed someone, killed as many of them as I could reach because there was more than one man in here, more than one of them, but then we must think, we must do a little thinking, because I'd come here with a cover and that was what I must use, the only weapon I had, the only one that could keep the mission running. I hadn't got this close to Nemesis in order to kill some people and get clear. I was here to go in deeper, right to the center. There was no place here for rage.

Flash—flash—flash.

Ignore.

"I might decide," I said, "to answer questions, and I might not. We'll see."

"... difficult."

"What? Listen, that thing's left my head buzzing, you ought to know that. You'll have to speak up."

"Who are you?"

"Hans Mittag."

"What business are you in?"

"Armaments. I buy and sell."

"What were you doing at the airport this morning?"

"None of your bloody business."

"I need to know."

"I was seeing someone off, but I'm not going to tell you his name. He's a business associate. Tell Klaus that if he wants what I've offered him he's got to pay for it. You'll never brainwash it out of me, you understand that?"

He didn't say anything for a moment. I let my eyes come open a little, and saw some shapes. They were floating behind the flashing light, because it had produced tears and they were still coming. I think there were three men here, and there was another face, beautiful, a woman's, Inge's.

"What?"

I thought he'd spoken. Perhaps he hadn't. I was still in

an altered state of consciousness, would be for a while, that was the object of the exercise, to disorientate before they started the questions.

"How long have you been an arms dealer?"

"Several years."

"How many?"

"Oh Jesus Christ, haven't you ever met an arms dealer before? We don't *start* at any specific time, it's not like reporting for your first day at a bloody *bank*, you don't just—" have to watch it, I mustn't get cross, it doesn't suit the cover, my head was still full of the most appalling noises, that was all, and I wanted to kill someone for doing that to me, kill one of these people, kill Klaus, Dieter Klaus, yes, well that's on the cards, isn't it, he's the target for the mission, kill that bloody—

" . . . You work in?"

"What?"

"Tell me what main area you work in."

"God, what a vague question, you mean what do I buy and sell or do you mean where do I go to do it? I buy and sell anything I can make a profit on and I go all over the world, is this the way Klaus normally does business with arms dealers, I thought he was an intelligent human being."

Don't get cross.

I suppose she'd asked Klaus if she could come here, Inge, in case they found I was some kind of spook and took me outside and tore me apart, and then she could play with the giblets like cats do when they've killed a mouse; her beautiful ice-blue eyes had been shining when she'd called out to him, *Can I be there too?* like a little girl asking Daddy if she could go to the party, bitch, she was a *bitch*, very thirsty now, I was very thirsty but I wasn't going to ask these bastards for anything, a pox on them, steady now, steady lad, get the nerves back in the basket or you're a goner, you'll blow the whole thing.

"Where do you go, for instance?"

"Go? China, for instance, wouldn't you? Look, there's been a tremendous proliferation of sources of matériel in the last few years because we've got all these lovely wars to keep going, but China's still very much in business—I'd put it about eighth on the list of the major world suppliers."

"Where else?"

He had a thin voice, and I believe a thin face: I could see it floating near the *flash—flash—flash* of that bloody strobe. He was wearing black goggles, welder's goggles, the bastard—*I could use a pair of those.*

"You don't have to go far, surely you know that. There are still over two hundred thousand Soviet troops hanging around in this country waiting to be sent home, and a lot of them are raiding their stores for anything they can carry. They—"

"But you deal in bigger things than that, don't you?"

"They steal *tanks,* aren't tanks big enough for you? Even Soghanalian deals in them, because when—"

"Who?"

"Sarkis Soghanalian, he's the biggest dealer there is, an absolute pro, a Turkish-Armenian Christian with Lebanese papers, lives in the U.S.A.—"

"What other dealers do you know?"

Flash—flash—flash.

I told him about Terpil, Korkala, people like that.

"What about the Turkish border?"

Flash—flash—flash.

I told him about the traffic in Semtex, the traffic in drugs.

The strobe wasn't inducing hallucinations as the piezo siren had done, but it was keeping me just below full beta-wave consciousness, and that was what he wanted, the man with the thin voice, the thin face, Gestler, no, Geissler, *Take him to the garage, give him to Geissler,* yes, he wanted me just below the surface, uncritical, unwary, and I'd have to be very careful, because—

"Go on."

161

"What? That bloody light's making me sleepy."

"You were talking about the exchange of sensitive information."

"That's right, I mean we meet a lot of top people on government level, and so we pick up some very valuable information, get a high price for it if we work it right, better than tanks, sometimes."

Flash—flash—flash.

Asked me about the U.S. scene.

Told him.

Asked me about a lot of other things, and sometimes I felt myself smiling, just as he had smiled, little Ahmed Samala when he was talking about his toys, the sweat drying on my face and the eyes still streaming, their faces floating in the rhythmic pulsing of light and dark, told him what he wanted to know.

"Where was that?"

"In the U.S.A, in Arkansas. An airman dropped a nine-pound socket from a spanner inside a Titan silo, and it punched a hole in the skin of a fuel cell and started a leak, and this is the funny bit, there was a seven-hundred-and-fifty-ton steel door on the silo and when that fuel went off it sent it two hundred feet straight into the air and dropped it a thousand feet away."

"You were there?"

"If I'd been there, I wouldn't be here. No, Soghanalian told me about it. These things happen."

Flash—flash—flash.

"Do you ever deal in nuclear armaments? Or components?"

I tried to look at him through the tears. "Do I *what?*"

"Do you ever deal in—"

"I heard what you said, but what the hell are you talking about? Didn't they tell you?"

"Tell me what?"

He was testing me out, that was all. He'd done a lot of that, asking me to repeat things to see if I was consistent.

"I'm offering to sell Dieter Klaus an NK-9 Miniver."

"And what is that?"

"Look, if Klaus wants to know the specifics, I'm willing to tell him, providing it's in a civilized environment. I'm not used to discussing an arms deal worth a million U.S. dollars in a garage. Now you'd better listen to this. You're behaving like a gang of thugs and it surprises me because Dieter Klaus has got a reputation for running a really sophisticated organization, but if you'll switch that thing off and get me out of this chair we can talk about things. I'm still ready to do a deal with Klaus, but he'll have to prove he's serious. All he's done so far is make me very annoyed."

The tears streaming on my face, nothing much more in my head now but the *flash—flash—flash* of the strobe, and then it stopped.

Not altogether. It went on, but only under my eyelids now, not right through my head.

"Release him," Geissler said.

People moved about, and someone came close, smell of tobacco. The handcuffs came off. Working, he was working on the strap now, the strap on my head. I couldn't hear too well, there was quite a degree of tinnitus, these bastards had been wearing ear protectors, must have been.

"What is the Miniver like?"

Geissler.

"I've told you, I'm not—"

"Just a brief description, nothing specific."

I opened my eyes, got out a handkerchief. The bodyguards who'd brought me here had gone, but there were two other people, both men this time, both with guns hanging from their hands. Inge was leaning against the redbrick wall, one foot against it behind her, arms folded, I couldn't see the expression in her eyes, things were still floating a bit. Geissler was quite tall, not your usual mobster, quite intelligent-looking, but then his questions had been like that, quite intelligent; I could see him holding a violin, or a baton, except for his eyes, which had as much soul in them as a steel trap.

He was waiting.

"It's a tactical nuclear missile," I said, "capable of being launched by a designated officer of high rank in the field at his personal discretion—or by anyone in his command, presumably, under his supervision, I'm not sure of the niceties. The Miniver can knock out an entire division, or as I told Inge, a sports stadium or the Houses of Parliament in London, what you will. That's all I can tell you."

I got out of the chair, and no one stopped me. They still looked like figures in some kind of netherworld, and I wasn't too steady on my feet, but that was to be expected. Presumably my cover had stood up, or the Stoph girl would be out there playing with my giblets by now.

"My name is Geissler," the thin man said, "Ignaz Geissler." He offered his hand. "I'll take you to see Dieter Klaus."

There was no one in the room.

"I'll tell him you've arrived," Geissler said, and left me. He didn't lock the door: I would have heard it, even though there was still some lingering tinnitus ringing in my head from that awful piezo thing.

The heavy silk curtains were drawn across the windows and I didn't part them to look out; on principle I don't like to offer a blatant target, though I didn't think anyone here was likely to shoot at me. They could have done that in the garage if they'd wanted to.

Geissler had ordered one of the men there to blindfold me again, and had apologized in his dry way, calling it an "inconvenient measure of security." Then they'd put me into a car and Geissler and another man had sat in the back with me, and I'd smelled gun oil. The garage had been somewhere south of Tegel Airport, because we hadn't gone far from the *Eissporthalle*, and on our way here I'd monitored the sound of the planes along their flight paths and the hooting of the tugs and barges on the Tegelersee, and I would have said the house was northwest of the airport but not far away, eight or nine kilometers, perhaps in Kreis Oranienburg.

The room was spacious, elegant: white-enameled fluted moldings, shot-silk wall covering, a twelve-foot ceiling, the furniture mostly reproduction Edwardian, the carpeting heavy, brocaded at the fringe. The magazines neatly arranged on the low polished table near the hearth were mostly German—*Stern, Quick, Brigitte*—and American—*Life, Time, Newsweek*—with some newspapers lying on the chair nearby, one of them Arabic, the Farsi-language *Jomhuri Islami*, with a picture of the President of Iran on the front page, which I thought was interesting.

There were no flowers in the room, and no bowls of potpourri anywhere that I could see, but there was a faint perfume on the air, as if a woman had been here recently, or came often.

I assumed they'd brought me to the headquarters of Nemesis.

It would please London, give them something for the board, pick up the bit of chalk, then—*Executive has maintained cover, infiltrated opposition headquarters*, three cheers for the poor bloody ferret in the field, that'd teach them to give me a clown like Thrower for my DIF, but we're getting petty, aren't we, a touch spiteful, that's the way it goes, though, in this trade—they've got so much raw naked *power* over us, those bastards in London, because the only way anyone can turn himself into a professional spook and work for an outfit as sacrosanct as the Bureau is to sell them his soul and submit to a degree of discipline that would put a regimental sergeant major straight into shock. We're expected to—

"So!"

Klaus.

I hadn't heard the door open. Perhaps he hadn't meant me to.

"We must shake hands, mustn't we, Herr Mittag, now that I know who you are. Sit down, please, sit down."

He wasn't wearing the smoked glasses now. His eyes were very dark, would look black in some lights: I thought he might be using colored contact lenses, because his hair was so blond in contrast. He sat on the edge of the settee, leaving me one of the silk-brocade chairs; he sat facing me directly, leaning forward with his hands on his knees. "We must have dinner later, and you'll stay the night, of course. Hans Mittag . . . I'm surprised I haven't heard your name before, if you're important enough to deal in the kind of armament Inge mentioned—we can speak freely here, of course."

Not really.

I said, "I use several names."

"That explains it, of course, I expected it to be the case, yes. Now tell me about the Miniver NK-9."

"Are you in the market for it?"

I didn't lean forward to face him; it was a wing chair, and comfortable, and I felt like taking it easy after that garage thing.

"I am in the market for it, yes," Klaus said, "otherwise I wouldn't have had you brought here. But I need details."

His face was open, attentive, but the bright obsidian eyes had an intensity that reminded me that although I'd come out of that garage with a whole skin my cover was still my only protection. For as long as I stayed here at the center of Nemesis I was a fly on a web, and one wrong word could send it trembling.

"I'll give you the most important detail first," I told him. "My price for one fully primed Miniver NK-9 complete with electronic detonator is one million U.S. dollars, cash."

He lifted his square, heavy-looking hands from his knees and dropped them again. I think it was a gesture of impatience.

"You must know," he said, "that the details I'm asking for concern the missile and its capability. We'll discuss the price later."

"Surely I don't need to tell you, Herr Klaus, what a missile with a nuclear warhead will do. I've already given Stoph and your man Geissler an adequate idea. You could reduce the *Eissporthalle*, for instance, where you were sitting tonight, to radioactive ash, if you wanted to, and turn the entire district of Charlottenburg into a wasteground for a century to come, if not the whole of Berlin. The funds must be placed to a Swiss account, by the way, within twenty-four hours of your decision to buy the Miniver if that's the decision you're going to make."

He said nothing, went on staring at me. That was all right: I wasn't in any hurry. It was quiet in the room; there were logs burning in the hearth but the flames were soundless, at least to my ears. I hoped the effects of the piezo siren weren't going to last too long: I needed the full use of my senses.

Klaus said in a moment, "I should tell you that I don't actually require the complete missile. I require only the warhead."

"The price is the same."

His hands lifted again, dropped. "I assume the warhead can be used by itself? It would become, in effect, a bomb?"

"Oh yes. It could be detonated electronically in just the same way, or by a conventional explosive charge or by remote control. Yes, we'd be talking about a point-one-megaton nuclear bomb."

And a first, a real first for Nemesis in the annals of international terrorism: a nuclear Lockerbie. He had a sense of the dramatic, Dieter Klaus. You didn't need a Miniver warhead to bring down a 747 with two hundred and fifty people in it: you could do it with a teddy bear. But it would attract a lot more attention to have the rescue crews and investigators go into the scene wearing protective masks and clothing and armed with Geiger counters.

"You mean," Klaus said, "one tenth of a megaton?"

"Yes."

"That is a lot of power."

"Yes."

I waited for him to put the next question. He hadn't moved since we'd started talking, just his hands; he was still sitting forward, right on the edge of the settee, giving me all his attention. The only difference I could sense, as we watched each other now, was an added vibration in him: I could feel its waves. He'd begun to want the Miniver with great intensity, to lust after it. But he still didn't put the question: how could it be taken aboard a commercial jet?

"And when could you deliver the warhead?" he asked me instead.

"When do you want it delivered?"

"As soon as possible."

In a moment I said, and with the greatest care, "You know, of course, that this kind of bomb has got its drawbacks. You couldn't, for instance, get it through an inspection area." It was as far as I could go. "It's not like a bit of Semtex." It was as far as I could go because Willi had told Inge that these people were planning a Lockerbie thing, and Inge knew that Willi had talked to me. I'd be lighting a short-burn fuse if I mentioned an airport.

"That's no problem," Klaus said.

I didn't show any surprise. The Miniver warhead wasn't all that big: it'd go into a suitcase; but you wouldn't get it through an X-ray unit. It worried me a little; Klaus was deviating from the script, and I didn't know why.

I asked him, "Will you need a conventional explosive charge to provide detonation?"

"No."

He'd got one already: teddy bear. "You can deposit the funds in Geneva within twenty-four hours?"

"Yes," he said, and got up suddenly and walked about, marched almost, energized by his newfound lust for that bloody thing. "Half down, half on delivery."

"Here in Berlin?"

"No. In Algiers."

Oh really.

"I haven't any plans," I told him, "to go to Algiers, so I won't be there at the delivery point."

He stopped his restless pacing and turned and faced me. "If we are to complete this deal, Herr Mittag, I'd prefer you to remain within my organization as a respected guest until delivery is made. Then if there are any problems you'll be there to take care of them and receive the final payment." He was standing very still, watching me. "I don't insist on it, but I would prefer it. What do you say?"

I got out of the chair and turned away from him, took a step or two, turned back, because it'd seem natural for me to want a little time, to give it a little thought. But I didn't need any time and I didn't need to think. It was a trap, because he was giving me a choice and he didn't have to.

There was no good reason why I shouldn't stay with his organization through the performance of the deal; it's often done in cases like this when the final payment is to be made at the delivery point. I could refuse, but if I refused he'd know I was frightened of something or that I wasn't on the level and it'd be tantamount to blowing my own cover and he'd forget the Miniver and tell Geissler to put a bullet into the back of the head and take me across to the East side and leave me there for the garbage collectors to pick up.

But if I agreed to stay with his organization until the warhead was delivered it'd be the same thing as going to ground: I'd be cutting myself off from my director in the field and from London, and Cone would assume I'd bought it and they'd put me down on the signals board as missing, missing or deceased, and it might not turn out to be a lot different from the truth because the strain of keeping to my cover in an organization like this one even for another twenty-four hours would be critical—get a word wrong or forget something I'd said and *finis, finito*.

He was waiting for my answer, Klaus. But I hadn't any choice.

"If that's what you'd prefer," I said, "I'll stay, of course. See the deal through."

169

Chapter 15

Volvo

Klaus went across to the door and pulled it open—
"Schwartz!"

There were guards, then, within call.

It would be difficult, difficult in the extreme, for me to leave this house during the night, if I wanted to. At the moment I didn't want to.

Klaus came back into the room, energy almost shaking him: he looked caged. But it wasn't that: I think I'd moved in on Nemesis at a time when their operation was ready to run, and had given it a sudden unexpected boost—the promise of nuclear augmentation. And Klaus was getting impatient now, wanted to press the button, see it all happen. Certain things about him seemed familiar to me, rang bells.

The man in the doorway fetched up short as if he'd run here.

"Herr Klaus?"

"Schwartz, I want a secure telephone line. How long will it take you?"

"Ten minutes."

"When you've got it, call me with the number, then bring the car here."

The man's heels came together and he ducked his crew-cut head as he swung the door shut.

"Will you drink?" Klaus asked me.

"Don't let me stop you."

171

He went to the bureau and poured some schnapps, tilting the glass toward me. "Your health."

"Thank you. I ought to tell you, Klaus, that if you're going to drop the warhead from a plane, you can't do it from less than five thousand feet without catching the flak."

"No problem."

"As long as you know." I hadn't got any idea what the actual safety distance was; I was trying to find out if he meant to drop the nuke on something from the air instead of bringing a plane down with it. "I imagine you also know that it's not something you can put aboard a commercial aircraft in the normal way. It's bigger than a bit of Semtex."

"What gives you the idea that I'd want to do such a thing?"

I shrugged. "It'd be trendy."

He gave a short laugh. "I don't follow trends, Herr Mittag."

I got out of the wing chair and wandered about, took a look at the bar. "In terms of weight," I said, "we're talking about forty-two kilos." I found some Schweppes tonic and poured some. "Cheers."

"You told me you wouldn't drink."

"It was discourteous of me not to join you. It's fairly rugged, but the detonator's rather fragile, have to watch bumps if you're going to take it overland across rough terrain."

"No problem."

And not much headway. It looked as if the plans he'd already got on the board would accommodate a Miniver warhead without any changes. I suppose that was partly why he'd begun lusting after it: the project wouldn't be held up.

I gave him a few more statistics and he wanted to know about critical temperatures, contamination zones, half-life figures. It was all in the faxed specifications I'd got from London. He hadn't asked me to get on the phone yet, because he wanted a secure line. He was efficient, Klaus, had been well trained, and the way he was talking, the way he'd handled me so far, had that familiar ring to it: I'd been handled like this before, and it had been inside Lubyanka.

The telephone rang and he went over to it.

He'd worn a uniform, once, had wielded authority, like the KGB colonel who'd put me under intensive interrogation in Moscow. Klaus had the same stamp: I put him down now as a reasonably high-ranking ex-officer of Stasi, the former East German secret police; five or six hundred of them had gone to ground after unification and Counterespionage were still looking for most of them.

"Yes," he said into the telephone. "Give it to me."

Some of them, the rabid Communists, had joined terrorist groups, mostly in Europe. This one had joined the *Rote Armee Faktion* and then broken away and set up on his own.

"Now bring the car here," he said and rang off, and I took in a slow breath because as soon as the stolen car reached here I would have to use the phone in it, and it was going to be an appallingly sensitive call and the whole of the mission would pivot on the outcome and could easily crash.

"So," Klaus said. "When can you deliver?"

I took a slow swig of the Schweppes. "You said you want it as soon as possible?"

"Yes."

"I'll have to see what we can do."

A wash of headlights came sweeping across the curtains while we were still talking, and Klaus nodded.

"We'll go down."

I saw three guards on the way, one on the second floor and two below. They watched us but didn't come close. Our coats were in the hall and we got into them and I told Klaus, "My partner's an Englishman."

"And he doesn't speak German?"

"None too well."

In good English Klaus said, "That is perfectly all right."

It was cold outside and there were bright stars pricking the glow of the city's lights. All I could see around us were trees, some of them with the last of the autumn leaves still clinging, trees and high walls and street lamps in the distance. But a plane was settling on its approach path, lined up with Sirius, and it confirmed what I'd thought before: the house was somewhere northwest of Tegel Airport, in or near Kreis Oranienburg.

The car was a Volvo 940 and Schwartz had the door open for Klaus and he got in and I followed. There was a pale blue headscarf on the seat and I put it into the glove compartment. The theft of the car was routine security procedure and I would have expected a probable former Stasi colonel to practice it. Up to a point he trusted me, but this house was his headquarters and any calls from it could be traced. Anyone trying to trace the call I was going to make wouldn't get any farther than a stolen Volvo, whereabouts unknown.

"You don't object," Klaus said suddenly, "to my listening in?"

"Of course not."

The man Schwartz hadn't gone back to the house; I could see part of him in the offside mirror, silhouetted against the street lamps. There would be other guards in the grounds. It was fifty yards, sixty, from the Volvo to the black iron gates I'd seen when we'd come out of the house, and they would possibly be locked, certainly watched. Dieter Klaus was young, thirty or thereabouts, younger than Krenz, the man who had died in the Mercedes, and he was athletic, Klaus, walked with a spring, turned quickly. But that particular strike, made with the requisite speed, is close to instantaneous in its effect, however young the target, however athletic.

"You have the number?" Klaus asked me.

"Yes."

He switched the ignition key to arm the ancillaries, and the telephone beeped and lit up.

And it's true of course that we are obliged, we the ferrets in the field, are obliged to take life solely in the defense of our own, and not, shall we say, in order to expedite the mission by removing the kingpin of the opposition, in order to save other lives by so doing, perhaps hundreds of other lives. We are required, by the strictest conceivable edicts of those who rule us, never to play God.

But temptation sometimes comes our way, and I sensed him beside me, Klaus, the kingpin of the opposition, the dark mind of Nemesis, could hear his breathing, could smell with a certain distaste the rather cheap cologne he used, would feel, if I moved my hand an inch or so, the pulse in his wrist, could destroy, if I moved my hand with the requisite speed, the source of its pulsation, life.

But then there were the guards and the gates and those pontifical bloody priests of the temple in far Londinium and we mustn't play God, must we, but there are times, my good friend, when we stay our hand, we the dirty little ferrets in the field, only because we know we haven't got a hope in hell of getting away with it.

Klaus was waiting.

Dial the number.

He watched me doing it, and could memorize the number if he wanted to, but it would have looked suspect if I'd shielded the grid with my hand: the semblance of trust must be maintained, was vital.

I held the receiver to my left ear, the side where Klaus was sitting. I couldn't tell how much sound he could pick up from the earpiece, how accurately he could make out words. It wouldn't have to be important; we would have to pick our way through this conversation, the Englishman and I, as through a minefield.

"Hotel Sachsen."

"*Herr Foster*," I said. "*Der Engländer.*"

We waited. Sound came into the sky, and the strobes of a jet flashed across the driving mirror through the rear window.

"*Bitte?*"

I switched to English, gave it an accent.

"Is that you, Charlie?"

Cone didn't hesitate.

175

"Yes. Who's that?"

"Hans. How's Mary?"

"She's fine."

There are certain classic words and phrases in the Bureau's prescribed speech-code that light up the board when they come in to Signals, and I'd just used two of them. *Is that you, Charlie?* indicates that the caller is either being overheard or is an actual captive. *How's Mary?* is a warning that the caller wants the conversation to be played according to the leads he'll give, or attempt to give. I didn't need to throw in a signal for Cone to move out of his hotel as soon as he put the phone down: the *Charlie* bit had told him there could have been someone watching the number I'd dialed. He'd get out straight away, and my lifeline to London would be cut until he called me back.

"The client," I said, "is willing to deposit half the funds tomorrow into the Swiss account, and I'm to receive the other half on delivery, which is to be in Algiers. Is that all right with you, Charlie?"

"If you're willing to go there."

"Oh yes. Sign of good faith. The thing is, when can we deliver?"

Cone tried his first question. "How soon do we have to do it?"

"As soon as we can."

"I'll check with Samala."

"Do that. Tell him we're only contracted for the nuclear warhead, not the whole NK-9 missile. Same price."

"Warhead only."

"Yes."

He'd be hunched over the telephone, Cone, his back to the blizzard he lived in, had probably lived in since childhood, when he'd been abandoned or orphaned or in one of a hundred ways cast out, hunched over the telephone now in a small Berlin hotel wondering what London would do with this, wondering as I was what London would do. They could wreck *Solitaire* if they didn't get this thing absolutely right.

The figures on the dashboard clock flicked to 10:14. It would be a few minutes before we rang off and Cone hit the mast at Cheltenham and his voice came over the speaker at the signals board and Carey or Matthews picked up the bit of chalk: *Executive contacted DIF 22:10 Berlin time reporting either as captive or surveilled, believed to have reached Nemesis center, requests delivery of Miniver NK-9 warhead, see printout of DIF's briefing.*

Croder would move in on a signal like this one or if he wasn't in the room then they'd page him and get him there, find him wherever he was. Croder had the soul of a piranha but he could think well, and there'd be a chance of keeping the mission alive until I could work as a free agent again and signal Cone and brief him. There'd be a chance but it was thin, terribly thin, because London might go for the obvious and decide to call in GSG-9 in Frankfurt and the counter-espionage service in Algiers and stake out the delivery point and risk exposure and blow the whole thing.

"It could take a little time," Cone said.

I used the chance. "You'll have to cut corners, Charlie. I'm talking about—wait a minute, our client's here with me." I turned to Klaus and I didn't put my hand over the mouthpiece. "He says it can take a little time, so give me your deadline."

He checked his watch. "19:00 hours tomorrow."

"That's tight."

"You offered me the missile." His eyes were black now in the glow from the dashboard lights. "If you can deliver it in that time, the deal is on. Not otherwise. Twenty-one hours."

It suited me, because every minute I spent at the center of Nemesis would be extending the risk of exposure; but I'd told him the deadline was tight because God knew how long it would take to persuade Army Ordnance to part with even an unarmed Miniver warhead casing. I was having to play the breaks as they came and make what choices I'd got: the longer I stayed with Nemesis the greater the risk, yes, but I was prepared to face that if the alternative was not to have delivery of the warhead made at all. I had to get it for Klaus if I could; I had to get closer to the deadline he'd been working on before I'd moved in; I had to know what he was planning to do before I could stop him.

"Charlie," I said, "the whole deal depends on the time of delivery, and that's our deadline: twenty-one hours."

"In Algiers."

"In Algiers. So you'll have to cut corners, as I said. Do we want to lose a deal like this?"

"No, if you put it that way."

Cone's German was fluent and he'd heard Klaus making the deadline but he couldn't tell whether I needed delivery as fast as that for my own sake or whether I was forced to let Klaus pressure me like this because he could be sitting beside me holding a gun at my head.

In the cold night air I was beginning to sweat because all I wanted was the chance of sixty seconds on the phone with Cone in private, thirty seconds, *Tell Control he's got to make the deadline with a dummy nuke and tell him that if he alerts GSG-9 or the Algerian counterterrorist service he'll risk exposing me and blowing the mission, tell him that and for God's sake make him understand.*

It was all I wanted, thirty seconds, fifteen, enough time to protect the delivery scene and make it worth my while to stay inside Nemesis and talk to these people and get it right, watching every word, every gesture, every reaction, every expression, so that they wouldn't sense a trembling on the web.

"How long," I asked Cone, "will it take you to make the delivery?"

"I can't say. It—"

"You've got twenty-one hours, Charlie."

"I can only do my best."

"Then it's got to be good enough. You want to work with

me again, you'll have to meet the deadline."

"It's very short notice—"

"Charlie, are you listening to me? Get that item delivered on time or it's the last deal we do together, are you *listening?*"

There was no speech-code involved but I was giving him private information. I'd started to threaten him and he'd picked up on it and started raising doubts to see what I'd do, and I'd pressured him and given him an ultimatum and the message was clear enough now: I wanted him to make the delivery for my own reasons, because if Klaus had had a gun at my head I would have started raising doubts of my own, pointing out the difficulties to him and pleading for more time.

It had been all I could do to spell things out.

"I'll get moving on it, then," Cone said. "Where is the point of delivery?"

I looked at Klaus. "Where do we deliver?"

"At Dar-el-Beïda."

The airport for Algiers.

"Who will receive the goods?"

"Five men will be waiting in a black Mercedes 560SEL at the northeast corner of Number Five Maintenance Hangar at the airport at exactly 19:15 hours tomorrow." He checked his watch again. "I'm giving your partner an extra two minutes, which should please him."

"Could make all the difference," I said.

He gave a short laugh. "We shall get on well together. I like your sense of humor."

"We need a name," I told him.

"When your people approach at that time, one of the men in the car will get out and meet them. His name is Muhammad Ibrahimi. The parole for exchange will be . . . would you like to suggest something?"

The parole for exchange. That was the vernacular of the intelligence field. He'd been in Stasi intelligence, then, perhaps under the control of the KGB in former East Germany.

"Mushroom," I said.

"I like that!" The short laugh. "Mushroom, yes. The freight will be put into the trunk of the car and the cash will be handed over immediately afterward."

"What currency?"

"You asked for U.S. dollars."

"Yes."

"Then you shall have U.S. dollars."

There wasn't anything else so I talked to Cone again and went over the whole thing twice and he said he'd got it. "It's just a simple exchange, Charlie," I told him. "Nothing we haven't done a hundred times before."

"Give it all I've got. Call you back at the same number?"

I checked with Klaus and he nodded.

"Yes," I told Cone.

"Anything else?"

"No," I said, "there's nothing else," and he rang off and I put the telephone back and Klaus snapped the driving door open.

"So! We will go back into the house. *Schwartz!*" The man's feet grated over the gravel. "Sit in the car here and when the telephone rings call me on my pager."

Headlights flooded the driveway as we left the Volvo, and the gates began swinging open.

"Who is that?" Klaus called out.

"His name is Khatami, *mein Führer.* He gave the password."

A black Porsche came into the drive and cut its lights and the gates were swung back as a man got out and came across to the house. Klaus didn't break his stride but shook the man's hand and told him to go on ahead. "I'll be there in a moment, Bijan. The others are waiting."

Klaus led me into the paneled hallway and touched my arm—"Everything looks very fine, my friend. I'm sure your associate realizes that delivery has to be made on time. I could have given you a more comfortable deadline if it weren't for the fact that my operation is running to a precise schedule, and I can't afford delays." His black eyes watched me steadily. "The next twenty-four hours, you see, constitute a countdown." A man was stationed near the wide carpeted staircase and Klaus called him over. "Fogel! Show Herr Mittag to his room." He turned away and said over his shoulder, "You'll find everything there—toilet necessities, a choice of pajamas, a small bar"—turning round for a moment—"Inge will entertain you if you wish—just mention it to Fogel here. We shall meet again to receive the call from your associate. I am very *pleased*, you know, that you have offered me this particular item at such a convenient time—I am *delighted!*"

His footsteps faded out along the corridor. Fogel showed me to a bedroom suite on the floor above and left me there, and I began thinking about the man who'd just arrived in the Porsche, Khatami. He hadn't been in uniform this time but I'd recognized him: he was the Iranian pilot I'd seen talking to Inge Stoph at the airport cafeteria.

Cone telephoned just after three in the morning and we went down to the Volvo.

"We can meet the deadline."

He was in a public phone box. He'd got out of his hotel and into another one but he couldn't phone me from there and he couldn't give me his new number because he knew I wouldn't be alone. He also knew that I couldn't call him back, wouldn't know where he was, couldn't hope to reach him again.

"Good for you, Charlie," I said, and put the phone down and watched the severed lifeline go snaking away in the dark.

Chapter 16

Sirocco

The sun was a pale disk in the haze, still low above the horizon. Its light glinted on metal and glass surfaces, on the mascot of the Mercedes limousine as it swung in a half-circle by the VFW-Fokker and halted. Klaus got out first and we followed.

There were two other cars already here, with people standing near them in a group, waiting for Dieter Klaus, watching him. His bodyguards—four women and two men—closed in around him as he walked toward the plane with that implacable energy of his. There was a small dog among the people who stood waiting. The pilot came down the ramp and saluted Klaus, standing aside and waiting for him to board the company jet. Klaus spoke to him and got an answer; I didn't hear any actual words but I suppose he was asking the pilot about the weather forecast: the haze was thick toward the horizon.

I joined the group, one of the male guards walking a little way behind me: I'd been under what amounted to close escort since we'd left the house, and I didn't expect that to change. Geissler, the man who'd interrogated me in the garage, had come with us in the limousine, and went aboard the plane soon after Klaus. The rest of us were following now, and ·the woman in the camel's hair coat gave me a flashing smile and said in English—"Hello, I'm Helen Maitland, and this is George, my husband."

"Hans Mittag. Delighted."

I'd caught sight of her earlier this morning, getting into one of the cars at the house.

"Dieter told us about you," Maitland said. "Most interesting." Then he hurried up the ramp, a short man, quick in his movements and with the same nervous tension in him that Klaus had.

The focus of this operation—Shatner, in the London briefing— is on a man named Maitland. Or rather, on his death. A week ago he was murdered, and his body taken away. His flat was broken into with some violence, and the police found evidence of massive blood loss. There were marks on the floor indicating that his body had been dragged out of the flat to the lift. The telephone was hanging by its cable—he'd been talking to a woman friend, who came forward, when the flat was entered. She reported sounds of the door being smashed in, an outbreak of voices and finally a cry.

Helen kept close to me as we went up the ramp, and I thought I heard her whisper, "I'm sorry . . . "

Maitland had sat down with Klaus in one of the forward seats behind the flight deck. The pilot had taken his place next to the navigator, and a stewardess was greeting us as we came aboard. Her smile, I thought, was overbright, as Helen's had been just now when she'd greeted me. No one was talking much; they seemed to be taking their cue from Dieter Klaus, from their *Führer*, and this morning he was totally changed from last night: in the limousine there'd been none of his brief outbursts of laughter. I took as long a look at Maitland as I could when I went past his seat: later I might need the ability to recognize some of the people here, perhaps quickly and at a distance.

Maitland, Willi Hartman had told me in the nightclub, had been interested in the Red Army Faction. *He began asking me questions about them. Then later I realized he was—how will we put it?—playing a kind of game with himself. He had a master plan, he told me once, about how to assassinate Muammar Qaddafi.*

A counterterrorist game, then? He fancied himself as an armchair counterterrorist?

I think, yes. George was a very unusual man. Very intense.

The twin jets began moaning.

He was neurotic, Willi had said with sudden force. *May I say that?*

Helen hadn't objected. *Oh, of course. Terribly so, terribly neurotic, yes. He fascinated me.*

The olive-skinned girl in the mink coat was the last to board; she'd been sitting next to Klaus at the ice-hockey game, and Inge had said her name was Dolores. She was last to board, I think, because her little dog had been giving trouble, scared by the noise of the jets, and as she pulled it through the doorway by the leash I saw Dieter Klaus swing his head—*"I told you I didn't want that thing on the plane!"*— and in the next second he was on his feet and the kick caught the dog in the flank and it went spinning through the doorway onto the tarmac with the leash whipping after it. *"Now shut that door!"*

The stewardess stood frozen for a moment with her mouth in an O as she stared out at the dog; then she reached for the security lever and pulled the door shut and made it fast and came quickly along the aisle looking at no one, her face white. The dog wasn't yelping out there; from my window I could see that its neck was broken.

Would you please fasten your seat belts, ladies and gentlemen, we are about to roll. Thank you.

No one was looking at anyone else. Helen sat with her head lowered, picking at her nails; the lacquer was already chipped. It couldn't, I thought, have been an easy decision to join George Maitland again when she found out he was still alive.

We listened to the exchange between the flight deck and the tower through the doorway as the wheels began rolling; then the stewardess came back and slid the door shut and sat down on the single rearward-facing seat with her head turned to the window, her eyes glistening. On the other side of the aisle I could see Khatami, the Iranian pilot, in a black bomber jacket and flying boots. He was sitting alone. His was the only face I'd seen when we'd come aboard that

185

hadn't looked tight, nervous. On the contrary, he'd looked in a strange way exalted.

We got the green from the tower and the full thrust of the twin jets came on and the runway lights began flicking past the windows.

Blood from a butcher's shop, I suppose, or they'd cut a dog's throat to give the scene realism. But why had they gone to so much trouble: couldn't he have just disappeared?

Picking at her nails.

Terribly neurotic, yes. He fascinated me.

That alone could have been why she'd gone back to him, had stayed with him even though she'd seen what it would have to mean—being absorbed into Nemesis, living among people like these. Perhaps she was easily fascinated by people like George Maitland with his neurotic intensity, by the girls in the nightclub, by anything or anyone illicit, by whatever dared to take its fill of the forbidden. It would be consistent with her character as far as I knew it, with her schoolgirl naïveté.

When we'd reached our ceiling and the power leveled off I asked her quietly, "Was it Kurt Muller?"

She turned her pale face to me. "What did you say?"

"Was it Kurt Muller who told Klaus you were in Berlin?"

He'd been the man who'd recognized her in the nightclub, the one I'd asked her about in the taxi when we'd left there. She hadn't hesitated, or not for long. *Oh, he was just someone I knew, a friend of George's at the embassy.*

"I'm not sure," she said. "It could have been. I didn't ask."

Muller must have been one of the few people who'd known that George Maitland was still alive, and he'd phoned him that night, told him that he'd seen his wife, that she was here in Berlin.

"He didn't *have* to do that," she said.

"Who?"

"Dieter."

Didn't have to kill the dog.

I said, "You're running with the wrong set."

How many hotels had Klaus phoned before he'd found her? He would have started with the big ones, so it wouldn't have taken him long. It must have put her into shock, a voice from the dead, *his* voice. But she'd gone to him, left her things behind, just walked out of the hotel and down the street and found a taxi once she was out of sight.

He fascinated me. Well yes, he must have, and still did. But there was something else she'd said. *I've only just realized how much I hated him.* But then hate is as close to love as laughter is to tears.

Five rows in front of us I could see Maitland and Klaus talking intently, their heads close. But I wasn't ready to believe that a neurotic embassy attaché with a feverish sense of adventure had mounted a one-man counterespionage crusade against an organization the size of Nemesis and persuaded a former Stasi colonel to put his trust in him.

I hadn't been able to do it myself, not completely, I knew that now.

"Aren't you running," Helen said in a moment, "a terrible risk?"

"It depends on what you tell them."

She turned her head quickly to look at me. "I won't tell them anything, of course."

"Then the risk I'm running isn't all that high."

Not absolutely true. Klaus had got the whole thing worked out and I hadn't been able to stop him because I'd had to stick with my cover and go with him to Algeria, to Dar-el-Beïda. It was possible that he believed in me, but it didn't make any difference one way or the other. We believe in what we want the truth to be, ignoring the evidence that would raise doubts, deceiving ourselves, and Dieter Klaus desperately wanted the truth to be that I was a bona fide arms dealer and could provide him with a Miniver NK-9 nuclear warhead. But he was a seasoned Stasi officer and he'd covered himself: if I made the rendezvous in Algiers and the NK-9 was delivered he'd be as happy as a kid at a Christmas tree—*I am very pleased, you know, that you have offered me this particular item at such a convenient time—I am delighted!*—but if there was no delivery he wouldn't be taking any risk: he'd still go ahead with his operation and he wouldn't let me walk away with all the information I had on him now. He would simply have me silenced.

"We're serving breakfast soon," the stewardess said. "Would you like to choose something from the menu?" Leaning over us, the smile fixed, fright behind it, she wasn't with Nemesis, she was just flight crew that went with the Fokker, MARLENE, the little brass tab on her uniform said, new to the job, hadn't had any idea what her employer would be like, "There are eggs Benedict, if you care for them that way," her heart still down there on the tarmac nursing a dog with a broken neck. "And we'll be serving champagne in just a few minutes." She took our order and moved on.

But the warhead would be there, and there on time: I wasn't worried about that. London would see to it.

He was quite adamant—we have to meet the deadline. Cone to Control. He would have got into signals the moment we'd rung off last night.

You feel that if we don't make this delivery it's going to jeopardize the mission?

And the executive.

Cone would have said that. He had a sense of the humanities, could be counted on to let them know they'd have a dead ferret on their doorstep if they didn't get it right.

Very well, then. We shall do what is necessary.

There would have been a lot of phones ringing in the dead of last night, at the bedside of the head of the Army's Quartermaster Office and Ordnance Stores, if necessary of the Minister of Defence, if necessary of the Prime Minister, to whom the Bureau was directly responsible. Red tape would have been slashed through, security units alerted at the Ordnance hangars, passes shown and metal doors rolled back, the instructions presented and transport called in, the crew of a civilian freight plane on Her Majesty's Service ordered

188

to report for special duty, their destination sealed in an envelope to be opened in flight.

So Klaus would get his toy and I would be paid off if he kept to the deal—unless London made the decision to stake out the scene, and *that* was why I was sitting here with the feeling that time was running out for *Solitaire* and that it was only a matter of hours, because I knew London and I knew their way of thinking and their way of thinking was that if they could send in the SAS and Germany's GSG-9 and Algeria's counterterrorist units they could do a better job of destroying Dieter Klaus and his whole organization than one lonely ferret in the field, and unless I could reach a telephone in time and persuade them to change their thinking then that was what they'd do.

Finis, finito.

Looking down over the snows of the Swiss Alps I told Helen, "I feel responsible for you. Did that occur?"

In surprise—"No. Why should you?"

"We brought you into Berlin to help us."

"It doesn't matter." Picking at her nails. "I could have gone home yesterday morning if I'd wanted to. He—just rang me up, and asked me if I wanted to go to him. I—said I would." She turned her head to look at me. "I can't help it, you see." With a note of bitterness—"You wouldn't think, would you, that there could be so much passion under such a placid exterior?"

I offered the obvious cliché. "Still waters."

"Yes, very still and very deep. Sometimes I frighten myself—but anyway, you don't have to feel responsible for me anymore. I'm a free agent."

"Are you?"

Her smile was quick, nervous. "All right, I'm free to trap myself in this—in this thing that's going on."

"Do you know what it is?"

She didn't look away. "No, I don't. Do you believe me?"

"Of course."

189

"They haven't told me anything," she said, "and I haven't asked. None of these people here know what Dieter's planning to do, except for George." A moment of hesitation, then: "I think he sort of switched sides."

"George?"

"Yes. I haven't talked to him very much since I went back to him, because Dieter's had meetings all the time and George has been kept busy; but obviously I had to ask him what all that drama was about, the murder scene at his flat, and he said Dieter had—I must get it right—had 'required it of him.' He wouldn't say any more."

Perhaps it had been a blooding, then, a ritual act of faith, of commitment. George had become excited by Nemesis and had wanted to go over—"switch sides" from counterterrorism to terrorism—and Klaus had demanded that he go through a symbolic act of self-immolation as his *entrée* into the organization. It could have appealed to Maitland's neurotic fancies: he could even have reveled in the idea of such grand deception. But he must also have brought something to Nemesis, something of value—as I had. He was already close to Dieter Klaus, on equal terms.

I asked Helen, "Why did Klaus accept him, do you think?"

"I don't know. He might have made some kind of proposal. He was always playing around with outlandish schemes in his mind."

Like assassinating Qaddafi, for instance. Possible scenario, then: Klaus had been planning a terrorist operation and Maitland had gone to him and said look, do it this way, it's better. Or bigger. So Klaus had taken him up on it and there wasn't going to be another Lockerbie, there was going to be something bigger than that, even more devastating. The purpose, after all, of any terrorist act was to attract attention.

The snows drew out beneath us, twenty thousand feet below. I thought I could make out the Matterhorn.

"These meetings," I said. "You weren't invited to any?"

"Oh, no. I'm just . . . here to be with George. But I heard

him talking to someone on the phone about *'Mitternacht Ein'* and *'Mitternacht Zwei,'* and I heard Dieter using the same phrases. My German's not good at all but they stuck in my mind: they were repeated so often."

They were obviously code names and possibly for deadlines and if one of them were for midnight tonight it'd be only five hours after delivery of the Miniver and they'd be running it very close.

She must have heard other things, a word here and there, things she'd half-forgotten because they hadn't sounded important, though I might see them as vital. I could coax her memory, as I'd done with Willi Hartman, and conceivably bring out information I could use; but it would be too dangerous for her. If anything she'd given me became the basis of my future actions and Klaus suspected the source . . .

"Look," I said, "I want you to forget everything you've told me."

"Forget?"

"You've seen what Dieter Klaus can do to a dog. He can do that to a man or a woman, to anyone, whoever they are." She was watching me with fright in her eyes, and that was good, she was paying attention. "If Dieter Klaus thought for one second that you were in his way, don't imagine that George could save you. He couldn't."

She looked down, and said in a moment, "You must think I'm terribly naïve, letting myself get mixed up in all this."

"I think you're playing with fire, and you don't know how easy it is to get burned, with a man like that."

Turning to me she said—"I'd like to stop everything, of course. I mean they're planning to do something quite terrible, and I know that. But what can I do? Should I walk down the next street and go up to a policeman and say my husband and his friends are going to kill a lot of people? Think of all the questions they'd ask me, the statements I'd have to make, before anyone could even lift a finger—if they believed a word of it, from a mere woman." She felt strongly about this. "Or suppose—"

"Don't raise your voice," I said.

Leaning close to me—"Suppose I phoned my MP, or Scotland Yard or someone like that—I don't know about these things—and told them the same story?"

"They'd get on to my department," I said, "and I'd be sent out here to do something, and here I am, so don't worry about it, of course there's nothing you can do. But be very careful. Don't show the slightest interest in what they're doing, not the *slightest*. And in a minute or two I'm going to find a newspaper and sit across there with it. If George asks you about me, tell him I've been boring you to death with my stories of armament deals, and you weren't really listening." She was watching me steadily, fretting with her nails. "And if we run into each other again we'll simply follow the social graces, mention the weather, that sort of thing." I got out of my seat and leaned over her for a moment. "What you have to do *above all* is to look after yourself."

The stewardess got me a copy of this morning's *Die Welt* and I sat down with it in a seat across the aisle and toward the rear, so that I could watch people. I could have stayed with her longer—if Klaus hadn't wanted me to talk to anyone he'd have put me right at the rear of the cabin with a guard— but there was no need to attract his attention: she and I must remain strangers.

Klaus was using the telephone again: it was his third call since we'd taken off from Berlin. Maitland went into the forward toilet and came out again and spoke to the stewardess for a few minutes, then looked along the cabin and saw Helen sitting alone and came aft to join her, and I caught the leap of excitement in her eyes.

I'd got a better look at him this time as he'd walked along the aisle; he was a short man, as Helen had told me—"He hates being short"—but he was attractive in a chiseled, sharp-featured way, with high cheekbones and imaginative eyes and a strong mouth, and I suppose that for a woman he'd pack a good deal of libido, which might explain his Svengali-like power over his wife. The houndstooth check suit was perfectly cut and he showed plenty of linen: he looked successful, experienced. One arm was round Helen's shoulders as he talked to her, his head close to hers, a sudden smile coming, a look of reassurance, this was my impression, *Dieter's not really a bad type*—perhaps—*it's just that he's got a hell of a lot on his mind at the moment and it's fraying his patience,* the same kind of thing he'd been saying to the stewardess, possibly, a few minutes ago.

Inge Stoph was sitting two rows behind Klaus, and after a while she got up and looked through a window on the other side, asking the stewardess something. Then she came along the cabin and talked to Dolores, three rows in front of me, then moved on toward the rear and stopped to lean over me, taut-bodied in a white sweater and slacks, her warm scent lacing the air, her ice-blue eyes reflecting the oval window and her brief smile brilliant.

"There's a bunk in the rear," she said, "if you want to rest a little. It has curtains. Would you like me to go with you?"

"At any other time," I said.

"Of course. Whenever you feel in the mood. It's part of Dieter's hospitality."

"He has great style," I said. "How long shall we be in Algiers?"

"At the palace?"

"Yes."

Her eyes darkened. "I don't know. Certainly overnight, because tomorrow we shall be celebrating. Has Dieter told you anything about it?"

"No. I wouldn't expect him to."

"You'll know," she said, "tomorrow. Everyone will know." She turned on her brilliant smile and went back along the cabin, stopping to talk to Khatami, the Iranian pilot, but not for very long: he seemed lost in his own world. I thought it should be telling me something, his trancelike preoccupation, perhaps something very important, but I couldn't get a fix on it.

We were over the Mediterranean when Marlene leaned over my seat, pitching her light voice against the sound of the jets. "We'll be landing in less than an hour, sir. Can I get you anything from the galley or the bar?" She watched me with her nerves still in her eyes. As soon as she landed at her home base she'd give in her resignation and apply for a different charter.

I told her I didn't need anything, and she moved on down the aisle.

"How was the champagne?"

Maitland this time.

"Excellent." I hadn't tried it.

He stood watching me thoughtfully. "How much do you know, Herr Mittag?"

"Very little." We were talking in German; he was fluent. "But I've great faith in Herr Klaus. I'm sure everything will go splendidly."

His eyes were flickering to the slightest degree, but I didn't think it was nerves. I thought he was holding back a great deal of excitement, was only just managing to contain it. "It will indeed," he said, "go splendidly. And your faith in Dieter Klaus is not misplaced. But the idea, you know, was mine."

"Congratulations."

I could smell the champagne on his breath but I didn't think he'd overdone it; I thought it would have had as much effect as Perrier: he was running on his own natural high.

"You'll understand what I'm talking about," he said, "tomorrow. We're going to make the headlines, you know. They'll be interrupting television programs, all over the world."

"I'm impressed."

"And you've made quite a contribution yourself, Herr Mittag—the icing on the cake. We appreciate that."

"Klaus did mention he was delighted—in fact I've got a question for you. Am I to be offered, shall we say, a grandstand seat when the balloon goes up?"

His mouth tightened. "Well, no, actually. There's only one man here who's going to have a grandstand seat." He straighened up. "Just came to chat, that's all, make sure you're all right."

"Civil of you. One more question—are we going straight to the palace from Dar-el-Beïda?" The airport.

"All of us except for you and Geissler. You'll be stopping off at the Banque d'Algérie, where he'll make the necessary transfer of funds to Switzerland." Touching my shoulder— "All is arranged, have no fear."

"I had none."

"Very good. The price was fair, I rather think. You didn't ask too much, and we didn't try to bargain. The true value is in fact incalculable: this is to be a *major* show."

"I very much hope nothing happens to stop your bringing it off."

His eyes went cold, and he waited a moment before he said quietly, "Nothing will happen, Herr Mittag, no. This operation has been planned with an attention to detail that will guarantee our complete success. *Nothing* will get in our way."

A ruff of white surf below us now, a fringe of coastal palms and then white buildings as we turned for the approach, a spread of white buildings and domes and minarets and beyond them the desert, the sands of the Sahara.

The undercarriage was down: I'd felt the slight vibration a minute ago. The noon sun flashed across the sea on the starboard side as we straightened, lining up with the runway, a degree or two of roll and then its correction as the flaps went down and we leveled off.

Mitternacht Ein, Mitternacht Zwei . . . Why *two* midnights, *two* deadlines—if they were deadlines?

Flareout, and the nose came up a little, the cabin tilting. The first of the runway markers began flashing past the windows.

There's only one man here who's going to have a grandstand seat.

Klaus? Why only Klaus? Or someone else here on board this plane? Maitland himself? Khatami, the pilot? Why only *one* man?

We're going to make the headlines, you know.

Because they were going to use what they thought was a live nuclear warhead? No. *And you've made quite a contribution yourself, Herr Mittag—the icing on the cake.*

The Miniver thing would be a dummy but they'd still have the "cake," and that alone was going to make the headlines for them.

Somehow I'd have to reach a telephone, signal London, stop them sending in a whole army to the delivery point, to the rendezvous, because they'd never take Dieter Klaus that way, he wouldn't be there, he was a former Stasi officer, KGB trained, and he knew that a rendezvous always carries a risk, *any* rendezvous carries a risk of exposure, can be a trap, can turn out not to be a rendezvous after all but an ambush, he knew that, so he wouldn't be here tonight at Maintenance Hangar 5, he'd just send some people with me to make the exchange, some people he could afford to lose if I weren't just an arms dealer, if I were there to blow Nemesis. And if the SAS and GSG-9 and the Algerian counterterrorist units came out of the shadows and made the snatch then I'd be dead, because those would be his orders, the orders from Klaus: in the event of any surprise, shoot Mittag, get him out of the way—and the operation would proceed as planned, exactly as planned, and tomorrow there would be headlines, because I wouldn't be there to prevent it.

First bump, and the cabin flexed.

So I must somehow telephone London, warn them off, let me do it, this is a job for one man on his own and right on the inside where Klaus can be reached, can be taken, can if necessary be killed.

Second bump and then the hot kiss of the tires on the runway as we settled, then a burst of sound as the jets were reversed and the brakes came on and we swung toward the terminal, sand against our faces as we left the aircraft, the sirocco was blowing, someone said.

Chapter 17

Viper

*U*ntil the thing with the snake it had looked like a scene out of a travel brochure, one of those poolside parties. There'd been a fountain here once, I suppose, in the middle of the shaded courtyard, and then they'd put the pool in for tourists. It was out of place; it must have been charming before, with the tall eucalyptuses brushing the sky above the white stucco walls and the olive trees framing the archways, one of the smaller palaces that in Europe would have been a country house.

Klaus was in the pool. I watched him sometimes from below the left lens of my sunglasses; I was sitting in a deck chair not far from the edge of the pool at the deep end, near the telephone. It had rung three or four times since we'd arrived here, and Klaus had always been the one to answer it; if he weren't near enough to hear the bell—the girls were making a lot of noise in the water—one of the guards would call him over. He'd answered in monosyllables every time, but I had the impression that the calls were from different people, that they were reporting in and he was coordinating things.

The sun was lowering through the afternoon hours, still warm on the skin. Tangerines and black olives lay rotting under the trees, and eucalyptus leaves floated on the surface of the pool. Inge and Dolores were making all the noise, diving from the board and giving little girlish screams as they splashed each other, vying for attention from Dieter Klaus, who wasn't interested. Helen stayed by herself, turning on her back sometimes to float with the sun on her face and her eyes closed. I watched her often, trying to share the calm she brought to the scene.

My guard had been changed; the new one was an Arab, not tall, but slender-looking in his kaftan; there didn't look room for a gun but that was an illusion. Klaus's bodyguards were dispersed around the courtyard, still in their black tracksuits, four women and two men. They moved very little, sometimes bouncing on the balls of their feet, swinging their hands together, never looking at one another, looking only toward the archways and the big redwood gates that led to the palace grounds. Two of them had gone with us to the Banque d'Algérie on the way here from the airport, where Geissler had wired funds to Intercom-Londres in the amount of U.S. $500,000.

I first noticed the snake soon after Klaus took the third telephone call; it was moving very slowly along the bottom of a wall, half-lost among the leaves and the fallen tangerines. It wasn't very big; I would have said it was a horned viper, a native here.

"Are you asleep?"

Helen was watching me, hanging on to the tiled rim of the pool, her slim body rising and falling in the water.

I said I wasn't, no.

"Isn't it nice here?"

I said it was. She was so different from the other two girls, apart from her quietness. Inge sported her rich blond body hair, lifting her arms a lot and shaking the water from her head, laughing into the sun as the models do in *Vogue* and *Elle*; Dolores was less active but swam with studied grace, her long muscles moving under the dark skin, her eyes sleepy as she looked across at Dieter Klaus. But Helen was just thin, bobbing in the water with one shoulder strap of her black costume hanging down and her slight breasts hardly noticeable. It was her innocence—even of this, the loose shoulder strap—that glimmered with a sexuality the other girls could never hope to express; and when she smiled it was heart-breaking, or so I found; what turns me on most in a woman is her unintended invitation to my tenderness.

"I expect I look rather gawky," she said, "in a bathing costume."

"Not really."

"It's something I shall always remember my father saying." The sun was in her eyes, and they were narrowed to slits of shimmering light as she watched me. "He was in the garden, trying to bend a croquet hoop straight, and I was going to tell them tea was ready in the summerhouse, and I heard him say to my mother, 'Here comes that gawky girl of yours.'"

"Quite a lot of fathers are like that," I said. "It's a kind of birth defect."

"You don't think I look gawky, then?"

"I think you look rather like the goddess of willow trees, though a bit younger perhaps."

A flush came to her pale face—and this is what I mean, she could still be moved by the clumsiest compliment—and she looked down, letting her long pale fingers slip from the tiles. "I think that's going rather far," she said, and swam away, not meaning it, hoping it might be just a little bit true. Beyond her I saw the snake move again.

Servants brought us things during the long hours of the afternoon, boys in kaftans and sandals, bringing us trays of tangerines, slices of ginger, *kab el ghzal*, mint tea, whatever we fancied, it was rather pleasant, he was a man of style, Klaus, regaling us with the fruits of the earth as the sun lowered toward the evening and the rendezvous and Midnight One. He couldn't do anything about the sand: it was everywhere, brought in by the light sirocco, gritty under our feet and the deck chairs when we moved them and even between our teeth, forming a pink film across the copies of *El Moudjahid* and the London *Times* and the *International Herald Tribune*.

The telephone was getting on my nerves, not because it

rang sometimes but because it was there, near the edge of the pool and almost within reach. Klaus had always answered it on the spot: he hadn't taken it out of earshot or lowered his voice, and I knew why. It wasn't that he trusted me; he knew I was safe, because if I had any reason to report to anyone, at any time, on anything I'd overheard this afternoon, I'd never be able to. I looked like a guest here, but I wasn't. I was a captive.

If I could use that phone, pick it up and call London and use speech-code, it could change the end phase of *Solitaire* from certain disaster to the chance of survival, even success. *Tell Charlie not to bring any friends: this is strictly a private party.*

In the signals vernacular of the Bureau the word *strictly* has the same weight as *fully urgent*. They both mean that *everybody* has got to listen, including Bureau One.

But it wasn't on because one of the bodyguards let out a shout in German when I picked the telephone up and Klaus jerked his head round—*"What are you doing?"*

Everyone else froze, watching me.

"It looked like getting splashed," I called across the pool to Klaus. I'd picked the whole thing up, not just the receiver. The receiver would have been *next* if no one had taken any notice. The guard who'd shouted had moved closer, was watching Klaus for any orders.

"Would you like," Klaus asked me, "to make a telephone call, my friend?" He had a big chest, a powerful voice: he could put a silkiness into the tone even at this distance.

"If I want to make a telephone call I ask you first, isn't that the drill?"

"I am delighted you understand."

He turned away and went on talking to Geissler. Inge Stoph gave a quick laugh and stuck her tongue out at me. I think she was peeved because I hadn't wanted to roll on the bunk with her on the plane; she couldn't have been used to refusals.

It was quieter now in the courtyard; the two women—"concubines" was the word Inge had used at the *Eissport-*

halle—had stopped splashing and playing for Klaus's attention. The guards weren't moving around anymore or bouncing on their feet; my own personal guard was closer to me now, his red fez making a blob of color against the white wall behind. I could hear a donkey braying, some way off, and Inge flashed me another look, a silent laugh, meaning perhaps that I'd been a donkey to try a trick like that with a man like Dieter Klaus, the *Führer*.

The smell of woodsmoke was on the air as fires were lit for the evening; it would be cool tonight in Algiers. A less attractive smell of chlorine came from the pool. I watched Klaus, Geissler, and the guards, simply to keep them surveilled as a routine: the ferret doesn't often have the chance of surveilling the chief of the opposition in every movement he makes without attracting attention, without attracting bullets for that matter.

On the board for *Solitaire* the bit of chalk moves in the floodlight: *17:06 hrs local time, executive maintaining close surveillance on opposition.* That ought to create a *lot* of interest in Signals, not to say a discreet degree of jubilation, an occasion perhaps for another cup of tea, providing the bit of chalk doesn't go on moving: *He is also their captive under guard and is liable to be shot dead tonight at the flashpoint.*

In most missions there's a flashpoint: it's when the executive is to perform a distinctly hazardous operation, to break into, for instance, the official intelligence headquarters of an unfriendly host country and try to get out again with something so classified that all the windows would blow out if anyone knew, or to get a wanted subject away from a fully armed mantrap outside Hong Kong Airport with the public and the police looking on, or to make a last-ditch break for the frontier ahead of a pack of war-trained Doberman pinschers, that sort of thing, flashpoint is what it says and the one that was coming up for *Solitaire* would be in two hours' time at the airport at Dar-el-Beïda, when the man from London stopped his car and got out and came over to the black Mercedes 560 SEL we were sitting in and the counterterrorist

units closed in for the snatch with their floodlights and assault rifles and the shooting started and the executive for the
mission went down first because those would be the orders
from Dieter Klaus, the prearranged orders, the ones he
would give before he left here this evening on his way to
Midnight One.

That was the flashpoint for *Solitaire* unless I could reach a
phone but they weren't going to let me do that, and I was
starting to feel the familiar tingling at the nape of the neck
as I sat here in my deck chair sipping hot mint tea because
the organism was going to need the sugar, sipping hot mint
tea as the boys in their kaftans moved quietly around the
pool in their sandals and the snake moved again *and this time
one of them saw it.*

He was sixteen, perhaps, seventeen, not one of the guards,
just one of the palace servants, and he was young enough
to enjoy playing a little prank now and then, especially if
there were foreign girls around to tease, and he put down
the tray and went over to the snake and grabbed it by the
tail before it could coil and swung it around in the air and
smashed its head against the wall and held it up for a moment
and then threw it into the pool with a bright boyish laugh.

The girls screamed and Klaus looked round and saw the
dead snake on the surface of the water and got to his feet at
once and went across to the Arab boy and shouted at him
in French, bringing his big hand across and across his face
until the boy's hand vanished into his kaftan and the blade
of a knife flashed in the sunlight and Klaus parried it and
tore the hilt free and slashed the boy's throat and pushed
him away as the blood came spurting. The bodyguards had
moved very fast when they'd seen the knife and were now
forming a ring around Klaus, their guns out.

"Get Ibrahimi!"

One of them turned and ran into the building.

"Where were you, then?" Klaus asked the others. "Was that
as fast as you can move? As fast as you can shoot?" An Arab
came through one of the archways with the bodyguard,

black-bearded, his robes flowing, and saw the boy sprawled across the tiles with his blood reaching the edge of the pool and trickling into the water, its rose-red color spreading.

"He attacked me!" Klaus told the Arab, not shouting now but with the hoarseness of rage in his voice.

Dolores had climbed out of the pool and was on all fours, hump-backed, retching. Inge was staring at Klaus with her ice-blue eyes shining as she absorbed the joy in the scene: her *Führer* had killed, as he would always kill any who dared oppose him. Helen had climbed out of the water and was lying on her back with her eyes closed, her face ashen.

"These people saw him attack me with his knife!"

Ibrahimi stared at Klaus, then at the boy again.

"Now get him out of here, take him to his family, tell them that if anyone breathes a word about this I'll tell the police what happened and shame his memory—*he tried to murder me*, Ibrahimi, you understand me, do you *understand*?"

The guards stood waiting, their guns at the hip. They might have been hoping—*must* have been hoping—that Ibrahimi would make some kind of move against Klaus, even a gesture of protest against the death of a fellow Arab, so that they could shoot him down and show this time how fast they could work. They were out of luck.

"Yes," he told Klaus, "I understand." He moved across to an archway, clapping his hands, and three or four boys appeared there, listening to Ibrahimi and then coming to the poolside, lifting the limp body in the kaftan and bearing it away.

"The mess!" Klaus called. "The *mess*, Ibrahimi!"

More servants came, one of them an old man with gaps in his teeth, his head shaking on its thin neck as he mopped at the blood with towels. I think he was going to wash one of them out in the pool, but caught a glance from Klaus; the surface was already clouded. He stood watching them, Klaus, in his gold-toned swimming trunks, big hands on his hips, until they went away with their towels and their buckets, leaving the tiles clean and shining; then Klaus turned away and rose on his toes and made a flat racing dive into the shallow end of the pool where the blood of the boy still swirled.

I went over to Helen and pulled a deck chair nearer. The time was right, now, to tell her; she might not have listened before.

"How do you feel?" I asked her.

She didn't look up at me, didn't open her eyes. Softly she said, "I must be mad. I must be mad."

Dolores, her dark skin yellowed, was telling a servant to wash the tiles near the diving board, where she'd vomited. No one else was moving except for Klaus, who climbed out of the pool and reached for a towel, saying something to Geissler that I didn't catch: they were too far away.

"Where's George?" I asked Helen quietly.

"He went into the *casbah*."

"Why?" I needed to know what everyone was doing.

"To take snapshots."

"Where's the Iranian? The pilot?"

"He said he was going to the mosque."

To pray, but to pray for what? Perhaps the blessing of Allah on Midnight One.

"If I can," I told Helen, "I'm going to destroy Nemesis. You know that. Have you thought about how it's going to leave you?"

"No. I just want to go home now."

That surprised me. "You're willing to leave George?"

"That's what it would amount to, wouldn't it?"

"Yes." She'd been doing some thinking, then.

I had to do some thinking myself, as the sun lowered and sent shadows leaning across the courtyard from the eucalyptus trees. I heard a car door slamming; the forecourt of the little palace was on the other side of the wall. George, back from the *casbah*? The pilot, back from the mosque? I might not have much time left.

"I haven't done anything wrong," Helen was saying, with

an innocence that would have touched me if she hadn't been in such appalling danger.

As gently as I could I told her, "You have been consorting with the most notorious group of left-wing terrorists in the world, and this is what you've got to say if you get arrested when everything blows up. You've got to say that when you went to Berlin to join your husband you hadn't the slightest idea he was mixed up with Dieter Klaus and his operation, and that by the time you found out, there was nothing you could do about it. You've been their captive—and this is perfectly true: they couldn't have risked your wandering off and giving them away, intentionally or otherwise."

Ibrahimi came through the archway at the far end of the courtyard. He wasn't a tall man but his robes gave him height and a certain grace, and his black beard added a look of strength. I needed to know all I could about him in the little time left before the flashpoint. He would be going there with me, to receive the Miniver warhead.

"Helen," I said, "I'm going to give you a couple of designations. How's your memory?"

She opened her eyes at last and sat up, turning to look at me, the shoulder strap still hanging down, her eyes narrowed against the late sunlight. "My memory's very good," she said.

That too surprised me, and I felt a touch of admiration for her. "That's the first time," I told her, "I've ever heard you say anything good about yourself. Do it again, get into the habit. It'll work wonders for you. Now listen, Klaus and George will be leaving you behind when they complete this operation of theirs, and back here the pressure will be off a little. If you can get away from here *safely*, take a taxi straight to the British embassy and ask one of the staff there to pay the fare. They get a lot of tourists running out of money and trying to get home, so tell them this is prime ministerial business and ask them to put you on the line to the Foreign Office in London. Just keep on insisting. When you're through to the Foreign Office, ask for Liaison 5. If some new clerk says she doesn't know that department, tell her to get her boss on the line and keep on telling them you want Liaison 5. But you shouldn't have any trouble: Liaison 5 is known to all senior Foreign Office officials."

It was the Bureau.

At the far end of the pool, Ibrahimi had begun talking earnestly to Klaus. He hadn't bowed when he'd gone up to him from the archway but it had been close. The German had total power over the members of his cell, whoever they were. He'd even killed an Arab and then told an Arab to get the "mess" cleaned up—*The mess, Ibrahimi, the mess!*

"When they put you through to Liaison 5, ask for Desk 19. You'll be given access right away." Desk 19 was Holmes. "The man at Desk 19 will recognize your name. Ask him to get you on a plane for London, priority. Now give me those designations."

"Liaison 5, then Desk 19."

I got out of the chair and looked down at her. "Go into the palace as soon as you can and write them down, keep them hidden away. However good our memory is, we can forget the most vital things in a crisis." She watched me with that stillness of hers, her eyes attentive, and I would have liked to stay talking to her, would like to think that one day, one fine day beyond the dark and ominous horizons of Midnight One, I might pick up a telephone and dial the number in Reigate and ask her if she'd like me to go round there for a cup of tea. That would be nice. "Don't take any risks," I said in a moment. "Wait for the right chance. And after all this is over for you, tell yourself again that you have a very good memory, just as you told me. And tell yourself all the other things your father's chosen to ignore, that despite his attempted sabotage you've managed to grow into a beautiful woman, poised and gracious and quite stunningly attractive. It's time to understand that now."

I turned away and left her, going across to a chair nearer the deep end of the pool, taking my time, talking to one of the servants who'd come back to stand near the walls, asking him where I could buy the best souvenirs among the *souks*. I was close enough to the group now—Klaus, Geissler and Ibrahimi—to hear snatches of French. It was the second language here and Ibrahimi was fluent; the two Germans were less at home with it.

I'd told Klaus we needed a name for when the delivery of the Miniver was made, and he'd given me one. *When your people approach at that time, one of the men in the car will get out and meet them. His name is Muhammad Ibrahimi.*

He would be there with me at the flashpoint, and what would happen, the way things would go, would depend critically on what kind of man he was and what I could do with him, if I could do anything with him at all.

Sand gritted softly under sandals, and two more Arabs came into the courtyard in plain white kaftans. Klaus went across to them straight away, and they greeted one another in the Muslim fashion, which I hadn't seen the German do before: so far he hadn't shown too much respect for Arabs. Then I recognized one of them. He was Khatami, the Iranian pilot: I hadn't seen him in native dress before. Perhaps they'd arrived in the car I'd heard just now. *He said he was going to the mosque,* Helen had told me. Klaus spoke to them for a few moments in his halting French; I caught only a word or two but it sounded like an exchange of courtesies, or it could have been more than that: he was asking them how they felt, rather than how they were—*Comment vous sentez-vous?* and not the formal *Comment allez-vous?* I thought this was interesting, because nothing had happened to them as far as I could see. But Klaus wasn't necessarily asking them how they felt *now*—after something had happened—but how they were feeling at this time when something was *going* to happen, as when we ask an athlete how he's feeling before a race. I played with it in my mind because I thought it was important, and might offer a clue; but I was desperate now for clues as we neared the flashpoint and it could have been simply that I was reading too much into things.

Klaus left them, touching their arms in a gesture almost of affection, and clapped his hands for servants. Two of them brought bowls and small muslin towels, and as the pilot and his friend—co-pilot?—sat at their ease below the leaves of an olive tree the boys knelt in front of them, bathing their feet with an air of ceremony; other servants brought fruit and a bottle of Vichy water and pewter cups. None of the Europeans here took any notice, but the Arabs—Muhammad Ibrahimi and the servants—seemed interested, glancing across now and then. The pilot, Khatami, had the same look of quiet exaltation I'd noticed on the plane, and so did his friend.

I made another routine check around the environment in case there was anything to be picked up. Klaus wasn't talking to Ibrahimi anymore: I assumed the Arab had come to report on what he'd been doing to keep the dead boy's family quiet—they would have been told to say his body had been found somewhere else, victim of an unknown assassin, something like that. Klaus would get away with it if the truth came out—he had a perfect case for a plea of self-defense in front of witnesses—but he was a busy man: today he'd killed only a dog and an Arab boy, but there were more deaths than that on his agenda, perhaps hundreds, on the stroke of Midnight One.

He was sitting alone now, leaning forward with his big hands interlaced, his eyes on the surface of the pool where the scimitar leaves of the eucalyptus floated, his mind absent, his fingers sliding together, sliding away, his whole body arched, flexed like a bow: he was in a form of meditation, deep in the theta waves, close to trance.

Inge Stoph watched him, her bright eyes idolatrous. Geissler was talking in low tones to Ibrahimi. The guards weren't moving, weren't bouncing cockily on the balls of their feet anymore: they'd been tested and found wanting, and I suppose would be fired and replaced, fired or left somewhere humped on the ground with an arm thrown out in mute testimony to their *Führer*'s displeasure—I'd seen today that in this small sovereignty of terror Dieter Klaus considered himself and was considered to be omnipotent, with the status of a god and the rights of a god over life and death. It was the only way he could run this show, the only way he could live.

Dolores had gone into the building after the scene with the Arab boy, and hadn't come out. Helen was lying down again, flat on her back, a sheen on her white face; I think she'd have liked to go into the palace too, or anywhere away from Dieter Klaus, but was afraid that if she stood up and tried walking she might feel dizzy and be sick.

George Maitland wasn't back yet from taking his photographs in the native quarter. I expected him soon now: he'd be here with Klaus as the time brought them close to Midnight One. From what Helen had told me, he was one of its architects.

One of the servants wasn't far away, and I beckoned him over. He was an older man with stubble on his dark, thin face; his eyes had a light in them, a glint of inner fires. He didn't look at me as he waited for me to speak; I think if he'd looked at me I'd have felt the heat of his ferocity: I was a foreigner, an infidel, and it was a foreigner, an infidel, who had killed the Arab boy.

I asked him in French, "Why are they bathing the feet of those men over there?"

He didn't turn his head. "It is holy water."

"I see. What does it signify?"

He was looking down, his dark head turned slightly away from me, as if to hear me better, but it wasn't that. If he'd looked at me he wouldn't have been able to resist the urge to spit in my face.

"It signifies," he said, "that they will die."

"When?"

"Before they sleep again."

Suicide run.

Chapter 18

Ibrahimi

*I*t was almost six o'clock, and the air was turning cool. The sirocco had died away from the south, from the Sahara; the leaves of the tall eucalyptus trees were still. Beyond them in the west the sun was low, the sky the color of blood.

Maitland had come into the courtyard a few minutes ago and spoken to Dieter Klaus; then he'd seen Helen by the pool and had gone over to her. They were talking now. He was in a dark jumpsuit and carried a padded jacket. He was talking seriously, no smiles.

I could hear the pilots, speaking to each other quietly in Farsi, a language I didn't know. The boys had taken away the empty bowls and the muslin towels. The water—the holy water—had made a puddle on the tiles.

A suicide run: hence the ritual and the look of exaltation on the pilots' faces. They were talking with their heads close together. Klaus watched them from across the pool, still crouched forward with his fingers interlaced. He watched the Iranians with a degree, I thought, of fascination. From the nearest archway I too was being watched, by my personal guard.

A suicide run, but that didn't tell me the target. The other Iranian could be a pilot too, or at least aircrew: they'd both been through the ritual of their preparation for their ascent into heaven, had possibly been taken through a more elaborate ritual at the mosque. So it involved a big aircraft, with a crew of at least these two. A bomber?

The evening prayer was being called by the muezzin from the minaret of the mosque; the voice sounded tinny: I think they use tapes these days, in the bigger towns.

Then the telephone began ringing again, and Klaus came over to it and picked it up. Two of his bodyguards had moved away from the wall, closer to him. This had become routine since the business of the knife.

"*Oui. Un instant.*"

He took the telephone to Khatami, pulling the long cable clear of a deck chair. "*Pour vous.*"

"*Merci.*" Khatami spoke into the phone. "*Oui?*" Klaus stayed where he was, on his haunches, arms across his knees. "*Non, c'est pas bon. Vous avez un crayon? Alors, écoutez. C'est précisément 26°03 au nord par 02°01 à l'ouest. Répétez. Bon, c'est bon. Ecoutez, il faut synchroniser les montres, hein? J'ai maintenant exactement 18:04 heures. C'est ça. A bientôt, oui.*" He put the receiver down.

I turned a page of the *Tribune* I was reading, got it creased, flattened it out, began reading again.

"*Tout va bien?*"

Klaus.

"*Oui. Tout va bien. Tout est en ordre.*"

Khatami.

I wasn't all that far away, a dozen yards or so, and I'd heard them quite clearly. But I don't think that Klaus even realized I was there; I don't think it mattered. I was under close guard and I was going to remain under close guard until the flashpoint out there at the airport, and whether the Miniver was delivered on schedule or not, whether London had sent forces in or not, my expectations were that I would be silenced at that time and in that place. Klaus would have ordered it. So it didn't matter what I overheard, what information I might pick up: it would remain safe for all time in the chill of the shriveling brain.

But it was interesting, academically. I had the target.

26°03 north by 02°01 west.

Much good may it do me, so forth, that man Muhammad

Ibrahimi had a bullet for me and he wouldn't leave anything to chance: if he failed to carry out his orders he wouldn't survive the day. I suppose it was the tinny ghost-voice of the muezzin wailing from the mosque that was giving me the creeps, that and perhaps the killing of the dog and the boy. The psyche was in despond, and this was dangerous, though difficult to change: time had started to run short. There was no—

The telephone rang again and Klaus answered it at once. *"Ja. Jawohl!"*

George Maitland came across from the edge of the pool and the pilots got to their feet. "They're ready," Klaus said, and his voice was charged. *"Allons-y!"* He went over to speak to Geissler and then made for the building, his bodyguards with him. The Iranians followed them, hurrying, their robes flying.

I noted the time: it was 6:14.

"I'm sorry you're going to miss this," Maitland said. His bomber jacket was hanging across his shoulder from one finger. He was smiling, if you could call it that; there seemed a kind of light on his face, in his eyes, and I thought he'd lost color a little. Yet I'd think he wasn't a man to get excited easily. "It's going to be something quite spectacular."

"Klaus didn't invite me," I said. "Should I ask him?"

He shook his head slowly. "He and I are the only ones going. Not even Geissler. Some of the minions, of course, but they're just monkeys, and won't be coming back."

I sensed Helen shiver, and she turned away. "It's getting cold," she said. "I must go and get some clothes on."

"Did you talk to her much?" Maitland asked. He watched me with his eyes shining.

"Not a lot," I said.

"Do you think she's attractive?"

"Very attractive."

"It's that innocence of hers . . . I find it extraordinarily seductive." He turned, looking across to the archway where she was just vanishing into the palace, long pale legs among the gathering shadows. "God knows," Maitland said, "what she'll think when she sees the media break. She'll know we're responsible. She likes power, you see, the kind of power she knows I can wield."

"Or enjoys her fear of it?"

"I've never thought of it that way."

He was dying to blurt things out; in times of great emotion we say things we know we shouldn't, can't possibly say. I think if I'd had him alone with me for a bit longer I could have got enough out of him to give *Solitaire* a final chance, reach a phone, bring London in. But there wasn't time, and it wouldn't get me anywhere: Klaus knew that as far as security was concerned I presented no risk, was already silenced.

Ibrahimi came across to us. "We shall be leaving in thirty minutes," he said in French, "for Dar-el-Beïda."

For the flashpoint.

I went in to change.

Scorpion in my shoe and I tipped it out and it scuttled under the bed.

I held my hands out and watched the fingers. They were perfectly steady. The nerves were singing quietly in that flat inaudible monotone that is simply a vibration, palpable but discernible to no other sense; perhaps it's what happens when a violinist tightens the string infinitesimally and hears, *knows*, that he has reached perfect pitch.

A woman was keening somewhere below, and I could hear faint voices. Perhaps she was the boy's mother. The scent of jasmine came through the open window with its iron scrollwork, and I saw two men in flying jackets standing in the forecourt near one of the cars. They were the Iranian pilots, changed and ready and presumably waiting for Klaus.

I put on the bomber jacket I'd worn in Berlin, where it had been cold. It would be cold here tonight, though less so.

There might conceivably be a chance of preempting the flashpoint and getting clear, turning the car over as I'd done once in Moscow and taking advantage of the confusion. But

I couldn't do that. It's not what we're for, the ferrets in the field. I could save my skin that way or by using some other crude but effective technique but that would mean abandoning the mission: I had *got* to stay with Nemesis for as long as I could in case there was the thousandth chance of blocking their operation, if possible destroying it. I couldn't simply bail out: to abandon the mission is against the most sacrosanct edicts of the Bureau, the Sacred Bull. If those bastards in London expect us to protect the mission with our lives—and they do, or they wouldn't give us capsules, they wouldn't hand out capsules like bloody Twinkies—it follows that they also expect us to stay with the mission until death do us part in the natural course of events, death from a bullet or a knife or a fifty-foot drop from a rooftop or a head-on smash or the last turning of the screw in the interrogation cell with the light blinding and the music blasting away at full volume—Brahms, they usually go for Brahms or Beethoven—death from whatever cause, then, it is in our contract, you understand, with the Reaper at our side we have said *I will*.

I put on my shoes. The scorpion was running inquisitively along the wainscoting, and it was in my mind to go over there and step on it, perhaps out of envy, because it was liable otherwise to outlive me; but I left it alone, reminded of Ferris, that inestimable but sometimes revolting director in the field who takes dark and perverse pleasure in stepping on beetles. With a full-blown Algerian scorpion he would have had a ball.

The guard outside my door was on the move: I heard his shoes squeaking on the marble floor—they were gym shoes, rubber-soled, making him sound athletic, impatient for me to do something wrong so that he could blow my head off and show the brains to Klaus in atonement for letting that Arab boy pull a knife. There was another guard below in the courtyard, watching the windows here.

I was beginning to sweat a little in the cool of the evening, and this worried me, and not only because sweat makes the hands slippery. I had good reason to be frightened as the minutes ran out to the flashpoint: I was almost certain by now that Klaus suspected my cover, beneath the lust in his breast to possess a real live nuke for the icing on his cake. If there was no delivery made I would be shot, but the same thing would happen if London hadn't laid a trap and the Miniver was handed over: after that I'd be worse than useless to Klaus: I'd be a danger, knowing too much.

The scent of woodsmoke was richer now as night began falling and more fires were lit and the *couscous* went into the beaten copper pans.

I got my jacket. It was the same kind as Maitland's, black, padded, Berlin style. I like them; they're good in cold climates and short, hip-length: you can't run in an overcoat, you can't turn, spin, kick, roll, rebound, dear God, my brain was working like a chicken's with its head cut off—those buggers had *guns*, it wouldn't matter what I was wearing, how fast I could run, they'd pick me off, concerted firepower.

I left my bathroom stuff and the flight bag where they were and hung the swimming trunks a servant had lent me to dry on the windowsill; then I went to the door and jerked it open and the gun was in his hand before I took another step, they were nervous, these people, didn't want to have Klaus shouting at them again. But I could have taken him, this one little peon, because I was alone with him and there are so many moves you can make if you've done it often enough; his weak point was that the gun gave him confidence while I was bare-handed, and I'd work on that. But I couldn't do it before he'd got the first shot out and even though it'd go wide of the mark it would make a noise and the others would come and Klaus would have me wiped out because I would have blown my cover and he'd know there wasn't a nuke waiting for him at Dar-el-Beïda, *finito*.

"*That way!*"

I was going down the arabesque staircase in front of him and took a wrong turn at the bottom and not by accident, I wanted to rile the little bastard, ease the resentment. I turned the other way and went into the open courtyard. It was quiet here, deserted except for Maitland: he was standing at one end of the pool, staring down into the water. It was still now, and no longer tinged with the blood of the Arab boy. The voice of the muezzin had stopped, and the only sounds beyond the high white walls were women's voices and the distant ring of cooking pots.

A ripe orange fell, on the far side of the courtyard, and burst among the dry scimitar leaves of the eucalyptus. I felt, for these few moments, a profound peace settling like gossamer on my soul, something close perhaps to what the two Iranians were feeling, and for the same reason: we weren't long for this world now.

"Hello." Maitland's voice came from across the courtyard, and I remembered how it had been when I'd first found Helen, this man's wife, standing as still as this on the frozen lawn in Reigate, the day before yesterday. She'd sensed my presence and turned and said, *Hello*.

"Where's Klaus?" I asked him.

"Coming. We'll be taking off at seven."

I went over to him, not hurrying, looking into the pool, watching his short dark reflection. "The deal I made," I said, "is for the exchange to take place at seven-fifteen."

"We're not taking the warhead on board." Maitland's eyes were still shining; his excitement was burning in him like a fever. "It's going on a later plane."

With the conventional explosive: with the teddy bear.

"Fair enough. I wouldn't want any last-minute complications—this is quite an important deal for me."

He watched me for a moment, his eyes bright, and I wondered if he knew what the orders were that Klaus had given Muhammad Ibrahimi: that I was not to survive the rendezvous. Maitland would probably know, yes, had possibly advised it, even insisted on it, for the sake of absolute security, and some of the unholy light in his eyes could be there because he knew he was talking to a dead man. I'd seen a degree of fascination in Klaus's look when he'd been watching the two Iranians.

"Dieter Klaus," Maitland said slowly, "hasn't planned this operation to include the risk of last-minute complications."

He didn't know I was English, this man, as English as he was. It'd be funny if we'd been to prep school together—he looked about my age. Not that it would have made any difference to our relationship. KGB Colonel Kim Philby had been an Englishman too.

"I'm reassured," I said, and then Klaus came into the courtyard with his four bodyguards and an Arab in a jumpsuit and a military-style jacket, compact and black-bearded.

"I don't think you've been formally introduced," Klaus said in French, "have you? Muhammad Ibrahimi—Hans Mittag. I know you'll get on very well. You'll be going to the airport with a driver and three guards for your own protection." He was in a black flying jacket with a fur collar, had a pair of military field glasses slung round his neck. "I'm sure your associate has taken every precaution"—his black eyes were locked on mine—"and that he too has protected the rendezvous from unwanted attention. Or am I perhaps overconfident?" His French was stilted but I got the message.

"The counterterrorist people," I said in a moment, "are quick off the mark these days. You know that. It wouldn't be the first time an arms dealer's come unstuck."

Telephone.

It was all I wanted: a telephone.

Klaus said at once—"You think there's the chance of a security leak?"

"Not really. I run a tight show, like you. But nothing in this life's ever certain, is it? I think you're right: I ought to phone my contact."

He became very still. I was running things terribly close, but it was so tempting, because if I could get London direct on the dial and use speech-code and warn them off the rendezvous they'd have time to signal whatever forces they'd

220

sent into Dar-el-Beïda and clear them out before I got there with Ibrahimi. I'd have a clear field with no one to mess me up if I could do anything useful.

"There's no time," Klaus said, "to phone anyone now." He checked his watch. "You're leaving here in fifteen minutes, and if your associate has left the rendezvous open to exposure it won't be my fault if you get shot. You understand me?"

"I don't need fifteen minutes to—"

"Do you understand?"

He was standing in front of me with the look on his face I'd seen when he'd killed the dog and when he'd killed the Arab boy, and I was ready for him to blow, had the angles worked out as a matter of routine, the synapses flashing throughout the system and devouring data and sifting it and presenting the analysis for the motor nerves, and if Klaus had made any kind of move I would have gone straight into the killing area and he would have started choking on his own blood as the bullets went into me from the guards.

I don't know if he knew I was ready for him, but I don't think so, because it would have been a challenge and he would have accepted it and come for me, just as a dog will do if you stare it down.

Adrenaline running in the veins like strong red wine: I could taste it in my mouth. He went on staring at me.

"Yes," I said, "I understand."

"I want that warhead."

"Of course. And I simply hate to sound tactless, but does Monsieur Ibrahimi have the funds?" I looked at the Arab.

"I have the funds," he said, "in cash."

"In hundred-dollar bills?"

"That is correct."

Klaus stood back, and Maitland joined him. "I hope all goes well," I said, "with the operation. It'll give me a certain sense of satisfaction in the morning when I read the headlines, to think I played a minor part."

Klaus left his eyes on me for a moment and then swung

away, didn't answer, knew I wouldn't see any headlines in the morning. Maitland went with him through the archway that led to the forecourt, where chrome glinted under the first faint light of the moon. Two of the guards followed them; two stayed behind. They were both men, both European, probably German; they were flat-faced, crew-cut, and had eyes with the indifference in them that we see in animals, but I made them change, moving my hand suddenly to tug the zip of my jacket higher, and they became the eyes of the animal that sees the prey.

"We shall make our way, then," Muhammad Ibrahimi said.

He walked beside me, the guards behind. No one else was in the courtyard now, and as our feet rustled through the fallen eucalyptus leaves and we reached the archway I had the feeling that a curtain would come down behind us.

Exhaust gas was on the air as we reached the forecourt; the taillights of a car showed among the trees where the driveway curved toward the road. Above the minarets of the palace the last of the daylight had gone from the sky, and with the coming down of the Sahara night a three-quarter moon was already silvering the chrome and cellulose of the 560 SEL Mercedes limousine that was waiting for us. An Arab driver and another European guard were standing beside it.

Ibrahimi gestured for me to get into the back of the car, then followed. Two of the guards got in and pulled down the jump seats facing us; the third sat next to the Arab driver. The last door was slammed and the hydraulic locks clicked home. I felt for the seat belt and buckled it. Ibrahimi folded his hands, leaving providence to Allah.

"The funds," I asked him, "are in the trunk?"

It was just to keep the polish on my cover. Five thousand hundred-dollar bills would need a suitcase, and I didn't see one here.

"Yes," he said.

He would have a knife, Ibrahimi, a knife rather than a gun. The European clothes he'd changed into hadn't altered his

222

image very much: with his beard and his hawk-beaked nose and his silences he was intensely Arabian, and would have been brought up with an affinity for the blade in time of need. It would be the same for the driver. The others would have guns.

Be not sanguine, my good friend, upon this inauspicious night, 'tis hardly meet. We are not superferrets, we the ferrets in the field, we are but ferrets, and subject to the laws of nature, red in tooth and claw.

Chapter 19

Limousine

South along the rue Khelifa Boukhalfa and across the
Plateau Saulière district, with the scents of the evening coming through the ventilation system: the smell of broiling lamb
mechoui from the Berbers' open-air kitchens, of jasmine and
donkeys and incense and bruised oranges and the acrid reek
of the leather tanneries in the *souks*. Our driver knew his job,
made detours around the congested areas where merchants
lined the streets with their loaded carts and their rickety
makeshift stalls.

"What is his name," I asked Ibrahimi, "the driver's?"

"I do not know."

We spoke in French, Ibrahimi and I, when we spoke at
all. I would have liked to know the name of the driver as a
matter of routine tradecraft: if you call a man by his name
you establish immediate intimacy by however small a degree—you are no longer a complete stranger. And in a scene
of confusion when other sounds are pervasive, call a man's
name and you'll get his immediate attention.

I didn't expect there to be any scenes of confusion on this
cool Saharan night. Klaus had things running with the precision of a Swiss watch. But habit was ingrained in me and
I let it work. It could save *Solitaire* at a pinch, given the advent
of a miracle to help things along.

I didn't expect miracles either.

From where I sat I could see the digital clock on the softly
lit dashboard of the Mercedes, between the shoulders of the

225

two hit men who sat facing me. The time was now 6:49: twenty-six minutes to the rendezvous, to the flashpoint. The airport at Dar-el-Beïda is twenty kilometers from the city, and we were now nearing the motorway. Since I could see the clock I wouldn't have to look at my watch. I didn't want Ibrahimi to know I was interested in the time. The hit men sat watching my hands. I didn't know if they spoke or even understood French, but it was unlikely. Ibrahimi wouldn't need to give them any verbal instructions. If I made a wrong move they'd go for me: they were robots with guns, knee-jerk reflexive. I didn't move my hands; I left them folded on my lap. If I were going to move them with malice afore-thought I'd need to do it very quickly.

The limousine accelerated onto the motorway, its head-lights sweeping over the moonlit landscape. There were twenty-four minutes to go. One thought kept obtruding as I looked over the options that were left: that fix I'd overheard couldn't be the target for Midnight One. 26°03 north by 02°01 west must be somewhere in the Sahara Desert, because London was the zero east-west meridian and almost due north of Algiers, and Baghdad was somewhere about thirty degrees latitude. Klaus hadn't mounted this operation to blow up a lot of sand. It would be nice to look at a map, one of the maps in the leather pocket at the back of the driver's seat, but I couldn't think of any excuse to ask for one.

Khatami, the Iranian pilot, had been quite insistent on the telephone at the poolside, making sure the caller got the fix correct and asking him to write it down and repeat it, even telling him to synchronize watches. But it couldn't be the target for Midnight One. Then was it the *location* of Midnight One? In the middle of the Sahara Desert?

There was a telephone set into the walnut console between the jump seats. It would also be nice to use the telephone, as well as a map, but I didn't think Ibrahimi would let me.

The only viable option I had left was to preempt the flash-point: move into some kind of action that could get me clear with a whole skin and leave *Solitaire* running. It would have to be calculated but it was going to be messy: that was unavoidable. One scenario seemed attractive.

There were five men with me in the limousine and they were armed, three with guns and two—I was going to assume—with knives. My immediate target would be Ibrahimi, and the technique would be an elbow strike to the throat, and lethal. To do it effectively and with the certainty of a kill I'd need to work up the optimum degree of catapult tension in the arms to lend added momentum to the strike. At the moment my hands were lying loosely on my lap and I'd have to move them a little and quite naturally, settling them again with my left hand holding my right wrist. I must then change the hold into an actual grip, tightening it and pulling my arms against each other to the point where the maximum tension was reached before muscle fatigue set in. Then I would release my hands, and the time it would take for my right elbow to reach the throat of Muhammad Ibrahimi would be in the region of one fifth of a second. This is the figure we've recorded in practice at Norfolk, where a lot of work has been done on this particular technique because it's quite often that an executive finds himself sitting captive in the back of a car.

Through the windscreen I could see a big jet sloping toward Dar-el-Beïda with its strobes flashing against the deep indigo sky. By the clock on the dashboard we were now nineteen minutes to the flashpoint.

So at any given time Ibrahimi could be sitting beside me with a smashed larynx and the blood flowing into his lungs: this is a death, oddly enough, by drowning. But the two hit men would also be fast. Their hands were resting on their thighs, a matter of inches from their guns, and I'd have to reach their eyes to blind them and inflict diversionary pain before they could fire, and that would take time, perhaps a full second, a second and a half, while my arms rebounded from the strike to Ibrahimi and I turned my hands into a four-finger eye shot as I drove them forward. It wouldn't be difficult: these men were facing me and even if they saw my hands coming and flinched or moved their heads I could change the eye shot into a claw hand with their eyes still the target and if they had time to reach their guns at all they'd have to fire blind and I'd be into a double outward rake to drive their hands away.

But there was a risk. He was the man up front with the driver.

The big jet was flattening out for the approach, floating above the black frieze of the date palms to the south.

"Have you known Monsieur Klaus," I asked Ibrahimi, "for very long?"

I didn't expect him to tell me. I wanted to know how far he was simply prepared to talk, because soon I was going to talk to him and it would involve London. He wouldn't know that.

"I have known him," Ibrahimi said, "some time."

Meant nothing.

The jet melted into the palm trees, vanished. The speedometer stood at a steady one hundred kilometers per hour, the speed limit on this stretch. At 100 kph a lot of things would happen if the driver lost control. He was no obstacle to me, the Arab at the wheel: his hands were tied and he must watch the road. But even supposing I could control the two hit men in the back of the limousine there was the third man sitting in front and he was a real hazard because I'd have to hit the seat-belt buckle release before I could reach him and in a car this size it was a long way from the backseat to the front and any initial momentum I could get from the upholstery wouldn't be enough to pitch me forward with the necessary speed to do anything effective: there wasn't the leverage. The third man would hear the action going on behind him the moment I started work and I wouldn't be halfway through what I needed to do with the other two before he spun round with his gun drawn and fired at the skull to drop me with a single shot. The timing, as it concerned that man in the front there, was brutal, impossible.

Rule out the idea, then, of preempting the flashpoint. There was nothing I could do before we reached the airport at Dar-el-Beïda, before we reached the rendezvous.

I could feel the adrenaline flowing into the bloodstream again, the resonance along the nerves as the digital clock flicked to 6:58 at seventeen minutes to the flashpoint. There wasn't a lot of time and I didn't see a single chance of doing anything even when we got there, anything effective. The most I could do would be to take Ibrahimi with me, Ibrahimi and the two men in the rear of the car, simply as a matter of principle. But if I could do anything at all it would have to be in a clear field with no disturbance: it was the only way I could work at the brink. So I'd better phone London, tell them to leave me alone, get their CT units out of Dar-el-Beïda before we arrived.

"I've only known Monsieur Klaus," I told Ibrahimi, "a few hours."

I shifted on the seat a little, half-turning to look at him, and the hands of the two men jerked.

"Relax," I told them in German. "I'm not going to hurt you."

They'd hate that, did it for a giggle.

"What did you tell them?" Ibrahimi asked straight away.

"I told them to relax. They're fidgety." His face was turned toward me, his black beard jutting, his eyes on mine in the shadows, a shimmer of black in the pale olive skin. "Only a few hours," I said. "I met him only last night, as a matter of fact, about this time. But I know he's difficult to deal with, as I'm sure you've discovered yourself."

He turned his face away from me, stared through the windscreen again, a glint coming into his eyes as headlights brightened from ahead of us in the opposite lane.

I wasn't waiting for an answer; it hadn't really been a question. I said, "You remember, probably, the difficulty I was having with Monsieur Klaus a little time ago, at the palace."

You think there's the chance of a security leak? Klaus, speaking in French. Ibrahimi had been there: we'd just been intro-duced.

Not really. I run a tight show, like you. But nothing in this life's ever certain, is it? I think you're right: I ought to phone my contact.

"I expect you remember," I told Ibrahimi, "that all I was suggesting to Monsieur Klaus was that I should get on the telephone and make quite certain the rendezvous at Dar-el-Beïda was uncompromised."

He would know the particular meaning of the word, in this context. I waited now, but he said nothing.

"Do you in fact remember, Monsieur Ibrahimi?"

In a moment he said quietly, "Yes."

Of course he did. Monsieur Klaus had been quite forth-right. *There's no time to phone anyone now. You're leaving here in fifteen minutes, and if your associate has left the rendezvous open to exposure it won't be my fault if you get shot.*

"I'm afraid," I told Ibrahimi, "that Monsieur Klaus was perhaps a little overconfident, when he refused to let me use a telephone. But then he's like that, isn't he? I admire con-fidence in people, but in this case he should have given a little more thought to what I told him." I waited, didn't expect an answer, received none. "Do you remember what I told him, Monsieur Ibrahimi? I told him that we can never be quite certain there hasn't been a security leak, during the process of an illegal arms deal. And I suggested I should telephone my contact. You were there, I remember, Mon-sieur Ibrahimi."

I waited again, just to give him time, sat watching him, the glint of headlights reflected in his eyes from the oncoming traffic. "I rather feel," I said, "that you're a more patient man than Monsieur Klaus, a more careful man. I hope so, because if there has indeed been a security leak since the Miniver warhead left Britain, and if I can't telephone to find out, this car could be surrounded by armed counterterrorist comman-dos the moment we reach the rendezvous, and we shan't have the firepower to shoot our way out."

I looked away from him, swinging a glance past the flat expressionless faces of the two hit men to take in the clock on the dashboard behind them. I had fourteen minutes left, which didn't worry me because I could do all I needed to do on the telephone in that time. But it worried me that London might not be able to call off whatever forces they'd sent in before we got to the rendezvous.

I looked back at Muhammad Ibrahimi and found his eyes on me. "But there's time," I told him, "for me to make quite sure we're not heading straight into an ambush, you and I. All I need is to use the telephone."

It would have been nice if I could have pressed him harder, told him he'd be a bloody fool if he didn't let me use the phone, so forth—it would have saved time. But that wouldn't be the right approach for a man like Ibrahimi; he was infinitely more refined, more subtle than Dieter Klaus, and he was involved with Nemesis, perhaps, not because he was in essence a violent man but because he had a violent antipathy, like most Arabs, to the West, and in this operation the West was probably the target.

"Why didn't Monsieur Klaus," Ibrahimi said at last, "permit you to use the telephone?"

"He didn't trust me."

"Why should I trust you?"

"You don't have to."

"You would agree to speak to your contact in French?"

"Of course. And we can leave the receiver on the console and I'll use the microphone." Doing it like that, he could listen in to London.

I waited, and through the windscreen watched a light aircraft making a turn on its way in to Dar-el-Beïda, the top of its wings flashing silver as it caught the moonlight.

7:02 on the clock. We were running it terribly close, but I couldn't hurry him, Ibrahimi.

Then he said: "You may use the telephone."

"May the wisdom of Islam be praised." The console was between the two jump seats and I told the guards in German,

"I'm going to make a call. Don't get excited."

As I leaned toward them to touch out the number they went for their guns at much the same speed as a striking snake and held them against their thighs with their fingers inside the trigger guards, a pair of Walther PPK .22s, all right at close range but not man-stoppers. The number I touched out belonged to the signals link unit in London that we use if we're being watched: it's untraceable even by British government agencies.

There was quite a bit of crackle going on, possibly because we were near a major airport. 7:03 on the clock. Then the ringing tone began and someone picked up almost at once.

"Hello?"

"Extension ninety-one," I said.

There's no Extension 91: I was simply telling them I had opposition company, and they would pass it on when they made the link direct to the board for *Solitaire* in the signals room.

It would be Carey on the board at this hour: he would have taken over from Matthews at six this evening, London time. I didn't know Carey but I wasn't worried: he'd be bright and fast or he wouldn't be in Signals.

"Yes?"

"Je voudrais parler à Monsieur Croder, en français."

"Hang on."

All the board crews knew a smattering of the European languages, enough to know which was which. Croder, as Chief of Signals, was fluent in French and German, and I needed to speak to him in any case because he'd have the authority to do what I needed done.

"Croder."

He'd got to the board very fast: I'd been cut off from Signals ever since I'd hung up last night after talking to Cone in Berlin, and they didn't know whether I was still operational or blown out of existence or running loose like a mad dog in the dark with the opposition closing in on me. I'd set up the Miniver rendezvous with Cone but when the executive is right in the heart of the opposition network anything can happen.

"Mr. Croder," I said in French, "I'm within twelve minutes of the rendezvous and I need to know whether you feel it's still secure."

It was an awful lot to hit him with because he knew I was with the opposition—he'd been given the Extension 91 bit and he'd have to assume they were listening to every word he said. I'd also spoken in what amounted to broad speech-code, and what I'd just said had got to be decoded as, *Have you sent counterterrorist forces there?* If he had, the rendezvous wouldn't be secure, and that was the key word in my question.

"One can never be sure," he said, "can one?"

He was filling in, asking for more data. He knew I was with the opposition but he also knew that I wasn't talking under duress: nobody was holding a gun to my head and telling me what to say. I was saying exactly what I wanted to, or I would have slipped in the prescribed warning straight off the bat: *Mr. Croder, I'm sorry to bother you, but I'm within twelve minutes . . .* so forth. I hadn't done that, so he knew four things: I was in the company of the opposition, I was not speaking to him under duress, I meant every word I was telling him, and we were both being overheard. This information was automatically going onto a tape and a printout sheet as we talked.

"You understand," I said, "that if there's been the slightest chance of a security leak, with the risk of police or counterterrorist or other forces waiting for us at the rendezvous, we can't keep it. Our client is concerned about it, and so am I. This is a rather important deal for us, but I'm calling it off unless you feel the rendezvous is absolutely uncompromised."

He now had the whole thing, and I waited.

Clock: 7:04. Eleven minutes.

Ibrahimi was watching my face, looking for any kind of giveaway as I talked.

233

The two hit men watched my hands, which were on my lap again.

The limousine rolled smoothly under the African moon, with the ruby marker lights on radio masts in the area winking against the sky.

Croder's voice came. "You shouldn't have anything to worry about."

I felt cold suddenly. He'd thought out precisely what he must say to give me the clearest signal he could.

He'd sent people there.

He'd told me I shouldn't have anything to worry about but that was very different from saying I *had* nothing to worry about. He would have said exactly that, if the rendezvous were clear. He hadn't. It wasn't.

His voice came again. "Do you feel you should cancel everything, then?"

He was throwing the ball to me and I tossed it back.

"Do you?"

I waited. He'd say yes or no. If he said yes it would mean he'd sent people there and couldn't get them out. If he said no it would mean he could.

I watched the ruby lights through the windscreen, letting them float through my mind, relaxing, because nothing must show in my eyes when Croder answered me.

His voice came.

"No."

The ruby lights floated.

"All right," I said. "We'll keep the rendezvous."

There was silence for a moment except for the crackle of interference on the line. Then Croder said, "Of course, you'll have to watch out for the airport police. I can't give you any guarantees: this deal is illegal."

It was a warning. He was going to call off the people he'd sent there—SAS, GSG-9, the Algerian units, whoever they were—but he couldn't be responsible for local forces. He could signal them that the rendezvous had been called off,

234

tell them to leave, but he couldn't make it an order. They weren't under his authority.

"We'll watch out," I said, "for the police."

He said good luck and shut down the call and I reached forward to touch the *End* button and sat back again and looked at Muhammad Ibrahimi.

"So what do you think?" I asked him.

In a moment he said, "Monsieur Klaus is eager to possess the warhead. Very eager."

And if Ibrahimi didn't get it for him his life might not be worth very much.

"Then you're prepared to go in?" I asked him.

"Yes."

The clock on the dashboard flicked to 7:05.

We had ten minutes left.

I said, "Ibrahimi, I'd like to know something. Whether the exchange is made or not, do you have plans for me?"

I waited.

The hit men watched me. Beyond them I could see in the far distance the floodlit control tower at Dar-el-Beïda.

Ibrahimi turned to look at me. "My lips are sealed," he said. "But you should make your peace with Allah."

Chapter 20

Flashpoint

A rose for Moira.

Through the windscreen I could see a twin-engined jet taking off, its splinter-sharp profile aslant against the brilliant haze of the starfields above the airport; it looked very like the company jet we'd flown from Berlin this morning. *We'll be taking off at seven*, George Maitland had told me at the palace. He and Dieter Klaus. Destination unknown, unknown at least to me.

You should make your peace with Allah.

It would be delivered to Moira, as specified in my will, a single rose, so that she should know.

7:11 on the dashboard clock, but what did it signify? That I should make my peace with Allah.

The driver took the Mercedes in through the gates to the freight area, showing the guard a piece of paper. He waved us through. A line of hangars made a black frieze against the horizon, and five or six aircraft stood at angles, big ones, freight carriers. I couldn't see any ground crews, any vehicles on the move.

7:12. It was three minutes to the rendezvous. Ibrahimi was checking his jeweled wrist watch.

"Wait," he told the driver in French.

The tires whimpered on the tarmac as the big car was turned toward the wall of a freight shed, and we stopped in its shadow. The three-quarter moon was twenty or thirty degrees high, bright in a clear sky; the sirocco had died away

237

toward evening as the air had cooled. There was traffic on the move near the main runway, the strobes of small planes flashing as they rolled.

The two hit men watched me from their jump seats. They hadn't put their guns away after I'd finished my call to London. They were aimed at me now, at the heart. The two men weren't watching my hands anymore; they were watching my eyes. They were well trained, and I knew from this slight but significant shift in their observation that they were expecting me to make some sort of attack on them, or on Muhammad Ibrahimi, very soon now, if at all. So perhaps they understood a little French, had heard what Ibrahimi had told me, and knew from experience that when the subject of an execution nears the moment of truth he tends to panic and strike out in a final attempt to save himself.

I haven't seen Moira for a long time, several months. She travels a lot, making those terrible movies, and of course I travel quite a bit too. I hope she is well.

Croder must have got his signals through extremely fast, but then we expect it of him: he has the attributes of a vampire and will draw blood in the instant if you cross him but when you're out in the field and he's in the signals room you've got infinitely more chance of bringing the mission home than with anyone else. I didn't know what units he'd sent in to the rendezvous or how many there were, but he'd cleared them out in nine minutes flat, phoning them direct or phoning their coordination unit and telling them the rendezvous was canceled, canceled or postponed or moved or whatever. Of course they could still be parked in one of the hangars over there or behind the freight shed. Nothing was certain.

He'd done a good job, Croder, and it looked as if I had an absolutely clear field for whatever last-ditch attempt at salvation I might try. This was what I'd wanted, asked for and got, but at that time I'd thought there'd be something I could do at the flashpoint, turn the car over or go for these people, these monkeys, *these stinking monkeys*, steady, you'll have to watch it, there's no room for emotion, no room for panic here, it's too dangerous, thought there'd be something I could do at the flashpoint, yes, but in fact there wasn't, take some of them with me of course but that was all, an eye for an eye, but what shall it profit a man when the mission is over before its time, what precisely is the point in taking life out of spite? Pride, yes, but that's no answer.

The mission had ended when that plane had taken off just now. My objective had been to infiltrate Nemesis and stay within it until I'd learned enough to be able to destroy it and get clear, but there hadn't been a chance and Klaus was airborne for Midnight One and tomorrow there would be headlines. Nothing would have changed if I'd let London spring their trap: they'd have got Ibrahimi, that was all. They'd hoped to get Klaus, thought he'd be at the rendez-vous. Nothing would have changed.

7:14.

One minute.

Adrenaline coursing through the veins, through the heart where the bullets would go. A feeling of lightness, of time slowing down, feelings that were familiar to me.

Ibrahimi told the driver, "Go to the hangar over there, the second from the end. Hangar Number Five."

We moved away, leaving the shadow of the freight building. I could see another vehicle on the move now, a dark-colored van. It was going toward Hangar Number 5, as we were. London is very good with timing, very reliable.

"That will be the van," I told Ibrahimi, "with the warhead."

"It is good," he said.

The moonlight flashed on the star mascot as the big Mercedes turned.

"Here," Ibrahimi told the driver. "Stop just here."

We were at the northeast corner of the hangar, not far from one of the big freight planes and a stack of crates with ropes across it. The tires whimpered again on the smooth tarmac, and we stopped.

The clock flicked to 7:15.

Fifty yards away, in the shadow of the hangar, the dark van halted.

Silence came in.

You should make your peace with Allah.

But I would rather stop the presses, stop the headlines.

Try.

"One thing worried me," I told Ibrahimi, "when I was talking to my contact in London. He warned us that we'd have to watch out for the airport police. Do you remember?"

He turned his face to me. "Yes," he said.

"I think he had a point. We're still not certain we can get through this rendezvous successfully. There could still be a trap."

I waited.

No one was getting out of the van over there.

"I'm thinking," I said to Ibrahimi, "of your personal welfare, at this point. There's no need for you to get out of the car yourself."

Across the airport a commercial jet came in, nose up and then flattening as the smoke rose in puffs from the tires. The sound hadn't reached us yet.

My hands were folded on my lap. The two men could see them in the moonlight that struck obliquely through the window. My hands were not folded with the left one holding the right wrist, gripping it. That technique couldn't work now, because these two had their guns out, didn't have to draw first. If I went for the elbow strike to Ibrahimi's throat it wouldn't connect with the tissues before the bullets came: they had their fingers inside the trigger guards, and like me they'd be feeling the adrenaline and would be fast, touchy.

The sound of the jet came in with a soft roar as it reversed thrust.

Ibrahimi had done his thinking.

"Order the man in front," he told me, "the German, to go across to the van and receive the warhead."

I'd known it would be the man in front he would send out

there, not one of the men in the back of the car, because they were watching me, protecting him.

I'd wanted the man in front to leave the car for two reasons. He was out of my reach, unlike the two in the rear, and Ibrahimi could conceivably walk across there into a hail of shots if in fact there were some people still hanging around here despite the call from London—and I wanted Ibrahimi to stay alive in case Allah was good to me and threw me a chance in a thousand and let me interrogate him. He was the last link I had with Nemesis, and might give me some information I could work with.

"He might speak a little French," I told Ibrahimi, "in which case you could give him the instructions yourself." I called in German to the man in front, asking him if he understood French. He turned his head and stared into my face.

"*Nein.*"

So I told him that Ibrahimi's instructions were for him to get out of the car and go across to the van. When he was halfway there, I said, someone would come out of the van and deliver the consignment into his hands.

He looked several times at Ibrahimi, who nodded to confirm what I was saying. When I'd finished he hit his seatbelt release and snapped the door open.

"*Jawohl!*"

"Wait," I said. "You will tell them you are here on behalf of Herr Ibrahimi. Mention his name: Ibrahimi. You will also give the password, which is in English. It is the word *Mushroom*. Pronounce it for me."

He tried.

"No," I said, "listen again. *Mush—room*. Repeat that."

He frowned, angered because he hadn't got his sums right, would have liked to put a bullet straight into my head. "*Mush—room.*"

"Good. Say it to yourself a few times as you walk across there. Now get moving."

He slammed the door and the echo came back from the

mouth of the hangar like a gunshot. We watched him walking across the tarmac, his right arm not swinging, not visible: his gun, like the others', would be left-side holstered under his coat. He didn't trust the people in the dark-colored van. He didn't trust his own mother.

I slowed my breathing, made it deeper, bringing down the tension in the muscles because there was sweat coming, and sweat is slippery on the hands, can make a critical difference in any kind of action.

But there wouldn't be any: the odds were too stacked and the timing was prohibitive: I couldn't reach those guns from this distance and hope to smash them away before they fired, not even with a double wave strike or downward blocks.

There were no options left, then. None.

The feeling of lightness came into me again, a kind of floating. I've known it before: I think it's when the conscious mind realizes that death is inevitable and allows the psyche free rein to survey the data on a subconscious level, where there may perhaps be insights, inspiration, where the spirit may redeem the flesh, offering a means of survival.

I gave myself to it.

Through the windscreen I saw a door of the dark-colored van coming open and a man getting out, then another. Between them they carried an oblong crate with rope handles. It looked heavy.

The German approached them, and when he was within a few feet of them they all stopped, and seemed as if they were talking. The German would be giving them the name of Ibrahimi and the password, *Mushroom*, and I suppose they were pointing out to him that this thing was too heavy for one man to carry, something like that, but then the whole scene turned silver in a flood of blinding light and the figures of men came running from the mouth of the hangar and two jeeps came swerving into the foreground with their tires screaming and Ibrahimi shouted something in Arabic and our driver hit the throttle and the Mercedes began slewing under the wheelspin until the treads found traction and we grazed the nearest jeep and rocked and steadied and got under way with a surge of acceleration that took us clear of the hangar and across the tarmac with the rear tires still whimpering under the acceleration.

Lights in the mirrors, bright lights, dazzling.

Ibrahimi was shouting to the driver again in Arabic. I didn't know what he was saying. The two guards hadn't reacted very much, were still watching me with their guns out, perfectly trained. Ibrahimi was turning sometimes to look through the smoked rear window, his face gray in the light coming through the tinted glass. He looked at me once, his eyes burning.

"Did you know of this?"

"No. But I warned you it could happen—and you're still a free man."

He looked away. The lights in the mirrors were colored now and flashing, and sirens began sounding. We kept a straight course until a fuel tanker came into view as a dark rectangle crawling across the taxiway, then we swerved and hit gravel and tore a radar scanner away from its base and straightened again with the automatic shift kicking down and giving us another surge of acceleration from the huge 5.6 liter engine, the sirens behind us howling and shots coming now as we crossed the central apron in front of the terminus with the digital speedometer moving through 150 kph, 160, 165 and the lights from behind us losing their glare and the sound of the sirens fading by a degree. But the shots were still coming and a rear tire burst and we slewed badly and then corrected, the huge shape of a commercial jet looming and swinging past as the tire was torn away from the rim and we began settling on the offside like a ship taking on water.

The driver was doing what I would have done: we'd got superior speed but not too much maneuverability at four thousand pounds so he was relying on putting all the distance he could behind us while the going was good, and we were closing in on some hangars at the other end of the airport and could even reach them and get into shelter and ditch and run if that was what Ibrahimi ordered.

Another vehicle was coming in from the side with its colored lights flashing and the siren going—it had seen the Mercedes and the speed it was doing and was coming across the tarmac to intercept, but either our driver had lost too much steering because of the rear wheel or he decided to make an oblique attack, because we swerved to the left and hit the vehicle at the front end and I saw it start rolling and the mirror on that side was lit up suddenly with an orange light and a second later we heard the dull thump of the explosion.

Shots from somewhere, from behind or from a new source of attention, and another tire burst and the tread began howling against the underneath of the fender and the stink of burning rubber came into the car and as we swerved again and hit something and spun full circle the whole thing took off and I smashed my hand down on the gun to my left and it roared and I felt for the man's throat and made the kill as the other man brought his gun up and fired wild and I went in very close and used a heel-palm and drove the nose bone upward into the brain as Ibrahimi screamed something and I saw the flash of a blade and blocked it and started forming a tiger claw but the car was barreling now and everything spun across the vision field and we smashed into something again and the doors burst open and I hit ground and rolled with Ibrahimi on top of me, forced him away and began dragging him clear as the tank went up and the whole of the night caught fire.

Chapter 21

Sahara

"Where is it?"

He began falling again and I jerked him upright.

"26°03 north," I said, "by 0.2°01 west. *Where is it?*"

He didn't answer.

The light of the burning limousine colored the wall of the hangar. Smoke was rolling, black smoke, and the emergency vehicles were moving in it, becoming lost in it. The smell of burning rubber was on the air, a sickening smell. The limousine, the mess, wasn't close: I'd run with this bastard for what had seemed a long time, possibly minutes, dragging him sometimes when he fell, pulling him up again, running again, cursing him in French, Ibrahimi, my last link with Nemesis, with the mission, with any hope of doing something to stop the headlines.

"What?"

I thought he'd said something, wasn't sure, there was a certain amount of dizziness coming and going, pain everywhere, understandable.

Center knuckle to the median nerve.

"Where is it?"

The fix.

It was all I had left.

He reacted to the nerve strike, opened his eyes and looked at me, but didn't see me, his eyes not focusing. Then I saw the blood: it had started dripping from the edge of his padded jacket, and when I pulled the zipper down I saw it had been

245

pooling inside, black in the moonlight, soaking. I suppose it had been friendly fire: the wild shot from the hit man on the right, opened an artery. I put my mouth close to his ear and asked him softly, "Where is that position, Ibrahimi? It's in the desert somewhere, isn't it? In the Sahara?"

Gunshot.

They hadn't been able to get one of the guards out of the Mercedes, then, perhaps neither of them, and their bullets were blowing up in the heat.

"Tell me, Ibrahimi, where it is."

His head lolled as consciousness slipped, then he jerked it up again and opened his eyes and looked at me with more focus, with a lot of effort. Then he spoke, but it was nothing to do with the fix.

"Help me to pray."

Bastard. He was dying, knew where that position was, perhaps knew something I could do to save a lot of other people from dying, stop the headlines. Was he going to pray for *them*?

A night breeze was moving the smoke still rolling from the Mercedes, bringing it across the huge mouth of the hangar, some of it clouding inside and bringing the sickening reek of rubber.

"Help me," Ibrahimi said.

"What?"

"I must pray."

So must we all. But I got him by the shoulders and lowered his body until he was doubled over with his hands on the concrete in front of him and his brow resting between them. I think he was too far gone to worry about facing east or west. He began speaking in Arabic, while the blood formed a pool around his spread fingers.

Making his peace with Allah. A luxury. I will tell you this— it was a luxury. We don't all get the chance to make what peace we can before it comes.

I got my handkerchief and held it against my face, but the stink of the smoke came through. I wondered how long he'd be, Ibrahimi, I hadn't got all night. There was blood on my hands, I noticed, but didn't know whether it was mine or his.

Then Ibrahimi rolled sideways, and I got him onto his back and put his hands across his chest and went along to the end of the hangar where I'd seen some sort of office when we'd come in here, not with doors or windows or anything, just some desks and a lot of paper and coffee mugs and a black plastic telephone on the wall.

I tried dialing direct but it didn't work. God knows what the problem was but it took minutes and the girl got stuffy and I had to keep my patience and it wasn't easy, because I didn't think I could do anything but I knew that if I could do anything it would have to be fast.

"Yes?"

This was the board for *Solitaire:* I hadn't had to go through the link unit because I was alone.

"Give me Control."

They knew who I was. Only the executive for the mission ever signals the board direct: it's his, it belongs to him.

"Control."

Shatner.

"Need"—I tried again, straightening up, getting things clear—"I need a DIF."

It was the bang on the head I'd got in the underground garage at Tegel Airport, I suppose, plus coming out of the limousine like that, pig out of a barrel, left me dizzy.

"He's in Algiers," Shatner said.

"Cone?"

"Yes."

It followed. The only information London had had when I'd broken off communication with my DIF last night in the stolen Volvo was that I'd be at the rendezvous in Algiers, so that was where they'd sent him.

I got one of the plastic ballpoints and used the back of a lading bill printed in French.

"Number?"

Shatner gave it to me and I repeated it and wrote it down in big figures because there was only moonlight here, coming in through the open doors, moonlight and the glow of the fire from the other end of the hangar.

"Look," I said, "you'll have to pull Helen Maitland out of this mess she's got herself into, see her safely back home. Put some people on it—we owe her that much."

In a moment, "Where do we find her?"

"Wherever the police catch up with Dieter Klaus, she'll be there. Look after her, that's all I ask, give me some peace of mind.

We're still running," I told him, and put the receiver back on the hook.

He'd have liked to debrief me but I hadn't got time; he'd have to wait until Cone signaled his report after I'd talked to him.

A yellow-painted jeep went hounding past the far end of the hangar with its emergency lights going. I wouldn't have thought there'd be any more need for rushing about; there were some bodies to get out of the Mercedes, that was all. But perhaps it was in the way or something, and they'd have to shift it. I wasn't worried that they'd start looking for me: they hadn't known how many people there'd been in the limousine and no one had seen me getting clear with Ibrahimi or they would have followed us into the hangar before now.

Local calls should work and I dialed the number direct again.

Three rings.

"Yes?"

"Executive."

He was at a safe house, then, not a hotel: we hadn't gone through a switchboard. A safe house or a sleeper's place, somewhere secure. That would help.

"Debrief?" Cone asked me.

"No. Write this down." I gave him the fix. "It's somewhere in the Sahara. I want you to have me dropped there. Can you do that?"

"When?"

"As soon as you can. It's fully urgent."

It meant he'd got to break every rule in the book if he had to, just get me the plane. Cone would do that. I'd been right, I'd been so *right* to get rid of that clown Thrower.

"Where are you?"

I told him.

"Can I phone you there?"

I gave him the number, got it wrong, not easy to read under the scratched plastic cover, gave it to him again, made sure, because this was the lifeline now for *Solitaire*.

"I've got that," Cone said. "Give me the picture."

"It's not a Lockerbie thing. It's much bigger. There are two Iranian pilots involved. I don't know what this fix means. It could even be a target zone but I can't think why. If it is, you'll know what happened to me, be in the papers, headlines, have—you'll have to—"

"What's your condition?" Cone cut in.

I pulled myself upright; I'd been lolling all over the bloody desk, papers on the floor, everything swinging round. I could not *afford* this.

"I'm operational," I said. "A few dizzy spells, there was a car smash. Listen, that fix could be totally remote, I mean that's the Sahara down there, so—so listen, if—" swinging again and I had to wait. "Listen, I want a two-way radio, you got that? I'll stay in contact as long as I can, but if—if you can't raise me by first light tomorrow you'd better send a search plane over the zone, I don't fancy dying of thirst out there." I held on to the edge of the desk and waited again, and the roof of the hangar swung down and tilted away again and I brought my weight underside and slowed the breathing, deepened it, and it helped. "Give me water rations for twenty-four hours, torch, the radio, hard tack, flares, the usual things for a desert drop, gloves, goggles, all right?"

"Yes. Have you lost any blood?"

"No. You got a map there, Sahara?"

"Yes. I'm with an a.i.p."

Agent-in-place. He'd know the territory, use the map, locate the bearing, adduce the range we'd need for the plane, the fuel capacity.

"Then fix me up," I said.

"Might take a bit of time."

"I've *got* to reach that zone before midnight."

Midnight One.

In a moment he said, "How long can you stay there by that phone?"

"As long as I have to."

"Do all I can," he said. "But you'd better know this: I'm not sure whether it's to do with a Lockerbie thing or not. There's a Pan Am flight reported missing, Berlin to New York."

Mother of God.

"What sorta girls they got there?"

I said I didn't know.

"So what you go there for?"

He was a Sicilian, Giovanni Scalfaro, spoke some kind of French, some kind of English, no German, sucked on some kind of chewing-gum which I suspected was laced, he flew dope, it was his living.

"To meet friends," I said. We were talking about the Safari Club in Tenerife, where I sometimes go between missions.

"You go there to meet friends," Giovanni Scalfaro said, "and you don't know what sorta girls they got there?"

Our heading was twenty-eight degrees west of south, with the moon high above the domed Perspex cockpit cover and the Sahara below.

"The friends I meet there," I said, "aren't that sorta girls."

We were an hour from the dropping point.

"Then what sorta girls are they?"

I've been given to understand that some Sicilians are like this.

But he was my friend, Giovanni Scalfaro. He could help

250

me to save *Solitaire*, stop the headlines. If it wasn't too late.

I'd asked Cone about Pan Am Flight 907.

"It took off from Berlin at six-seventeen," he'd said, "and went off the screens twenty minutes later. The flight plan was New York via London. No radio contact since, still nothing on the screens. Pan Am have alerted their Emergency Procedures Information Center and they're waiting for reports of wreckage."

I didn't understand.

The object of this operation, Willi Hartman had told me in Berlin, *is to place a bomb on board an international flight scheduled by one of the major U.S. airlines.*

Last night, when it had looked as if Nemesis had planned something bigger than a Lockerbie, I'd thought that Inge Stoph must have got it wrong when she'd told Willi about their plans. She smoked grass, and could have been high when she'd said that, wanted to shock him, Willi.

It didn't fit. The two Iranian pilots didn't fit into any plan for a Lockerbie operation. *It signifies that they will die,* the Arab at the palace had told me, *before they sleep again.* But it had been a Pan Am plane and they hadn't been flying it; we hadn't left Khatami behind in Berlin: he was here in Algeria. Nothing else fitted—Midnight One, the bearing, the zone somewhere in the Sahara—nothing.

It could be a coincidence.

I don't believe in them.

When I looked at the clock on the instrument panel again it read 22:00 hours—ten P.M. I would be dropping in fifteen minutes.

"It's eight hundred and fifty miles," Cone had told me when he'd telephoned the hangar. "The Aero L39 cruises at four hundred and fifty-four mph at sixteen thousand, four hundred feet." The smoke had been rolling through the doorway, tinged with the glow from the fire. I'd thrown tarpaulins over Ibrahimi's body in case anyone came through there on a routine security check; then I'd holed up in an empty crate until the phone rang. "He's using tip tanks and reserves, so he can drop you over the zone and swing back and put down in Adrar to refuel. There's an airstrip there."

We'd taken off at 8:16. Cone had been very fast, hotting up all the telephone wires in Algiers. The agent-in-place would have known the territory, where to find couriers, interpreters, weaponry, locksmiths, how to pull strings at the embassies, where to find transport, boats, planes, pilots, how to hire them, how much to pay.

Ten minutes ago Giovanni Scalfaro had pointed downwards and to port. "Adrar," he'd said. There'd been a few lights, that was all. Now we were flying across darkness below, into the wastes of the Sahara. It would be like dropping, I thought, into midocean.

"Did you hear," I asked the Sicilian, "about the Pan Am flight?"

He swung his head to look at me—"Yes!"—and crossed himself.

"There's nothing been found yet?"

"Wait," he said, "I ask Rome," and moved a hand to the radio.

Rome said there'd been some wreckage sighted in the North Sea, but it hadn't been identified. Pan Am Flight 907 hadn't come back on the screens, hadn't resumed radio contact.

"We will pray," Scalfaro said. "We will pray for them."

You'll understand what I'm talking about, Maitland had said, *tomorrow. We're going to make the headlines, you know.*

If that wreckage were identified as belonging to Flight 907 there would be headlines, yes, tomorrow. But Klaus had talked about conventional explosives, had wanted a nuclear warhead. It couldn't have been anything to do with Flight 907.

At 10:05 Scalfaro looked at the INS reading. "I'm gonna use partial flaps to bring the speed down to one hundred and twenty, okay? Gonna drop you off at nine thousand feet, okay with you?"

I said it was.

"We'll be over the drop zone in ten minutes. You better get all that stuff hooked on."

I got the military knapsack and the water bottles from behind the seat and buckled them to the chute harness. "Will there be sand blowing down there?"

"Maybe some." He looked through the dome. "Maybe a little, sure. We didn't see too many lights back there in Adrar, but then it's a pretty small place, couple of thousand people. Could be some blowing sand, though."

I got the goggles out of the knapsack and slung them round my neck.

At 10:12 Scalfaro looked down through the dome again. "It's none of my business, but you know what you're doing?"

"Not necessarily."

"Tell ya something, my friend, you're going to be lonely down there."

I looked through the Perspex, saw nothing below, just a waste of darkness. "What about wind currents," I asked him, "between here and the ground?"

"There shouldn't be any, this time of the year and at night. You won't be drifting much."

10:14 on the clock.

The roar of the Titan turbofan was muted as Scalfaro brought the throttle back another notch. He had his head turned to watch me.

"You feel okay?"

He'd noticed me lurch a bit on the tarmac at Dar-el-Beïda, wanted to know what the problem was, told him my shoes were pinching, none of his bloody business.

"Feel fine," I said.

"Okay." He slid the canopy back and the windrush slammed across our heads. *"Go for it!"*

Drifting.

The sound of the plane had died away minutes ago, and there was just the whisper of the shrouds above me. The air was freezing against my face.

The starfields were brilliant in the dome of the night sky. Below me the darkness wasn't total: the moon was spreading its light across a vast ocher-colored haze: the Sahara.

I felt isolated, minuscule.

Tell ya something, my friend, you're going to be lonely down there. And earlier Scalfaro had said when we'd boarded the plane, *Maybe you're just crazy, I dunno. But I mean, where you're going, a hundred and sixty miles from Adrar, there's just desert. There's just sand, is all, the Sahara. I mean that's all you'll be too— just another grain of sand down there. I just hope you know what you're doing.*

Perhaps. Perhaps not. It was all I'd got left of *Solitaire*, the fix, 26°03 north by 02°01 west, a point in the night, in the desert. And now I was there.

Drifting.

I looked at the glow of my watch face again. I'd dropped six minutes ago, with a minute left before I hit ground. The ocher color was lighter now, by a degree. Fine sand was pricking the left side of my face, and I put my goggles on and took a quick look above me. The moon's rim had lost its sharpness: there was sand blowing, close to ground level.

I looked down, waiting, as the desert rose against me in the final seconds of the drop and I sensed zero and pulled on the lines to break the impact and saw shapes in the distance through the blowing sand and felt hard ground under my boots.

It was fifteen minutes since I'd come down, and I had walked something like a mile across the violet-red clay surface in the moonlight, the fine sand blowing against my goggles and the scene ahead of me shifting as the wind came in gusts, so that the shapes out there took on substance and vanished again. Sometimes I could hear voices calling.

I'd tried to signal Cone on the radio but there was nothing but squelch. There was a power generator running somewhere, jamming the set.

I walked more slowly, trying to identify the shapes ahead

of me, and heard another sound coming in now, a faint whistling. I stopped, trying to identify it, then without warning the generator was gunned up and the whole scene took on brilliance as a flarepath bloomed across the desert floor and lights flooded from the sky and I dropped into a crouch as the massive shape of an aircraft came drifting through the haze and settled onto the ground with a roar as it reversed thrust and I saw the blue and white Pan Am insignia on the tail.

Chapter 22

Flight 907

*F*igures moved through the haze.

I was in cover, concealed by a stack of crates. The time on my watch was 11:14. I still had my goggles on. Others were wearing them too, as they worked in the blowing sand.

The last of the passengers were coming off the Pan Am plane. The Nemesis team was herding them into a huge group, two hundred of them, perhaps more; it looked a full complement. Their voices came thinly through the night. The flare path had blacked out as soon as the plane had come to a halt and then turned, facing the way it had come. The generator was idling now.

This was a dry lake bed, not salt but clay, with a fine powdering of sand on the surface. It felt hard under my boots, brick hard. There were three other planes on the ground, smaller than the Pan Am jet. I recognized one of them as the company plane we'd flown from Berlin to Algiers. Klaus would have landed here in that, with Maitland and some of the guards. The second aircraft was a twin-engined freighter with no insignia. It would have brought these stores here, the crates. Not quite stores—they had markings on them, and lettering in French, with the skull and crossbones prominent on the cylinders where they showed through the slats. Most of them contained explosives; some contained gas.

The third aircraft was a tanker, and its generators were throbbing as the Pan Am plane took on the last of its fuel.

It was going to take off again, and I knew when. It would take off at midnight.

Midnight One.

It was a time and a place, Midnight One. There was another time and another place in the Nemesis schedule: Midnight Two.

That would be the target.

Voices came on the wind, the passengers complaining, asking questions. I could hear children crying. Six guards stood at intervals with assault rifles leveled at the hip. Floodlights washed over the crowd, over their pale faces. I saw Klaus, standing halfway between the Pan Am jet and its passengers, fifty yards from where I was now. He was shouting orders, his arms waving with the precision of a traffic cop's. Maitland was nearer the jet, talking to the two Iranians, their figures floodlit by the lights of the tanker. A camouflaged jeep was on the move, providing liaison.

We're going to make the headlines, you know. They'll be interrupting television programs, all over the world.

I tried the radio from time to time, got nothing. If I could raise Cone he might be able to alert the Algerian Air Force in time for them to intercept the Pan Am jet before Midnight Two, before it reached the target. It would be the final chance, if I could reach him. So I tried, every few minutes, but the generators were throwing out too much interference. There wasn't, quite clearly, anything else I could do.

There's a Pan Am flight reported missing, Cone had told me. *It took off from Berlin at 6:17, and went off the screens twenty minutes later.*

So it had been airborne for nearly four hours, airborne and off the radar screens. When it had landed here and the jets had whined into silence and the forward passenger door had come open, Dieter Klaus himself had greeted the first two men off the plane, throwing his arms round them. They would be the hijackers who had gone on board in Berlin.

There would have been no way to get Flight 907 off the screens except by losing altitude over water and getting below the radar, and that was what the pilot had been ordered to do: follow the English Channel and turn south across the Bay of Biscay and then east across Morocco into the Sahara. Morocco would have picked up the jet on its screens but wouldn't have been able to identify it.

The sand blew against my goggles; the air was cold against my face. They would be coming across here very soon now, to start loading the cylinders onto the Pan Am plane.

Two men were standing near the company jet. I think one of them was the pilot. Another man was crouching below the belly of the freighter, checking the undercarriage: perhaps it had been a bumpy landing. The tanker had people around it, watching the fuel going into the airliner. If I could break cover without attracting attention and go across there and get into any one of the aircraft I could send a Mayday call giving the position of Flight 907 and reporting it as hijacked, alerting the Algerian Air Force. But they couldn't put any aircraft down here before midnight unless they had a base nearer than Algiers.

Tried the radio again and drew blank.

So I had successfully infiltrated Nemesis, the target opposition network, and I had stayed with it all the way to the operation zone and I was there now, watching the steadily running procedures as the time ran out toward zero, but there was *nothing* I could do to stop them. So *Solitaire* was going to be the first mission I couldn't bring home, couldn't follow right through to the end phase, signal London and tell them to pick up that bit of chalk and put it on the board: *Mission accomplished.*

But I'd had to give it a try and I'd had to go it alone: there'd been no choice. I hadn't known what I was going into, but I know that in any ultrasensitive situation you can't send in support without risking confusion in the field, and sometimes I can persuade London to understand this: I'd got that clown Thrower recalled on that very point. In Algiers my director in the field couldn't have given me more than half a dozen people at the most at such short notice, and even if they hadn't been seen dropping out of the sky all over the place they couldn't have got this close, as close as one man could come—had come. And even if London could have raised a whole bloody platoon and armed it to the teeth there'd have been a war on down here the minute they landed, and half those passengers over there would have been caught in the cross fire and there *still* wouldn't have been any guarantee that the Pan Am plane wouldn't take off on schedule at Midnight One.

There'd been no choice.

11:22.

The wind blew cold, penetrated my bomber jacket, penetrated to the spine, because there were going to be headlines, yes, after all.

The refueling crew were hauling the flexible pipe away from the last Pan Am wing tank and stowing it on their plane, and the jeep started up and drove across to where Klaus was standing. He must have been a touch pissed off, Herr Klaus, had been expecting a nuke to play with, but it hadn't arrived. He was answering a question from the driver of the jeep, nodding emphatically, and some of the guards piled aboard. The jeep would turn, I believed, and head in this direction, toward the stack of crates that were giving me cover. It was time for the cargo to be loaded into the airliner.

I waited.

It seemed, somewhere in the shadows of my mind, that I had been waiting a long time for this moment to come, longer than hours, longer than days, as if in the past I'd been given a glimpse of the shape of things to come. I think this was because I'd just realized that there might be something, after all, that I could do to bring Klaus down before he could reach his target, Midnight Two, wherever it was.

A woman screamed somewhere among the crowd of passengers, having got to the point of hysteria, I suppose, and understandably. The scream touched my nerves, for an instant froze them, because I knew quite well that if I started to do what had come into my mind there'd be no calling it off, no chance of getting back.

Carpe diem.

I went on waiting.

Seize, yes indeed, the day.

My cover was good, here: the crates were stacked higher than a man, and I could move with freedom. Personal cover was also satisfactory: most people here were in black bomber jackets like mine: it had been the fashion of choice when we'd set out from Algiers for a winter's night in the desert. Three or four of the men on the jeep wore goggles, as I did, against the discomfort of the blowing sand; and we all wore padded gloves, *de rigueur*. I wouldn't have been noticed in the front row of the chorus: someone would have to tell you I was the fourth from the left, just above the bald-headed violinist.

In the distance the jeep turned and gunned up, its head-lights swinging toward the stack of crates.

I didn't move.

You won't get out of this alive.

Shut up.

It's a suicide run, you know that.

Christ's sake *shuddup.*

Then the jeep slid to a halt on the dry sand and the men dropped off it with a clatter of combat boots and started work on the crates with their jimmies, breaking away the slats to get at the cylinders, two of them moving around to the sides, so I kicked at the slats of the nearest crate and prised them away and hauled one of the cylinders out and stooped and got it onto my shoulder and joined the chorus line, lurching with it across to the jeep, another man beside me, the one just above the red-haired lady with the trombone, the sweat running on me because I was committed now and beyond the point of no return, because if I could get *this* far I stood a chance of bringing the mission home.

That or the other thing: *finis, finito.*

I slid the cylinder onto the back of the jeep and found a spare tire lever and went back to the crates and worked on the slats and dragged another cylinder out. There were two Arabs here but the rest were German, by their speech.

"Remember the orders," one of them said, "and don't throw these bloody things around. Knock 'em together a bit too hard and we're goners, *kerbooom*, so for Christ's sake be careful."

"He's leaving it late," someone said, "you know that?"

"He knows what he's doing. Shuddup and get the job done."

I checked my watch at 11:39 when we'd shifted more than half the cylinders, making five trips with the jeep fully loaded.

The two Arabian pilots had moved: they were standing with Klaus as we passed him on the final run. One of them was laughing, the sound carrying on the wind. They looked at their ease, hands on their hips and their heads thrown back as Klaus slapped their arms, telling them in his terrible French that they were heroes: I caught snatches of it—"You will have streets named after you. . . . You will go down in history as the saviors of Islam. . . ."

It was not good news. This was not good news.

Unless he was wildly exaggerating, this concerned more than just a megadeath in a football stadium. It concerned Midnight Two, something big enough to earn them a place in history.

The mental sense of powerlessness is enervating: my legs felt weak, my arms incapable. I needed help with my last cylinder as I staggered with it onto the Pan Am plane.

"You all right?"

"Bloody things weigh a bit, that's all." The cabin was swinging across my eyes, and I had to hold on to a bulkhead to steady myself.

The men were shouting at the entrance to the cabin, behind the flight deck.

"How many more?"

"Three."

"Look sharp, then."

I moved back to give them room.

"Okay, that one on top of those two."

They moved about. I could hear them. I couldn't see them anymore, because I'd slid down on my haunches behind the stack of cylinders: I think I was in one of the forward galleys, because there was a curtain drawn half across, and the smell of coffee. It was comfortable here with my back against a panel, and I closed my eyes.

Voices from outside the cabin, speaking in French. Because of the curtain I couldn't hear them clearly.

They're on a suicide run, and now you're going with them.

Shut up.

You're out of your fucking mind.

Shuddup and leave me alone.

The wind blows across the desert, across the clay of the dried lake bed, flinging sand against the windows of the cabin. I listen to it.

I look at my watch.

It is 11:57. We have three minutes left.

Then I can hear voices again, this time speaking an Arab tongue. They come from inside the plane. Then there is the soft rushing of the jets, and vibration comes into the airframe. I can feel it against my back.

Now there is a roaring, the sound of huge power. The big metal cylinders begin a discordant tintinnabulation as the cabin trembles, and then it dies away as the wings lift and we are borne into the sky.

Chapter 23

Airborne

01:13.

It was the first thing I looked at, took an interest in, when I opened my eyes: the watch on my wrist. We had been airborne an hour and thirteen minutes.

I had slept. The decision had been made for me by the subconscious when the beta-wave levels had been phased out by shock, by the accumulated shock of the mission that we file under the simple name of mission fatigue. It is not simple.

I felt quite good, felt refreshed, clearheaded again. Thought came easily now, and I was becoming aware of what had happened. But there were certain troubling aspects, because the decision my subconscious had made for me was totally illogical.

I could hear them talking up there on the flight deck through the open door, the two pilots. They were speaking in Farsi, presumably: I couldn't hear any specific words, wouldn't have understood them in any case.

Totally illogical, then, the decision that had been made, that I was *stuck* with. I could either have stayed where I was on the ground or I could have stayed on board the plane and taken off with it. If I'd stayed on the ground I could have joined the tanker crew or the freighter crew and hitched a flight back to Algiers. They wouldn't have recognized me, had never seen me before, would have accepted me as one of the team. Once in Algiers, communication, immediate communication: telephone Cone and tell him the situation, let him signal London and tell them to alert and inform Pan American Airlines. But there wouldn't have been anything they could do. Flight 907 would by then have been airborne for more than two hours, invisible in the night, untraceable, on its way to the unknown target, Midnight Two. If it hadn't already reached there, if there weren't already headlines running through the press.

It would have been an exercise in total futility, calling up my director in the field and having him signal London and all that tra-la, an exercise in *total bloody futility*. All it would have done would be to put the matter down in the records: *Mission unsuccessful, executive safe.*

So there wouldn't have been any point in staying on the ground in the desert. It wouldn't have achieved anything. But there'd been no point in taking off on board this aeroplane either because I was in a strictly shut-ended situation. I had no argument that would persuade the Iranians to put this aircraft down somewhere and call the whole thing off, and if I got control of them I couldn't put it down anywhere myself: I'd had no training on anything half this size and it'd have to be brought in like a feather on the breeze or we'd blow up the airport.

Teddy bear.

The subconscious, then, is not always reliable, is not always so bloody clever. You would do well to remember that, my good friend. It can send you to your bloody *doom*.

Teddy bear on the floor. Dropped, I suppose, by one of the children when they'd all been herded through the exits. Or was it perhaps a *naughty* teddy bear that would blow my head off if I picked it up, blow the whole plane to bits? But it wasn't worth worrying about: the stuff in these forty-eight cylinders we'd stacked in here was measurable in mega–teddy-bear power.

There were two kinds of label on them, both in red and white and with the skull-and-crossbones symbol. At least four of the cylinders contained trinitrotoluene and carried another vignette, an explosive flash in red. There might be more of these in the stack; I didn't know, because the labels weren't all visible. The labels on the other cylinders read NITROGEN TETROXIDE and carried four symbols: the skull and crossbones, the explosive flash, a man's head with a gas mask on the face, and a coat on a hanger symbolizing protective clothing.

As an explosive, nitrogen tetroxide is dramatically potent. When Geissler had put me under the strobe in the garage last night I'd repeated the story Samala had told me: *An airman dropped a nine-pound socket from a spanner inside a Titan silo, and it punched a hole in the skin of a fuel cell and started a leak. There was a seven-hundred-and-fifty-ton steel door on the silo and when that fuel went off it sent it two hundred feet straight up in the air and dropped it a thousand feet away.*

It was 1:32 when I checked my watch again. The time was important, because I would very soon have to do something definitive.

The empty cabin made a sound box for the soft rush of the jets. The lights had been left on in here, turned low on the rheostat. Something was rolling on the floor, pinging against one of the cylinders, and I picked it up. It was a lipstick, and I put it onto the counter of the galley, and bent again to pick up the teddy bear—*freeze*—but it was all right, nothing happened, and I sat him on the counter too, with a sense, I suppose, of restoring order while I sipped my coffee and thought things out and eventually reached conclusions, deadly conclusions.

Solitaire was in the end phase, and if all went reasonably well I could bring it home, though only metaphorically. I would remain somewhere in the Atlantic, distributed piece-meal on its surface to be plucked at by fish—and I say this without bitterness, because I'd rather have them than the worms. In the end phase of a mission when we realize the executive's status is terminal it's rather like drowning, in that we look back over the events that led us here, and at this particular moment I found myself thinking of that clown

Thrower and hoping that Shatner would learn from his mistake and not send him out again unless it was to direct a shadow who could work comfortably with a bloody schoolmaster. I also thought of Helen Maitland, and hoped that one day she would shatter the self-image she'd been stuck with, and start fresh again; and as I considered these things I came to know what was happening: I was putting off the moment when I must set in motion the necessary procedures, because they would bring my death, and the sweat was crawling on me and the adrenaline was firing the motor nerves as I drained the cup with the Pan Am crest on it and put it into the sink.

Polaris had been high on the starboard side when I'd checked our heading through one of the windows and the time was now 1:46, so we were somewhere west of Morocco and over the Atlantic.

Procedures.

Three of the nitrogen tetroxide cylinders were stowed vertically just aft of the galley and secured with straps, and I loosened a buckle by one notch and pulled a cylinder away from the others and let it fall back. It had the deep musical sound of a bell.

Did it again.

Remember the orders, don't knock these things around. He'd been the leader of the work group, the jeep's driver. *Knock two of these together a bit too hard and we're goners, ker-booom, so for Christ's sake be careful.*

Did it again.

Boom ...

This was all right, I wasn't knocking them about.

There was a shipping label on the loose cylinder, half torn away, printed in French. It had been shipped—they had all, then, presumably, been shipped—out of Libya.

It's believed that Dieter Klaus has the substantial backing of Colonel Muammar Qaddafi. It had been in my Berlin briefing.

Boom ...

The voice of one of the pilots cut through the rushing of

the jets. He was telling his friend, I would have thought, that he was going to take a look: there was some cargo shifting, so forth.

Boom . . .

I saw his shadow now, moving across the wall of the cabin on the other side. I let the cylinder fall again and backed away, staying close to the galley bulkhead. The Iranian reached the three cylinders, and saw what the trouble was.

I searched him and found a gun and emptied the chamber and dropped the bullets into the trash container in the galley and put the gun into the refrigerator. The edge of my right hand was throbbing but that was normal: the strike had needed great speed and great force so that he didn't have time to cry out. He'd started falling toward the cylinders and I'd steered him away and let his body down gently, then dragged it behind the galley bulkhead.

Then I straightened up and tightened the buckle on the strap securing the cylinders and went forward onto the flight deck.

The pilot said something, asking what the problem was, I suppose, and I didn't answer so he looked up and his face opened in surprise and he brought his right arm across his body and I waited until the gun was in his hand and then broke his wrist and worked on the gun and threw the bullets into the cabin and shoved the gun into my coat, bugger was throwing up, for Christ's sake, the bugger was lolling over the control column with his face white, all right, there's a lot of pain with a broken wrist but you don't have to go into histrionics, do you, and I told him in French:

"Get that control column, watch what you're fucking well doing!"

A lot of anger coming out, it had been suppressed for a long time now, and there was some fear in it, I knew that, because the chances of getting out of this thing alive were so terribly thin.

I pulled him upright, slapped his face, got him more or less conscious again, I suppose he'd got a low pain threshold, some of us are like that, it's a matter of sensitive nerves, but

I didn't want him messing about when he was meant to be flying a jumbo load of explosives through the dark.

I said in English: "What's our destination?"

He looked at me with his eyes trying to focus. "Come on, for Christ's sake! What's your target?"

There was 15° north of west on the compass but that didn't tell me enough.

He shook his head.

It looked all right. I was going to use a *lot* of English in a minute or two when I hit the radio, and I didn't want him to understand.

In French: "Where are we heading? Wipe your mouth, for God's sake, get a handkerchief. *What is our destination?*"

He wasn't quite with me yet, kept looking behind him into the cabin. "Where is Hassan?" he asked me.

I reached and slid the door shut without taking my eyes off him. If I told him I'd killed his friend he'd go crazy and try something and I didn't want any milling about, we could break an instrument, kick a control out of whack. I wanted, in any case, his cooperation.

I didn't think I'd get it.

"What is our destination?"

He glanced down and across, wasn't fast enough mentally yet to stop himself, and I saw the briefcase on the co-pilot's seat and picked it up. Then I looked into his eyes and said quietly, "Khatami, if you give me any trouble, I'm going to kill you. Do you understand that?"

He watched me, some anger of his own coming into him now as he thought of his friend.

"Did you kill Hassan?" he asked me.

"As long as you understand, Khatami."

"You are a pilot?"

"Yes."

"You fly these planes?"

"Yes."

Otherwise I couldn't kill him and he knew that.

He wasn't a small man; he looked strong, fit, probably did

a lot of aerobics, athletics, to keep in shape doing a sedentary job. But he was an airline pilot, and hadn't undergone any special training, or he wouldn't have let me take his gun away. And the difference between any given athlete, however strong, and an agent who has been trained for years at Norfolk and by exhaustive experience in the field is immeasurable, when it comes to effective close-combat techniques. This man was also in a lot of pain, his face still bloodless, and I didn't think I'd have to work on him again until he started feeling better.

He began wiping himself down with his handkerchief and I moved behind him and sank onto my haunches, facing his seat with my back to the bulkhead, where a cup of coffee had been spilled, splashing against the vinyl, the empty cup smashed on the floor, this was when the two hijackers had pushed their way onto the flight deck past the stewardess, she'd been bringing a fresh cup for one of the crew.

A teddy bear on the floor, a lipstick and a smashed cup, the small signs of great crisis, of the process of an act of inhumanity.

If Khatami moved, I would see it in the periphery of my vision field.

I took out the first sheet from the briefcase and let my eyes make leaps across the paragraphs to get the gist. The first of them were in French and one pulled me up short.

. . . You will insist that you have a fire in the cabin and that you cannot risk going on to Dulles International. Remind Air Traffic Control that you have a full complement of passengers and that you must get them onto the ground as soon as possible and regardless of all other considerations. . . .

There were three more paragraphs in Iranian and some figures that looked like radio call signs. I took out the second sheet.

It was a map for airline pilots: *Washington D.C. (VA). Washington National, River Visual Approach for Runway 18.*

I began taking slow breaths. The image of Khatami's seat had moved, the whole silhouette had moved against the lights of the instrument panel. I didn't want any more of that *bloody* dizziness at a time like this, I couldn't afford the luxury, nobody could afford it, the President of the United States couldn't afford it, I knew that now.

You will make your approach to Runway 18 from the northwest, following the lights and landmarks of the Potomac River. You should pick up the river just after passing through 10 DME 6 at 3,000 feet. The American Legion Memorial Bridge will be on your right. You will pick up the lights of the Chain Bridge just after 10 DME 6 and you should now be down to 1,800 feet.

I felt the vibration of the bulkhead against my shoulder blades, could smell the stale coffee that had been spilled, and Khatami's vomit. The lights and the LEDs shimmered below the darkness of the windscreen, some of them steady, some of them flashing red, green, amber, white. I had to look away from them; they were starting to swing a little in front of my eyes.

Never neglect concussion. It was in the medical section of the *Manual* at the Bureau, and Doc Dibenidetto can be trusted to know whereof he speaks. It had happened in the underground garage at Tegel Airport, and pitching out of the limousine in Algiers had aggravated things.

Slow breaths.

And make haste, great haste now.

The Georgetown Reservoir will be coming up on your left and you should now be down to 1,200 feet. At this point you should request confirmation of your permission to make an emergency landing from ATC, so as to reassure them that your situation is genuine. You should be through 3 DME 6 and over Key Bridge at 900 feet. Continue your approach above Roosevelt Bridge and Arlington Memorial Bridge as scheduled, with the Washington Monument now on your left. At this point you will break off your approach path and make a 70° turn to line up with the White House and complete your run in to the target.

The lights swinging at the edge of the vision field, around the edges of the map, the rush of the jets diminishing a little.

I waited, had to wait, until I thought I could get onto my

feet and stay there. I think it took only a few seconds, and when I finally managed it I had the feeling I should have waited longer, not rushed it.

"Khatami," I said, "get on the floor."

He looked up at me, down at the map in my hand.

There wasn't any point in talking to him about this. I hadn't got a gun that I could have pressed to the back of his neck while I told him where to fly this thing, where *not* to fly it, but I had enough stamina left to kill him if I had to. But he was beyond threats to his life: he'd already surrendered it to Allah, and nothing could touch him now. This is the strongest weapon of the kamikaze: he's got nothing to lose, nothing you can threaten to take away from him.

He was still looking up at me, Khatami.

"You killed Hassan," he said.

"Down on the floor! Face down on the floor—move!"

He held my eyes for a moment and then dropped from his seat and lay prone, I think because he'd seen I was ready to kill him if he didn't obey, and that would mean he'd have no chances left of overcoming me if he could. That was all he wanted to live for: my death and his final run in to the target.

I put my foot on his neck so that I'd feel any movement, any attempt to get up. Then I hit the speaker switch of the radio so that I wouldn't have to reach for the headset, and raised the board for *Solitaire* in the signals room in London.

"Can you hear me?"

Yes-yes.

The voice-activated tapes would be starting to roll.

"I am on board Pan American Flight 907."

Croder would be there, Chief of Signals. During the end phase of a mission he will never leave the signals room. Sometimes a camp bed is brought in there for him.

We have that.

I felt a chill: I'd paused longer than I'd thought, and they were having to prompt me.

The radio display was blurring, clearing again, blurring.

273

I'd got up too soon, off the floor too soon, pushing it, this was pushing things, no good, this was dangerous.

Said, I said: *My position is west of the Moroccan coast and south—southeast of the Azores.*

We have that.

Oh Jesus *Christ*, this wasn't—I wasn't doing this *fast* enough—

"Listen—this aircraft must not be allowed—must *not* be allowed—"

Lights went out, the lights of the display went out, dark now, not the lights, my eyelids closing, that was it, have to open them, *open them*—"This aircraft must not be allowed—"

The lights swung in an arc and a flash of pain shot into my right shoulder as I crashed down on it.

Chapter 24

Fireball

In the dream I heard a voice.

It was screaming at me.

Heat in my shoulder, white heat. It didn't bother me. I listened to the dream, because that was all it was, a voice. It was screaming at me, but I didn't understand the words.

I went on pushing.

The lights were beautiful, circling above my head, red, green, amber, white, circling around the starfields in the windscreen, went on pushing, running down my arm, there was something running down my arm—*Oh Mother of God this is—*

Screaming at me about Hassan, I could hear the name *Hassan.*

I pushed harder. I wasn't going to let him do this. He had a knife, a long knife with red on the blade.

Come in, please. Come in.

That was in English.

London.

Hassan, Khatami was screaming, then he seemed to remember and switched to French—*You killed Hassan . . .* and went on screaming, something about *le grand Satan,* he would die, the Great Satan, yes, a seventy-degree turn from the river—*Jesus Christ I've got to—*

Pushed *very* hard, but my hand was slipping because of the blood, it was dripping against my face.

Come in, please, come in.

275

London, waiting.

I had things to tell London, very important things: *This aircraft must not be allowed to approach the eastern seaboard of the United States. It must not be allowed to approach land at all.*

Tried—tried to shout it out so they'd hear, nothing happened.

His face was above me, Khatami's, dark, enraged, in the center of the swirling vortex of lights, one clear thought burning in my head, one clear thought, *If I don't tell London, this whole bloody thing is going to hit the target,* the one thought burning in my head.

Come in, please. Come in.

Calm—his voice sounded very calm, but they knew what was going on, they could hear this bastard screaming, could understand his French.

Come in, please.

Blood in one of my eyes.

You killed my brother Hassan.

Tried shouting again and got a word or two out but then the blood was in my mouth and I began choking on it and that was going to make things worse so I pushed *very hard indeed* and felt his arm swing away as I twisted from under him, choking, choking for breath and hanging there like a bloody dog but the adrenaline was firing the muscles and I reared and smashed my head into his face and the screaming stopped, felt for his knife hand and reached it and got my feet braced against the bulkhead and lurched forward, lunged forward and smashed my head into him again and did it again and turned the knife, turned it, pushing it through the dark, the red roaring dark, pushing it into the softness, deeper and deeper, pushed it as far as the hilt, coughing up the blood that had got into my mouth, choking for breath but it had stopped, the screaming had stopped and I lurched forward again and hit the bulkhead near the radio console and heard something break, a panel, making a brittle sound but it seemed all right because they were talking again.

Come in, please. Come in.

Choking still, but I could breathe now, things much, things much better, he wasn't moving, I could see him with one eye, the knife sticking up like a bloodied erection, went on choking again and got the last of it out of my throat, leaned against the console, the sweetness of air in my lungs.

Come in—

"Listen—this is—this is my situation."

No need to tell them now that this aircraft must not be allowed, so forth, because this aircraft wasn't going anywhere after all, he was dead, I believed, Khatami, or if he wasn't dead he wouldn't be able to get at the controls again, there was a lot of blood coming out of his groin, creeping toward the smashed coffee cup that was lying there on the floor. I did some more coughing and it helped.

"This aircraft is loaded with explosive but I am in control." Odd, an odd way to put things, in control of what exactly, a flying coffin, yes. "What I mean is, I'm going to have to ditch, and blow it all up, you got that, have you got—"

Yes, we have that. Then another voice came on, and I recognized Shatner. *Control. Let me have your position.*

My left eye was streaming with tears and the blood was getting washed away, but I couldn't see the instrument display very clearly yet. "I can't tell you. Not accurately. West of the Moroccan coast, southeast of the Azores, possibly more like due south by now—" broke off to do some more coughing, but things were much better now and I could breathe quite well between bouts. It was my wrist, where the blood had come from, he'd sliced a vein. "The target was the White House, but listen, the passengers of Flight 907 are being held in the Sahara Desert and this is their position: 26° 03 north by 02°01 west. Need to get them out of there. Terrorists guarding them with assault rifles, need to be careful."

Gave myself a short rest, needed more air in my lungs, they felt constricted. But the tapes were running in London and there'd be signals going out already to alert people—the British ambassador in Algiers and through him the Algerian Air Force and Army Desert Reconnaissance, GSG-9 in Germany because Klaus was out there—

"Listen," I said, "Dieter Klaus may still be there when the rescue aircraft reach those people or he may fly out before they arrive. If he's still there, I advise the use of utmost caution. He is vicious, ruthless, and determined, and I suggest they shoot him on sight, have you got—have you—"

I have that, Shatner said. *That position you gave me—is it an airfield?*

I told him it was a dry lake bed, had a flare path, told him its distance from the nearest town, Adrar, gave him the whole thing while the starfields crept across the dark of the windscreen as we headed west through the night.

I was beginning to feel lonely.

Are there other aircraft there in the desert?

Said yes. Told him what kind they were. I knew now from what I'd found in the briefcase why Klaus hadn't used a cargo plane for this operation: Washington National wouldn't have let it land there. They would have told it to go the extra distance into Dulles. But a Pan Am carrier with a full complement of passengers would make a difference: the potential loss of life would have been far greater if the situation had been genuine.

Beginning to feel lonely, yes. The night-black ocean was below me, its crests touched with silver by the moon. This huge aircraft was like a mote of dust compared with the vastness of the Atlantic. I'd thought, when I'd made the drop into the Sahara, that it was like going down into an ocean, but that had been an illusion. This time it was real.

When you can give us your exact position, do that.

I leaned away from the console, overdid things and lost my balance and had to throw out a hand to save myself. I think I stayed like that, swaying on my feet, for a long time, quite a few seconds.

What is your condition?

"I'm trying to see. Give me a—"

—Your condition. How much strength have you got left?

"Oh. Enough to ditch this thing, I mean it can do that for itself, but I've got to get it off autopilot and then we've got to steer clear of the Azores and the African land mass. I don't—"

Have you lost blood?

It wasn't wholly telepathy. In the final hours of the end phase there's often a bit of blood drawn by someone or other. This place looked like an abattoir.

"Yes. But I don't need long."

I worked my way round to the front of the left-hand seat and dropped into it and buckled the harness on and the instrument array swung into an arc and I blacked out, gradually came back.

... In terms of morale?

Oh Jesus Christ they wanted to know about my bloody morale when all I needed was the strength left to hit the auto switch to manual and bring the control column back. I did that. "Listen," I told Control, "I'm going to bring her down and make a—"

It was like hitting a wall.

Stars whirling through the dark, through the silence.

She watched me, one shoulder strap hanging down, her eyes innocent, her skin cool, with water droplets on it from the pool.

I hope we'll meet again, she said.

I know where to find you, I told her, and brought my head away from the instrument panel with a jerk as the roar of the jets slammed back.

Come in, please. Come in.

The display lights swam and steadied and I looked for the altimeter and the shock went through me and I brought the control column back and locked my arms round it, feeling the g-force as the huge mass of the aircraft pulled out of its dive.

Asked London: "How long was I out?"

Seventeen minutes.

"I lost altitude. I'm down to three thousand feet."

What is your position?

"36°04 north by 25°02 west."

What is your heading?

"160°."

You are approximately 150 miles south of the Azores and will pass them to the northwest if you maintain your heading. What is your altitude now?

"Still three thousand."

I'd kept her steady at that level since I'd pulled her out of the dive.

You're well placed to put down in Ponta Delgada.

The airport in the Azores. It sounded comforting, an island in the night, in this vast sea. But I was not in point of fact well placed to land there.

"I can't put this thing down anywhere at all. I've got to ditch it."

What have you flown before?

"The nearest thing to this was a single-seat jet fighter."

Then you're familiar with the basics.

"The basics are," I said, "that I've got enough explosive behind me to blow the Azores out of the Atlantic, if I mess up the landing."

Silence for a bit. They were putting their heads together, Shatner, Croder, perhaps Loman, I didn't know how many of them were in the signals room now but there'd presumably be quite a few because it wouldn't go down terribly well with the Portuguese government if I wrote off their seagirt real estate.

"Listen," I said, "there's nothing—"

Oh Jesus Christ.

I'm ordering you to land your airplane in Ponta Delgada.

It wasn't London. There was a U.S. Air Force F-15 right alongside, sleek and pointed and with the moonlight flashing on its wings.

This is Major J. F. Franklin of the United States Air Force. If you wish to avoid attack, you must land your airplane immediately.

There was another one sliding up on the port side. I was flying in formation. They'd picked up my radio call to London and they'd heard me say that the White House had been the target and they'd got off the ground in the Azores or they'd been on night-flying exercise from Spain and they were up here to start a war.

"I can't do that," I said. "I've had no training with this aircraft. If—"

I will give you one minute to alter your course for the Azores. Your failure to do this will bring an immediate attack.

Hadn't believed me, thought I was playing for time.

"Major," I said, "let me give you a little advice. If you attack this aircraft you'll blow yourself out of the sky. I'm carrying the equivalent of a small nuclear bomb."

I could see his helmet through the cockpit cover; his face was turned toward me.

You will alter course immediately for the Azores.

Had the White House on his mind, I could quite understand. He—

Major Franklin—London—this is the British Foreign Office. Good morning. We can vouch for the identity of the person flying the Pan American plane. This is the flight that has been missing since early last evening from Berlin, Flight 907. The pilot has seized control from Iranian terrorists, but has not flown this type of plane before. The British government would be most grateful for your assistance in any way possible.

I think he said a bit more but I went into another coughing fit, clearing the last of the blood out of my throat. It was nice to have company up here with me but there wasn't anything they could do. They were pallbearers, that was all.

Please identify yourself.

"What? Oh. Name's Locke."

I couldn't think how it would help, could have said I was Moses.

London was quiet, waiting for some kind of answer from Major Franklin.

I watched the instrument panel. We were still at 3,000 feet, airspeed 350, heading unchanged.

Shut my eyes for a bit. I knew what I'd got to do and I wanted to do it and get it over. The radio was quiet; I suppose they were both thinking things out, the U.S. pilot and London. Then another voice came on.

This is Walter J. Cummins, the American ambassador in London. Can you hear me, Major Franklin?

Yes, sir.

Now *that* had been very fast work. Control had told someone at his elbow to get the ambassador on the phone as soon as he'd started talking to the U.S. pilot, in case he refused to accept the authority of the British FO. They'd got him on the phone at his bedside and told him the brief position and patched him in through the signals-room amplifiers: he sounded as if he were speaking into a bucket.

I can vouch for the authenticity of the gentleman speaking to you from the British Foreign Office. You may therefore accept what he has just told you about the person at the controls of the Pan American airplane. I'm not completely clear about the situation apart from that. Is there any assistance you can give Mr. Locke at this time?

The U.S. pilot still had his head turned to watch me. *Okay, sir, I guess it's over to him. What are your intentions, Mr. Locke?*

I told him I'd got to ditch.

I understand you're not familiar with this type of airplane. We could try talking you down into Ponta Delgada.

The display lights had begun swinging again, and I braced the control column in my arms. The sound of the jets had started fading. I said, "Look, you'd better stand off a bit in case I let things slip. We don't—we don't want any collisions. Tell—tell your friend too."

What kind of shape are you in?

"Bit snuffed. Listen—" then it started again, and the whole thing blacked out.

. . . Mr. Locke? Can you hear me?

"Yes. I think—"

Why are you losing altitude?

I looked at the instruments. We were down to two thousand feet and the needle was still falling. Pulled the control column back, overdid it, felt the plane shuddering. There was a ringing sound from the cabin behind me: the cylinders had started shifting under the vibration.

Knock two of these things together a bit too hard and we're goners, ker-booom.

The U.S. pilot had asked me something about altitude but it wasn't important. The important thing was to stay conscious for long enough to put this thing down, get it out of the air, out of harm's way.

"Look," I said, "I'm going to ditch now. You'd better keep your distance."

I could talk you down into the Azores. I think we should do that, Mr. Locke. It's not all that tough, if you've flown a jet before. We—

This is Air Traffic Control, Ponta Delgada. You are not permitted to land at this airport. Please acknowledge.

There was something I should be thinking about.

Please acknowledge.

He had a thick accent.

"Would you repeat that?"

Yes. You are not permitted to land at this airport. Please acknowledge.

They'd picked up the stuff about the explosives.

"Right. I can't land at your airport."

I ought to be thinking about what Major Franklin had said, not to be taken lightly, perhaps. About talking me down. I mean if I was going to put this thing in the sea, maybe we could do it gently, take the thousandth chance.

We regret. Azores. There is risk of damage because of the explosives. But we have dispatched two air-sea rescue helicopters and we would like to know your present position, altitude, and heading.

I checked the panel and told them.

Okay, Mr. Locke, so we'll talk you down onto the sea.

The major.

I kept the control column braced in my arms. The sound of the jets had faded again, but I realized it was because the two air force planes had done what I'd said, moved away a bit in case of accidents. Through the windscreen I watched the Atlantic below me, not far away, black and endless, glittering in the moonlight, flecked with crests.

Not hospitable.

Mr. Locke, can you hear me?

"Yes. Thinking."

The ringing from the cabin back there was still going on, like the bells of a temple in Tibet.

Blood in the mouth, I couldn't get the taste of it out.

Black water below.

We were at fifteen hundred feet. I'd been letting the control column go.

I said, "Yes, all right. Much obliged."

Okay, this is going to be a gear-up, flaps-down landing. Leave—

"Look, when I hit the sea, you'd better keep your distance. I'd make it at least a couple of miles."

Will do. Thank you for your concern. Now get your flaps down.

I saw the two fighters sliding away on both sides, becoming small, becoming silhouettes.

This is Ponta Delgada. Your position, please.

Gave it to them.

That is good. Heading, altitude, airspeed, please.

Gave it to them. The sea was close now, lines of white crests across black water. The starfields dipped and rose in the windscreen, I suppose there was a wind blowing, perhaps a gale, I couldn't find the instrument that would give me the windspeed.

Okay, now let's have your landing lights on.

I began looking for the switch. There were hundreds.

We are still with you, if you need us.

London, Shatner's voice. Support, I suppose, moral support for the ferret in the field, correction, ferret in the sea.

We need those lights on. There should be a group of switches, maybe on your—okay, you found it, great.

Suddenly the sea was close, floodlit, the waves glittering, the troughs running deep. I used the controls, moving into a turn, bringing the aircraft into line with the swell.

That's great. That's really great. You're looking good. Now start checking your radio altimeter.

The needle was at nine hundred feet.

I could feel the weight of the aircraft under the controls, the vibration in the seat as we lowered toward the waves, the bulkheads creaking, the bells sounding all the time from behind me. A strap had broken somewhere, and there were some cylinders loose.

Sweat running on me suddenly, a feeling of heat as the organism reacted chemically to what the mind knew.

How d'you feel?

"Fair to middling. Does this look all right?"

Okay, get the nose up a little, say five degrees, can you do that?

Five hundred feet on the radio altimeter, four hundred, three hundred.

I pulled the control column back a bit, felt the mass of the plane shift, heard the bells, loud now, sounding the alarm, not used to this aircraft, the sea vanishing below the windscreen, tilting back as I corrected, *Jesus* we were—

Trim her back a little, back a degree.

Two hundred feet, one hundred.

Huge troughs in the black water, the crests breaking, foaming under the ashen light of the moon, a big sea running—

Nose up, bring the nose up, get it up now, bring—

The whole aircraft slackening, the crests breaking dead ahead through the windscreen, the dark mouth of a trough opening and the screen going white as the foam was flung against it, a shudder through the airframe and then a kind of silence, a hole in the night where nothing happened, then a second shudder and the bells ringing wildly back there as we hit water and the harness made a wall and I leaned into it and the sea broke over the screen and it blanked out and I stayed there with the deceleration forces clamping me against the straps, nothing I could do if I moved, couldn't move, stayed there and waited, the lights of the instrument panels swirling past my eyes and the sound of the jets dying and the sound of the sea taking over, the waves rising under the cabin and dropping again and the wind bringing white water off the crests.

Are you okay? Are you okay?

Hit the harness release and got up, got out of the seat, the bells ringing back there, the cylinders moving to the force of the waves now, caught my foot on something, the dead Iranian, tripped and crashed into the rear bulkhead and found the door and slid it open and heard a low screaming from the cabin, gas escaping under pressure, great pressure, we've got to be quick, very quick.

Freezing water, black and silver in the searchlight, the blades above me chopping at the night as the machine lifted and the net cleared the sea and I swung free of its crests and darkness drew down across my eyes, and I was aware only of a void that held me somewhere in it until I came to again and a mile away the black water broke to a blinding flash and a fireball rolled and billowed against the starfields, blotting them out.